M000198705

Necromancy the Musical

DEBBIE HIBBERT

MONSTER IVY PUBLISHING

Cover design by Caleb Staker and Lenore Stutznegger

Interior images from Pixabay

To Ryan: Your love is my superpower. Together we can conquer anything.

THE MORGUE: MONDAY NIGHT

I fidget in the passenger seat of the unmarked police car and glance at the clock. 11:07 p.m. *Ugh!* Cold air pours from the vents, and I relish the relief. On a mild day, New Orleans' heat and humidity are intense enough to curl hair and straighten clothes. Today is a scorcher.

Downtown passes by in a blur of historic buildings and bright lights, and while I normally love admiring the best city in the world, tonight, I have other things on my mind. My fingers tap the armrest, and I instruct time to stop. It doesn't listen. 11:08.

Glancing at my driver, AKA Dad, I tap the armrest a little harder. "I don't have time for the morgue tonight."

"We don't have to stay long, CeCe, but this is a weird one." Dad pulls at his tie, his perpetually wrinkled suit even worse at this late hour.

"A normal dad wouldn't take his sixteen-year-old to visit a murder victim," I say.

"A normal daughter wouldn't be able to talk to the dead."

He has a point.

I sigh dramatically, which seems appropriate, considering I leave for drama camp in the morning. "But early o'clock comes fast, and I haven't finished packing."

He doesn't respond, his focus on the road. Or maybe on the case. As a detective for the NOPD, he often falls into the long don't-ask-what-I'm-thinking-about stare. And since I try to be a good daughter, I don't.

Pulling out my phone, I text Portia, my BFF, and the chips to my salsa. More like I'm the chips, and she's the spicy, flavorful salsa that should come with a warning label.

ME: Still awake?

The three typing dots appear. Clearly not sleeping.

PORTIA: CeCe! 5 days. 1 suitcase. How?

The drama camp guidelines say one suitcase. They might as well have told Portia to pick a favorite out of her five brothers and sisters. Although, sibling roulette might be easier than packing a week's worth of glam into a single bag. Her love of fashion can only be rivaled by the way French fries love salt. She's tall, dark-skinned, gorgeous, perfectly trendy, and never looks bad a single day of her life. For me, dressing up means making sure my t-shirt doesn't have stains.

ME: Didn't you get a big suitcase? The Hide a Dead Body size?

> PORTIA: 1. When one of us kills, there's no hiding the body. We bury that stiff deep. 2. Sure did.

I giggle, my thumbs flying over the screen.

> ME: 1. I'll have extra room and will share. 2. Who are we killing?

> PORTIA: You downgraded murder to point 2? Our life of crime means so little??

> ME: Your clothes were 1.

> PORTIA: Forgiven.

Dad pulls into a parking space. Country music plays on the radio, some sad song about sleepless nights due to lost love. I can relate. Not about lost love, but lost sleep. There's no way I'm getting to bed before 1:00 a.m.

> ME: I'll call you when I get home.

> PORTIA: Doing your Sherlock and Watson thing?

> ME: Yep, the game is afoot.

Ever since I accidentally raised my dog from the dead ten years ago, Dad and I have cracked more cases than the greatest mystery-solving pair.

I'm Dad's pink-haired secret weapon. Emphasis on the secret. Only Dad and Portia know I can talk to the dead. I hide my necromancy, like a skeleton in the closet, living a strange double life of Everyday CeCe vs. Magic CeCe. Of all the places in the world, The Big Easy might be more accepting of supernatural things. But what I do goes beyond party tricks and sleight of hand.

Most days, I wish I was normal.

Dad waits for me by the building, and I run to catch up, my magic bag in hand. Not that my bag is magic. But calling it the-bag-holding-supplies-I-use-to-perform-necromancy seems a bit much.

We head downstairs to my home away from home: The morgue.

Our footsteps echo in the otherwise quiet hall, the only other sound a dull hum from the air conditioning. As we enter the room, a chemical scent irritates my nostrils, the pungent bouquet of formaldehyde and death. It always takes a few minutes to acclimate and regain the ability to breathe deeply. Until then, I inhale shallow, choking spurts that burn my throat.

"I've never seen anything like this, baby girl." Dad opens the refrigerator drawer, and the steel table glides out. "The wounds seem to come from the inside."

"That is strange." The chilled room fogs my breath. I clutch my jacket closer, glad I remembered to bring one. The NOLA heat often makes me forget the freezing temps down here.

"After the autopsy, Rivera almost lost his lunch," Dad says. The happy-go-lucky cop always wears a smile and I try to imagine him hunched over a bucket. Mental note to tell Portia about the vomit escapades, greatly exaggerated, of course. Maybe her crush on Dad's partner will fade after a few cookie-tossing stories.

Dad hands me a file containing information about the victim. I ignore the case number, cause of death, and physical descriptors. Those don't help me at all. But having a name; that's important.

Henry Guillory. I know a couple of Guillorys at school and wonder if they're related.

Dad unzips the body bag, the metal tines buzzing, and he exposes the head. I set out my supplies, starting with a green candle. Striking a lighter, I touch it to the wick and turn it to flame. Next, I take a pinch of graveyard soil from my pouch and mix it with water, spreading the muddy paste over Henry's closed eyelids. Finally, I pour a wide circle of salt, Henry Guillory on the outside, Dad and me standing together on the inside. It only took one haunting for him to realize the importance of standing in the protective barrier.

"What's the—"

"Waxing gibbous," he interrupts, knowing exactly what I need. I forget to follow the moon cycle, and he picks up the slack.

"Waxing gibbous it is." I drip the hot, green wax from the candle in my hand, and it stings my palm. The paraffin hardens, the color lightens, and I mold it into three-fourths of a circle. Moon token complete. But blood holds the true power, and I use my pen knife to poke the tip of my pinky, rubbing a small amount on the token.

Stepping over the salt circle, I place the moon token on Henry's forehead, then nab a hair. Luckily, Mr. Guillory has a full head of hair, so it's easy to pluck one. At times I've had to take hair from an armpit, a leg, and an even less desirable location that shall never be named.

I shudder at the memory.

"Are you ready?" I ask my dad, walking back into the circle.

His answer is a grunt, which could mean anything from

Yes to *I'm sorry for dragging you to the morgue when you need to pack and get ready for drama camp.* I take this one to mean yes.

I sit on the floor, crossing my legs, and burn Henry's hair in the candle wick. The flame turns blue, and rather than radiate heat, this new glow emits cold. A frosty touch courses over my skin.

"Henry Guillory." Death magic runs through my veins, and I close my eyes. "Show me your killer, and you can rest."

A breeze surges through the room, papers rustle and drawers rattle. The salt circle remains intact, the wind unable to affect anything inside.

"Henry Guillory," I repeat. "Show me your killer."

The moon token keeps his body weighted down, and the wet soil keeps his eyes shut. His corpse struggles against the magical restraints, but he won't rise tonight. I only need to see. His words become mine, his thoughts my own.

My focus narrows, and an alley comes to mind, a sidewalk behind some bar. I observe as if hovering above, my view limited to the immediate area. Trash litters the ground despite the dumpsters pressed against the brick façade. Henry faces the wall, relieving himself. A noise startles him, and he turns, tucking in and zipping up in a quick movement.

"*Who's there?*" We say at the same time, me from the morgue, Henry in his memory.

He looks back and forth, his wide eyes a bit too drunk to be observant. The sky clouds over, a heavy cover blowing across the moon. It blocks the ambient light and my vision. The world darkens. I hear movement and, strangely, fabric tearing. He screams, and I scream with him.

"*Tataille,*" We yell the word, and it echoes. "*Tataille,*" we say a little softer. Until it fades to a whisper, "*tataille.*"

Dad shakes my shoulders, and I flop like a bobblehead. "CeCe, what happened?"

My eyes fly open, and I gasp. It takes a few breaths to calm my racing heart. "I don't know. I just..." I pause, thinking about the way the moon and my mind both became clouded. "I couldn't see his killer."

Dad grunts, and using my brilliant skills of interpretation, I know he means, *that's weird. Nothing like that has ever happened before.*

"I know it's weird. Everything went black."

"And you didn't see the monster?" he asks.

"What monster?" The guttural fear choking Henry has me checking over my shoulder. Of course, no one's there.

"Tataille is a Cajun word. Means monster."

"No, I didn't see anyone else. Sorry I wasn't more help," I say.

Another grunt. My dad, a man of many words.

A lingering terror keeps me on edge, and the scene runs through my mind again. I center on the slight sound I heard, trying to decipher the only discernible clue—ripping fabric. Could the noise have come from the attacker? Or...

"Did Henry have any torn clothing?" I ask.

"No. Why?"

"I thought I heard material tearing. It's probably nothing."

"I'll keep that in mind." He nods and gets to his feet. "Come on. You have to get home and pack." As if he needs to remind me.

I lean over the candle. "Henry Guillory, you can rest now." The cold presses in, more intense than before, and I blow out the blue flame. "It's over."

Dad grabs a broom to sweep the salt, and I collect the supplies, throwing them in my magic bag. My steps slow as exhaustion sets in, my body heavy with fatigue. I wipe the mud from Henry's eyes and take the moon token. It weighs more now since the green wax caught the overflow of my power. When I use necromancy, an excess of magic ekes out, and it needs somewhere to go.

After Dad zips the body bag, rolling the table in and closing the fridge, we head out. Taking my elbow, he steadies me, matching his pace to my slower shuffle. We get to the car, and the trembling starts. "Necro-shivers," as Portia calls it. A side effect of using magic. My body shakes, and I slide into the passenger seat. Dad helps me buckle up and grabs a blanket from the back, tucking it around my shoulders. Cranking the heater on high and aiming all the vents in my direction, he drives home.

My teeth chatter, and I bundle further under the soft quilt, letting my eyelids drift closed. Henry Guillory invades my thoughts. I couldn't feel his pain, the magic doesn't work like that, but I felt his fear. It charged the air, a current of panic raising the hairs on the back of my neck. The need to run burned in my chest as the monster waited to attack. But I didn't see anyone else in the alley. The killer either wore sophisticated camouflage or came at Henry with inhuman speed. How is that possible? In all my years talking to the dead, I've helped Dad catch dozens of murderers. This time I drew a blank.

By the time we pull under the carport, the necro-shivers have eased. I force the confusion and concern of Dad's case aside, needing to focus on the important matter of drama camp. Tossing off the blanket, I run into the house.

My suitcase won't pack itself.

CHAPTER
TWO

MY HOUSE: EVEN LATER MONDAY NIGHT

The Young Entertainers Conservatory is an acting and music training program held at Tulane University in May, after their semester ends but before high school breaks for the summer. I signed up to compete in two events, and a nervous gut boulder forms just thinking about it. I've practiced my dramatic monologue to the point I could give it in my sleep. And for the pop duet, I'll have Portia by my side to help calm the tension. But still: the gut boulder.

Cell phone in hand, I hit the number one spot on my favorites. After half a ring, Portia answers.

"Hey, girl. Red wedges or turquoise ankle boots? I don't have room for both." She puts me on speaker and rustles around. I imagine her throwing clothes and shoes in a storm of color.

From under my bed, I pull out a suitcase and throw it open. "Take out the black combat boots, and you can fit both."

9

A gasp of true pain wheezes from her end. "You know I love those boots. I could never leave them behind."

"Sa-cri-fice, sa-cri-fice," I chant.

"Why do you hate them? Is it the chunky heel? The chains hanging from the sides? The way they make me a good eight inches taller than you?"

I don't answer, and she tries to out-silence me in a battle of she-who-talks-first-loses. But I'm an only child with a dad who speaks in grunts. She starts conversations with strangers on elevators to make the fifteen-second ride less awkward. I've got this in the bag.

"You win," she says. As if there was any doubt. "I'll leave the combat boots behind. How many pairs of shoes are you bringing?"

My eyes shift, looking at the black and white checkered Vans on my feet. "Are you implying I should pack more than one pair?"

"I'm giving you a three pair minimum. And make sure at least one of them has a heel." She often designates herself as my fashion advisor which...fair. I totally need one. "You're also taking The Dress. There's a fancy dinner on the last day."

I gasp. "You don't mean that."

"Oh, I do. The Dress has been in your closet long enough. It's late 90's vintage. Perfectly minimal. Cut like a dream. Time to let that beauty out." She zips her suitcase closed, sealing the finality of her words.

The Dress. A beautiful white-to-aqua ombre fabric that hugs me like a clingy boyfriend. The deep v in the back exposes enough skin to make me blush. The length hits me right above mid-thigh; translation: extra work shaving my legs. It was my mom's and is the only thing I have left of her. I used to try it on all the time, playing dress-up, the shimmery material pooling around me. Now I've finally grown into it.

"Fine. I'll pack it."

"Good—" She cuts off with a startled shout. "Penelope June, get out of my closet, you little sneak."

High-pitched giggling echoes on the line and I listen to their muffled conversation. Portia, telling her youngest sister to go to bed, *"why are you still awake?"* And Penny's laughter, shifting to sobs as she cries, *"you're going to be gone forever."*

While Portia calms her down, *"it'll just be a few days, Pen,"* I dig out the moon token from my magic bag. Plugging in my wax melter, a ceramic vase with a heated bulb, I throw the moon token on top. The waxing gibbous melts, the green growing darker and liquifying, vanishing into a small puddle.

Henry Guillory's spirit is free of my magic.

The phone rattles and Portia comes back. "Sorry about that. Crisis averted."

Opening my closet, I grab stuff to fill my suitcase, including a pair of shoes with a heel and The Dress. Portia will be proud. "Poor Penny. Being seven is hard. Especially when your favorite sibling leaves for days."

"I love my family, but I can't wait to get out of here. A break where all I need to think about are hot guys and which lipstick to wear." The longing in her voice echoes on the line. "Moving on. How's Antigone? Are you nervous?"

"I have a gut boulder." I chose Antigone for my dramatic monologue. It's the scene where Antigone defies the king to ensure her brother receives a proper burial. Civil disobedience and death at its finest. "But I'll be ready."

"Of course, you'll be ready. Don't be all work and no play, though. We're going to have fun. Preferably, the what-happens-at-drama-camp-stays-at-drama-camp kind involving some hot ta-males." She doesn't pronounce the word as tamales, but rather ta-males, emphasis on the *male* syllable.

"Please, no. Hooking up at drama camp is so cliché." I gag, letting her know I'm serious. Nothing says *I mean it* like the sound of fake vomiting. "You might as well fall in love at first sight and have an easily-explainable misunder- standing."

"Whatever, CeCe. Just wait. You're gonna find a boy this week who will change your mind." The glint of being right shines in her voice, and I can't wait to prove her wrong.

"Don't count on it."

THREE

DRAMA CAMP: DAY ONE – TUESDAY MORNING

"Him," Portia says.

My note-taking pauses, and I blink a few times to pull myself from the lecture on physical comedy. "What?"

"Him." She points a few rows ahead and to the left. "Red shirt, blond hair, perfectly formed biceps that flex when opening stubborn pickle jars."

The red shirt stands out, and I catch a glimpse as the guy tips his head and laughs. "When did you see him open a pickle jar?"

"I was speaking from my imagination."

"Good to know." He's attractive in a way that makes me want to mess up his hair. A little too perfect. "What about him?"

"He doesn't stand a chance." Ah, the famous words she utters whenever she goes after something. Role in a play? It doesn't stand a chance against her acting skill. Landing a job at an exclusive consignment store? No chance she loses that with her determination. So Red Shirt should be eating out of her palm by the end of the day.

Class ends, and I get my backpack from the floor. "I liked the..." I realize I'm alone. Portia vanished in a puff of pheromones, magically reappearing next to her target.

She wears loose orange and white striped pants and a tight white shirt, showing the tiniest strip of stomach. Her black skin is smooth and flawless, and her dark curls go wild. Her hair is shorter in the front, longer in the back, mullet style, and on anyone else, it would look bizarre. On her, it's amazing.

The perfect dude appears a little less perfect standing next to her.

I amble through the crowd. My jeans and black Tee with the words, "Bless Your Heart," seem more like an episode of What Not to Wear compared to Portia.

"CeCe LeBlanc?"

My body stills, the way an animal might when it senses danger. I paste on a smile and turn, my voice holding an extra cup of sugar. "Julie Jolley."

Yes, that's her real name. Nature decided to play a cruel joke by giving evil incarnate a surname conjuring images of Santa. For a while, she tried to go by Julie Ann, but the world sensed her deceit, not buying the wholesome girl-next-door vibe.

Her posse stands guard, the J-Crew, being Jaelynn and Gemma. Jaelynn, who's about my height and wears her hair in long box braids, narrows her brown eyes at me. And Gemma, who pretends her name starts with a J, plays with the flower clip in her hair, looking like the real-life inspiration of Moana.

"I see you entered the dramatic monologue contest."

Julie sticks out her forked tongue, licking her top lip. "What a coincidence, I did too."

"That *is* a coincidence." It's absolutely not a coincidence. Ever since I beat her for a role in the musical earlier this year, she's tried to prove her superiority. "A contest that has almost fifty people, and we both entered. Wow."

"And you're doing Antigone. How cute. It's brave to perform something from such an outdated play." The light catches on her nose ring and it glares at me like a smirk. Jaelynn and Gemma glance at each other and giggle.

Inadequacy bubbles up somewhere between my esophagus and my ego. "A classic is a classic for a reason."

"Personally, I've chosen something super modern and relevant. I'll be playing an unhoused, street-performing orphan from the wrong side of town, who just found out she's coming into money."

"You're doing something from Annie?" Portia's behind me, and I close my eyes in relief. Only two people intimidate Julie Jolley, Satan himself and Portia Landry. "I love Annie. I played Miss Hannigan in fourth grade. Killed it."

Julie frowns, her cheeks going red. "It's not...I'm not..."

"It'll be great. The judges prefer the classics." Portia links her arm with mine, pulling me from the war zone.

"It's not Annie!" Jaelynn yells after us, and I laugh, burying my face in Portia's shoulder.

We walk into the hall, far enough away that Julie's heated glare no longer singes. "I love you so much."

"Of course you do, and I love you back." She leads me out of the crowd to find a secluded corner. "You need to stop letting Julie get to you. Yes, she's talented and beautiful. But so are you."

I start to protest, and she quiets me with a finger pressed to her lips.

"I'm going to show you something." She takes her phone out, opens the screen, and turns it around. It's an image of me in an I-might-pee-my-pants-I'm-laughing-so-hard moment. My mouth is wide open, and tears gather in my eyes. "See this girl? Not just anyone could pull off pink hair. Julie would look like a demented Strawberry Shortcake."

A reluctant chuckle escapes. "The color's cherry-dipped rose gold."

"It's pink." She shakes her head, but the humor lurks in her smile. "And you have the most vibrant green eyes. You make leprechauns jealous."

"Really?" I purse my lips. "Name one leprechaun you know."

"The Lucky Charms guy...Lucky. He's jealous." She puts her phone away and places her hands on my shoulders. "The point is you're gorgeous. You're talented. You're CeCe freakin' LeBlanc. Don't forget it."

"Thanks, Coach," I tease.

"Anytime. Now suit up, and let's get back on the field."

Every hour there are four learning sessions to choose from, and this is the one I'm most excited about: Dramatizing Magic & Characterizing Mysticism.

For obvious reasons, I'm intrigued.

"How was the guy in the red shirt?" I ask as we find seats in the lecture hall.

"Ah, Devin." She sighs and stares into the distance, the weight of her family responsibilities fizzling under the interest of a hot guy. Being the oldest of six, and with two working parents, she plays the role of mom, maid, and taxi driver a lot. Too much. "We're meeting for lunch by the pond."

"The pond?" I squint, trying to figure out where she means. "Are you talking about the toxic waste dump?"

She tsks. "It's a retention basin. They even get fish in there."

"With five eyes."

"Har har." She playfully jabs me with her elbow. "You can see for yourself since you're coming too."

"That sounds like fun. Because what good is a tricycle without its third wheel?"

"No tricycles, silly. Devin has a friend." She waggles her eyebrows. Yes, those crafty eyebrows of hers.

I'm not really up for a double date at the toxic waste dump, but the hope in Portia's pleading face makes me mutter the most ridiculous statement. "I can't wait."

Pulling out a notebook, I relax in my chair. A woman walks to the front. Long blond hair curls down her back, and she wears a full-length floral print dress. Our magical and mystical instructor.

"Let's go ahead and get started. My name is Jennifer Black." She speaks loudly, her voice carrying over the chatter. "Double double toil and trouble."

The lights dim, and fog drifts from machines on the floor. Thunder rumbles through the room, a convincing sound effect in stereo. Some girl squeals in overreaction, a reminder this is drama camp.

"Now that I have your attention, let's talk about some plays." Ms. Black opens her arms, encompassing the crowd. "The Crucible, Brigadoon, Wicked, even our favorite cursed play, Macbeth. What do they all have in common?"

"They're old?" A guy on the front row calls out.

"Shut your mouth, son," Ms. Black laughs, and we join in. "Wicked is practically a baby when it comes to Broadway. What else could it be? Especially considering the title of this class."

"They all have magic." Julie Jolley. Of course, she came to this class. The teacher's pet answers in true form with a sure voice and know-it-all grin.

"Exactly. In these productions, we have witches, characters pretending to be witches, and mythical cities appearing every hundred years. The stage has always been a place to portray magic, because..." She pauses, gazing at her rapt audience. For a brief moment, our eyes meet, and I hold my breath. "Magic. Is. Real."

She says the words slowly, emphasizing each syllable. Recognition burns in my gut. The kind of understanding shared when two people have read the same book or watched the same series on Netflix. Not many people believe in magic. Most don't know it exists. I have the feeling Ms. Black is a believer.

"Magic is real," she says again. "At least when you're on the stage. It's your job to convince everyone else."

Her message runs through my brain like a catchy commercial jingle. *Understand the magic, study the history, know who you are.* I can't get it out of my head. Although she relates the idea to playing a character, I apply it to myself. Necromancy is something I've tried to hide from. Maybe I need to take my magic more seriously.

Time passes quickly, my pages filling with her words. I get far more out of the class than I expect. Enough to distract me from the impending double date.

Almost.

I glance at the clock. Noon. Lunch.

"You ready?" Portia stands and stretches, her gold hoop earrings swaying with the motion.

"Off to the radioactive wasteland?"

"Retention pond," she corrects. Biting her bottom lip, she dances from foot to foot. With thoughts of Devin on her mind and a deep peach color on her lips, she has fully adopted the role of carefree Portia. "I really like him, CeCe. He's so cute, he oozes charm."

"If he's oozing, the toxic dump is a wise choice for a meetup." I put my notebook away, trying to hide my suddenly sweaty palms.

I'm not great with guys and haven't had a boyfriend since Anthony Zamata in sixth grade. I offered to raise his grandma, who had just died, and he dumped me on the spot. He started dating Becky Christensen the next day. Since then, taboo topics include my magic, raising others' relatives, and Becky Christensen.

I don't date much. And I definitely don't meet strangers at a possibly noxious retention pond.

"You're going to be fine." Portia knows me too well. My necromancy *and* my neuroses. "Devin's friend is awesome. I don't remember his name, or anything about him. I was super wrapped up in Devin, but amazing people have amazing best friends. It's a fact."

I laugh, shaking my head. "You make a convincing argument."

"Give it a chance," she says, and I reluctantly nod. Because nothing bad ever happens following those words.

Right.

CHAPTER
FOUR

DRAMA CAMP: DAY ONE – TUESDAY AFTERNOON

Heat blasts us as we walk outside, the humidity so thick it weighs down the air. I regret my decision to wear jeans. The heavy material sticks to my thighs, a gluey adhesive making me awkward-squat every few feet to gain some breathing room.

The unimpressive retention pond looms ahead. Green moss floats on the stagnant water and thin vines poke through the surface. A stench of stale weeds and fishiness hangs in the gentle breeze. The perfect atmosphere for a romantic meet up.

Two guys stand by the toxic waste, and Devin mostly blocks his friend, my date, from view. I fall behind Portia, and we stop like we're preparing for a duel, the two shooters lined up front, and the two seconds keeping watch, ready for the carnage.

The whole scene is ludicrous.

"Hey, beautiful." Devin looks at her the way a gator

stares down dangling feet in a pond. "I've been thinking about you."

"Hey, Devin." Portia's shoulders "squee," the tightening shrug caused by a cute boy's attention.

"Your pretty brown eyes distracted me all morning." He moves forward. She matches him step for step. Something passes between them—a magnetic energy. And then, inexplicably, they come together, their lips meeting, their arms flying and wrapping like loose tentacles.

The duel just turned into a PSA on PDA.

My eyes go wide, and my gaze hits the ground, needing to give them privacy. And to find my dropped jaw. Carefree Portia really means business. The last time I saw her this undisciplined was over the summer when she took a week off work and stay-cationed at my house, ignoring her phone and eating her weight in Zapps Voodoo-Heat Potato Chips.

But this instant affection isn't like her. Sure, she kisses guys. Not minutes after meeting them. Nor to the point I worry about her intake of oxygen. So, this is new. She either really needed a break or Devin is a lip incubus. If such a thing even exists.

Devin's friend walks over, avoiding the drama camp hook-up playing out in front of us. "Uhh...hi," he says.

I glance at him and give myself whiplash to get a better look, realizing I stand next to a superior male specimen. Tall—taller than Devin—with dark hair and eyes so blue they put the sky to shame. He holds his hand up like a blinder, his focus on me.

Hi, I'm CeCe, I think, and imagine myself reaching out to make an introduction.

That's not what I do.

"Your friend's a player." The words pop out of my

mouth of their own volition, slinking away to mutate in the radioactive waste.

The fine guy tips his head, slowly lowering his hand. "Excuse me?"

"Your friend's a player," I say. "And I don't like him."

"Because your friend assaulted him with her mouth? Or because he reciprocated?" His lips quirk, the most adorable side smile distracting me.

"Because..." I trail off. What are we even talking about? He has dimples. Like, actual dimples. A sculpted masterpiece deserving of a museum display.

"Did you want me to guess the rest of that sentence?" he asks, his blue eyes staring me down and giving him an unfair advantage.

"Honestly, I don't even remember what I was saying." Laughter bubbles in my chest, and I let it go, the giggles and my nervous energy. We aren't really going out, despite Portia calling it a double date. Just two strangers caught in the middle of a drama camp moment.

"Probably for the best," he laughs. His accent hails from the south, but not deep Louisiana. This boy is not a born-and-bred New Orleanian.

"Can we start over?" I stick out my hand, my silver nail polish glittering in the sun. "I'm CeCe LeBlanc."

"Zach Wren." The warmth of his smile could melt butter.

We shake, and something passes through me, a flow of electricity. My smile freezes as my body heats, a buzz traveling my veins. Surprise lights his expression; he feels it too. Taking back his hand, he wipes it on his pants.

I don't know much about Zach Wren, but I know he has magic.

CHAPTER
FIVE

DRAMA CAMP: DAY ONE – THE MOST AWKWARD
LUNCH EVER

The supernatural pulse that hums when I use
necromancy trembles between us now. His is a
little different than mine but still has a distinct
vibration. I've never met another magic user. Do I ask about
it? Is it even a civilized conversation?

I'd rather pretend everything is normal.

He tucks his hands in his pockets. "It's funny when
people say, 'let's start over,' because you know I won't
forget you think my friend's a player."

Apparently, we're not going to talk about magic. I
approve.

"The polite thing to do is *pretend* you forgot. It's in the
Southern Gentlemen's Cotillion handbook. Article fourteen,
subheading three." With the talk of magic tabled, and the
awareness that we're *not* actually dating, tension lifts from
my shoulders. My words come easier.

He walks a few feet away from our friends, and I follow,

happy to leave the sounds of kissing behind. "You just made that up." He gives me the side eye. Very suspicious. "I don't remember an article fourteen subheading three."

Now I give *him* the side eye. "Did you really attend Cotillion?"

"Of course. All good southern gentlemen do." He swipes at his shoulders, dapper-like. "But the real question is, what do you want for lunch?"

"Lunch?" The change in subject slows my brain function.

"You know, the meal between breakfast and dinner, eaten around noon."

"Ah, *that* lunch." I laugh and roll my eyes.

"Yes. And you'll have the tough choice of a ham or turkey sandwich." He runs a hand through his hair, which falls effortlessly back into place. "Hey, Devin," he calls out. "We're heading to the dining hall."

"I don't think they're particularly interested in sandwiches." I clear my throat, facing the prospect of being alone with Zach. Welcome back, Nerves.

He glances at Portia and Devin. "They can catch up."

"Maybe, but Portia's easily side-tracked by a cute face."

"You think he's cute?"

I think you're cute. I almost say it. The words play on the tip of my tongue. But I'm not bold like Portia. My style falls more in the harbor-a-crush-for-months kind. "I think he's a player."

Zach laughs, and, welcome back, Dimples. "I thought we started over."

"My mistake. Starting over, take two." I slap my hands together like a director's clapboard.

"Shall we?" He tips his head, inviting me to walk with him.

It should be a simple decision; go to lunch or say no. It feels bigger than that. His magic still lingers on my palm, and I worry this is a guy I could like. Really like. I stand on the precipice of getting to know Zach Wren better. Someone who has magic and also happens to be total eye candy.

A sprinkling of freckles dot his nose, and I focus on that. "Yes," I say. "Let's grab lunch."

"Great." He steps over the precipice with me.

On the short walk to the dining hall, the sun attacks. Sweat pools in the small of my back, rolling to catch on the waist of my jeans. I imagine multiple deranged scenarios where he suddenly needs to touch me there. Like, a blue heron swoops low and Zach's fingers fling in the filmy moisture to keep me from kissing the pavement. Or a bike messenger plows down the sidewalk, and Zach spins me out of the way, his hand sliding under my shirt and into my puddle of perspiration.

As Portia would say, I'm acting kooky.

"What school do you go to? What grade?" He walks by my side, making no move to touch my sweat.

"I'm a sophomore at New Harmony. What about you?" The scent of honeysuckle fills my nose, and I breathe it in, enjoying the perfume of early summer.

"I'm a junior at Marshall."

Marshall. My rival high school. Mostly in sports. The two schools switch off football titles often enough I never remember who the current champ is.

"Will we start a war by having lunch together?" I ask.

"I think we can keep our reputations intact. Unless you're a cheerleader?"

"Nope." I laugh. The extent of my cheerleading experience includes watching the movie, *Bring It On* and dreaming I resurrected a girl with pom poms. "Are you a football player?"

"No. Football's not my religion." He opens the door to the dining hall, holding it for me. "Maybe we can trigger the collapse of Friday night lights another time."

"I'll add it to my to-do list." I pantomime holding a pen and air-drawing a checkmark.

The swarm of bodies inside makes us pause our conversation, and we work our way to the front, where brown sacks sit on tables. We each grab one, turkey for me, ham for him, before surveying the seating options.

My CeCe senses alert me to the presence of evil, and the cold grip of terror prickles my spine. Only one thing causes this fight-or-flight instinct to pump my adrenaline.

Julie Jolley.

Despite my earlier reluctance to touch Zach (i.e., tingling magic palms and overactive sweat glands), I grab his arms and duck behind my improvised human shield. The lunch sack crinkles, and the hum of magical energy zips at the contact.

"CeCe." His head turns, exorcist style, in an attempt to see me. "Do you make a habit of ripping arms from sockets?"

My fingers dig into his skin hard enough that I leave claw marks. I relax my hold. "No."

"Good to know." His voice carries a hearty dose of amusement. "Why are you hiding?"

"CeCe LeBlanc?" The high-pitched cackle of Julie Jolley assaults my ears. It's rare to see her in the wild without the J-Crew, and yet, here she is. Her long, dark hair falls in perfect beachy waves, and her toddler-sized shirt stretches tight.

We always dance around, playing this game of passive-aggressive hate. And I don't intend to lose. I step from behind Zach and press arm to arm, letting her know he came to lunch with me.

"Julie Jolley," I say in a syrupy tone.

Her gaze shifts to the very impressive blue eyes watching our exchange. "I'm Julie Jolley."

"I gathered." His lips remain flat, much to my relief. Julie would leech onto his dimples like a medieval blood-letting.

"What's your name? Are you competing? CeCe and I both entered the dramatic monologue," Julie says.

I roll my eyes. Of course, she would bring that up. *You're doing Antigone. How cute.*

"I entered the pop duo," he says.

"Oh yeah?" I shift to look at him, ignoring Satan's evil twin. "I did too. With Portia."

"May the best duo win." His smile turns up, and I watch in slow-motion horror, knowing those dimples will join us. Knowing Julie will attack. I don't even think about my actions as my hand flies out, covering his mouth.

My palm touches his lips, his breath a light fog against my skin. Embarrassment begs me to walk away and never show my face in public again, but I can't move my hand with his dimples still engaged.

This might be the most awkward I've ever felt.

Julie points out my cringiness. "What's wrong with you, CeCe? He can't talk with your hand over his mouth."

An army of the undead couldn't force me to pull away. "He's self-conscious about his smile. I'm just helping."

She mmm-hmms, totally not buying my lies. I don't care. My focus stays on him, and I hope my laser beam stare conveys my apology. Millimeter by millimeter, I lower my hand, hoping the dimples have disappeared.

"Thanks, CeCe," he says, completely straight-faced. "I almost let a smile slip."

Zach Wren just owned drama camp. I bite my cheek to keep from laughing. Even then, my breath quickens with the urge to let it out. "No problem."

"I'm sure you have a beautiful smile." Julie tries to recover, sidling up next to him. "No need to be shy, especially around me."

"CeCe and I are going to eat lunch now. Maybe I'll see you around." Not even a tiny smirk escapes.

"You can count on it." She winks and runs her talons down his arm.

We walk outside, leaving Julie, and the noisy dining hall, behind. The hot air brushes over me, and the sweat returns. But this time, my nerves produce just as much as the heat. He'll probably ask questions. Questions I'm not prepared to answer.

He turns to me, his confident, dimpled smile blooming fuller than the honeysuckle. "I played along, so according to the Cotillion handbook, you have to explain what just happened."

I see a spot of shade on the grass under some hulking willow trees, and head in that direction. Sadly, as I sit, the ground doesn't swallow me up and get me out of this. "That was Julie Jolley. She's sort of my nemesis."

"I figured that out." He lowers next to me and opens his lunch. "What I don't know is why you lied. I'm not self-conscious about my smile."

"Oh, that," I laugh and dig into my bag as well. Sandwich, apple, chips, water bottle, and a cookie. Yep, all the basics are here. Just a regular sack lunch.

He stays silent. Even the rattling of his bag stops. I

glance up to find him watching me. "Don't forget the Cotillion handbook," he says.

"You know I made that up, right? There's not really a Cotillion book of rules." Or maybe there is. I have no idea.

"Then let's call it the handbook of not throwing you under the bus in front of your nemesis." He tosses his red apple and catches it without taking his eyes off me.

My skin heats several shades to match the apple. Is it suddenly hotter? I pull at the collar of my t-shirt. My sweat throws a pool party, inviting all the glands to join in. "I didn't want Julie to see."

He leans in, genuinely confused. "See what?"

That your dimples win an Oscar for best performance of a face. I open my mouth. Close it. My suddenly dry throat makes me cough, and I take a drink from my water bottle. He patiently waits for me to get control. I take a few breaths for courage, nearly hyperventilating with the amount of air I take in.

I can't believe he's going to make me say it.

Be like Portia. Be bold.

"Your dimples," I say. "Julie's the worst. She once sabotaged an audition of mine by switching out the scripts. And another time, she put tabasco in my water, and I took a drink right before I got up to sing. You deserve better than some soul-sucking drama girl to...." I trail off. Embarrassment seizes my tongue, and the red apple has nothing on the color of my cheeks now.

"See my dimples?" He finishes.

"Exactly."

Yep. I put it out there in the universe, or more importantly, out there for Zach to hear. I covered his mouth so Julie Jolley wouldn't see his dimples. I stare at my turkey sandwich. The plastic wrapping crinkles under my trembling fingers.

"CeCe, look at me." Zach's hand settles over my sandwich mangling, and I feel it, the magic zinging. I lift my gaze, meeting his eyes. Those adorable freckles dot the bridge of his nose. "I promise I will never smile at Julie Jolley and let her see my dimples."

That does it. Zach Wren is my favorite leading man.

CHAPTER
SIX

DRAMA CAMP: DAY ONE – TUESDAY NIGHT

Portia is missing. The friend in me figures she hit it off with Devin and lost track of time. The daughter of a cop in me worries she got kidnapped by human traffickers. I look at my phone, re-reading the last several texts.

> ME: Zach and I are going to the Shakespeare class.

> ME: Zach is Devin's friend if you forgot.

> ME: Y'all coming to any more classes?

> ME: I'm alone in dramatic readings. Saved you a spot.

> ME: When are you coming back?

> ME: Portia?

10:00 p.m. means lights out, which, according to the clock, gives her three minutes. Devin didn't strike me as an ax murderer or a serial killer, but crazy comes in all kinds of packages. I would know. I've helped Dad solve murders for a decade.

The dark thoughts turn darker and memories of the dead flip through my head like a picture book. Corpses I talked to. Gruesome victims waiting for justice. My imagination betrays me, replacing their faces with Portia's. My best friend on a steel slab at the morgue.

No!

Bile climbs my throat, and I sit on the edge of the bed, hanging my head and sucking in deep breaths. I can't lose Portia. Especially not now that I know what real grief feels like.

A year ago, my grandma passed away. The pain of losing Mawmaw hollows my chest, the sorrow a melon baller scooping out pieces of happiness while everyone else remains oblivious to the devastation. And I starve for one more day, one more conversation, one more hug from the person who meant everything.

I've thought about raising her, so many times the memory almost seems real. But I promised I never would.

Death is good for the soul, she said.

The door flings open, and Portia rushes in, her hair wild. She carries her shoes, and the bottom of her orange and white striped pants brush the floor. "Made it, with seconds to spare." She flops on her bed, dropping her ankle boots, and laughing. "I had the best day. How about you?"

She notices my expression and sobers, sitting up. "What happened? Did Julie Jolley do something?"

Moisture tickles the corners of my eyes, thoughts of

Mawmaw and relief at Portia's return releasing the emotion. "I texted all day. You never answered."

"CeCe, I'm sorry. My phone died." She moves to sit by me on my bed and wraps her arm around my shoulders. "I assumed you'd be enjoying the classes, but I should have checked in."

The anxious worry shifts to frustration. "I thought we were going to have fun this week. The Two Amigos. And you dumped me for a guy you just met."

"I didn't dump you. Nothing has changed." She tightens her arm, pulling me closer. "We have so many adventures racked up. Sometimes I want a different adventure involving a cute boy who's charming and funny and randomly breaks into song. Who makes my toes curl when he kisses me."

That got oddly specific, very quickly.

"But I like our adventures." My soft whisper hides the hurt.

"I like our adventures too." She shifts on the bed and ruffles my hair. "Devin and I are going to the workshops tomorrow, so we can all hang out together. Deal?"

All? Is she referring to Zach too? "Deal. I guess."

She kneels in front of me and holds my hands. "You will always be my best friend. When we leave here, we'll still be the Two Amigos. But I need a break more than you know. Things at home...." a long sigh leaves her lips.

I slide to join her on the floor, and we prop our backs against the bed. "What's going on?"

"You know we've had the stomach flu circulating. Penny got it first. Then Pace. Then Piper. My parents can't afford to miss work, so I've been cleaning vomit chunks and barely sleeping. The house smells like sour milk and

Bourbon Street. My fingers are permanently pruned from Lysol." Her eyes glass over, tears trembling on her lashes. "I'm exhausted."

"Portia," I say softly. "I didn't know it was that bad."

"I don't want to talk about it right now. This week is about having fun." She swipes the sadness away and tips her head to look at me. Taking my hand in hers, she squeezes. "Listen, I don't know what'll happen with Devin. Just...let me have this. For the next few days."

Her soft brown eyes plead, and my frustration melts. I love Portia way more than I love my annoyance.

"But y'all are going to the workshops. Right?" I lower my head, adding my best *you better not leave me again* tone.

"Absolutely. And we still have our duet that we'll rock." She waggles her eyebrows and adds, "Plus, I'd never miss watching The Exhibition with you. I've heard there'll be actual Hollywood scouts this year. Too bad we can't get a piece of that action."

The Exhibition. Capital T, Capital E. Several of the teachers present one performance piece and most have it cast before arriving. Others hold an audition, and the competition is fierce.

"I might not kill for the opportunity to do an Exhibition scene, but I'd definitely maim. Bribe, for sure." The joking comes easier now. My smile is natural.

"I'd pool my money for that." Rising from the floor, she brushes off her pants. "Now it's lights out. This girl's gotta get her beauty sleep."

We change into pajamas in the dark, and she fills me in on her day of talking, making out, walking, making out, laughing, making out. And a little bit of making out on the side. Maybe Devin *is* a lip incubus.

Settling into our beds, we both go quiet, and I stare at the ceiling, fatigue drawing me in. The bed isn't particularly comfortable, but between the busy day, the heat, and my worry, sleep pulls at me.

"So...Zach, huh?"

My eyes spring open to see Portia's cell bathing her face in light as she catches up on text messages.

"We hung out a little." I make sure to sound completely neutral. No need to create illusions of becoming the dating foursome of drama camp. She'd be all over that like shrimp on grits.

"And...?"

"He's pretty cool." I try to stop the smile in my voice, but it slips out. The boy promised not to show his dimples to Julie Jolley.

"You like him!" Portia swings to a sitting position, her legs hanging over the side of the bed.

"Don't get any wild ideas," I warn.

"Every wild idea I've had turned out awesome."

I laugh. Loudly. "Do you need a list? We're lucky my dad's a cop, or last summer could have ended—"

"Okay, okay." She cuts me off, joining in with my laughter. "You make a good point. But you do like him. Right?"

"My dad? I love him."

"Har har." She throws her balled-up pants across the room, and they hit the wall by my head. "You know I'm talking about Zach. Drama camp double couple!"

"Don't start that. Too soon to tell."

"Sure. I believe you." Her tone says differently.

I doze off thinking of Zach, but I dream of something else entirely.

My sleep self drifts through the window to float

outside. Wind blows in the trees, and the rattling leaves sing like chimes. Something compels me to move, a cord pulling me, leading me away from my dorm room.

And I go.

The bright moon guides me through the hub of New Orleans, highlighting the mansions of the Garden District. Their gas lanterns flicker, the tiny flames quivering inside the metal lamps. Tall houses and taller trees give way to the cramped streets and graffitied spaces of Central City. Historic church buildings dot every other corner with their aged bricks and shimmering spires. And on I go until I arrive at the morgue, the same one I visited with Dad last night.

I hover above, looking over the room. Traces of my necromancy linger, but another magic taints the space—a magical oil slick coats the air in thick grease.

A person stands in a protective circle, this one made of ash rather than salt, which adds to the dark and heavy feel. The magic caster hides behind a murky, supernatural veil, making it impossible for me to see him. Or her. I can't tell gender, age, or anything distinctive.

Henry Guillory's drawer hangs open, the table rolled out. He looks the same as before, except sharp needles stick in him like a human pincushion. Dozens of pins with red tips protrude an inch from his skin. Two in each eye seal his lids closed. Two in the middle, meaty part of his forehead. A line of them travels down his nose and chin, leading to his chest where they fan out in a spiral. I'm not sure what this person wants to do with Henry Guillory, but they won't be able to. I released his spirit.

And I need to leave.

Pulling back, I try to return to my dorm, but drift closer to the caster. No matter how hard I put on the brakes, the strange leash drags me until I end up right outside the circle of ash. A gloved hand reaches to grab me by the neck, and darkness oozes into me at the contact. I gasp and struggle, not even sure how the grip holds. This is just a dream.

"CeCe LeBlanc, I need your magic." The mysterious voice whispers in the air around me. Terror makes me fight harder.

This person knows my name. They know I have magic.

The Caster remains shrouded in shadow, and we fly out of the morgue. We retrace the same route I took, the path highlighted in a foggy red line. My fingers scratch and tear at the clamped hand, but it's different in this spirit state, unsteady. Like trying to clutch a fistful of water.

The longer they hold my neck, the more I feel tainted by dirty magic. Hoping I have any ability in this dream, I center myself and call on my necromancy. The iciness of death magic builds on the fingers of my right hand and spreads all the way to my left hand. I let it fill me, and I pull at the vice around my throat. The power pushes against The Caster and slows us down.

Tulane looms in the distance and instinct tells me I can't let us get there. My physical body sleeps inside. Portia's with me. I have to protect us both.

Stop, I scream in my mind and shove at them with my power. *Stop now!*

I jolt awake, gasping for breath, tears trickling from my eyes.

Portia kneels next to the bed, shaking my shoulders. A glow radiates from the lamp on the nightstand, silhouetting her in soft light. "Are you okay? You screamed."

"I'm not sure. I had a nightmare..." I trail off and touch my throat, now tender where The Caster held me.

Weird.

Something Mawmaw used to say comes to mind. *Not everything is meant to be understood. Just accepted.* But I'm pretty sure she didn't mean being spirit kidnapped.

"Do you need anything? A glass of water?" Portia asks.

"No thanks." A chill ripples in my core and spreads outward. Necro-shivers. They come on fast, and I cuddle deeper under the blanket, pulling it to my chin.

"Did you use magic?" Motioning for me to scoot over, she squeezes onto the twin bed.

"I guess." My teeth chatter, and the two words carry a few extra syllables.

"You guess?"

"I thought it was a dream."

"You screamed and used magic. That doesn't usually happen in your dreams." She adjusts to get under the covers and wraps her arms around me to take some of the cold.

As I snuggle into Portia and wait for the trembling to ease, I think about the dream. I feel the oily magic like a residue of filth coating my insides. My neck aches from the press of The Caster's fingers. Could it have been real? If it was, there might be evidence left behind at the morgue.

"I need to talk to my dad," I say.

She glances at the glowing numbers on the alarm clock. "He'll love the three a.m. wake-up call."

"I know. But something happened at the morgue." I sit up, and she moves with me, both of us resting our backs against the wall. The blanket bunches around my waist, and I pull it to cover my shoulders.

She grabs my cell and hands it to me. "The hard life of being the parent of a necromancer."

Have truer words ever been spoken?

The screen lights up as I hit Dad's number. It rings

twice before he answers with a grunt. Being a policeman, he's used to middle-of-the-night calls.

"Hey, Dad." My eyes begin to moisten, and I worry they might leak. Dad's not a particularly sensitive sort, but my waterworks want to make an appearance anyway. Portia pats my leg and leans on my shoulder.

"Am I killing someone or burying a body?" His sleepy croak rumbles in my ear.

"I had a strange dream, but it could have been real." I take a breath and start over. "I was at the morgue."

"You went to the morgue?" The sleep clears from his voice, and his tone changes from Dad to detective.

"No, in the dream. Someone was there doing magic. Not necromancy, though. Something worse."

His grunting reply means *I have no idea what you're talking about.*

"They used my name, Dad. Told me they needed my magic."

"Who did?"

"The person from the dream. The Caster." Is he even listening? Granted, I'm not making a lot of sense, but he needs to put in some effort to fill in the blanks. "Can you look at the morgue and see if anything's out of place?"

"Tonight?"

"Yes. Please." I take Portia's hand and squeeze. She gives me an encouraging nod. Having her next to me helps me finish my thoughts. "I think this person is trying to find me."

"You think, or you know?"

CeCe LeBlanc, I need your magic.

I gently touch my neck and prod at the aching skin. "I know."

"I'll head to the morgue. See what I can find."

I'm grateful he believes me. No skeptical questions. No grunts of doubt. Just Dad being Dad.

"Thanks. And one more thing," I glance around the room, deciding how to rearrange it to pour myself a protective barrier. "Can you bring me salt tomorrow? Like, a lot of it."

CHAPTER
SEVEN

DRAMA CAMP: DAY TWO – WEDNESDAY MORNING

I took a little extra care in getting ready this morning. Flat ironed hair? Check. Concealer to cover the lack-of-sleep eye baggage? Check. A light dusting of powder over the faint bruising on my neck? Check. Doing all this for a boy? Absolutely not.

And my nervy stomach has nothing to do with seeing Zach again.

Portia and I walk into class, and she spots Devin immediately. Today, he traded his red tee for a bright orange one, which should make him look like a traffic cone. But with his blond hair and tan skin, he looks ready to film a beach volleyball scene. She texted with him all morning, making plans to meet, which classes to attend, the location of their dream honeymoon. The important details on day two of a relationship.

We walk down the aisle, and I concentrate on not tripping while my gaze stays on Zach. He looks just as good as I remember. His still wet, dark brown hair swoops perfectly

41

across his forehead, managing to highlight the bright blue of his eyes. A grin tugs his lips as I approach.

"Morning." He ignores the cuddle fest between Portia and Devin.

"Did the player make it back before curfew?" I ask.

He grins, close to dimple exposure, but not quite. "Barely. I almost locked him out."

Gesturing toward our seats, his arm brushes against mine. The magic buzzes, a different feeling from last time. There's something new I can't quite put my finger on. A sort of urgency making my magic really want to know his better.

My heartbeat picks up speed and I reach for him, wanting longer contact to understand the change.

He takes a sudden step back. "Actually, I'm gonna sit with my other friends for this class." His forehead crinkles, wariness etched into the lines. Without waiting for me to say anything, he quickly strides to a group of people across the room.

What just happened?

I take my seat, completely confused. My arm tingles where we touched, and I run my fingers along the skin, wondering if he felt the difference in magic.

"What'd you do, Pinky?" Devin speaks loud enough to get a few stares. "You chased off my buddy."

"Her name's CeCe." Portia smacks him on the arm and sits next to me. "Ignore him. He's annoyed I told him no making out during class."

The teacher begins talking, leaving me to stew in relative peace.

I wonder if Devin's right. Did I do something to push Zach away? We seemed to hit it off yesterday, despite my embarrassing move in covering his mouth—thinking about it makes me turn a couple of shades of sunburn. Maybe I imagined our connection, and he only ate lunch with me so I wouldn't be alone. Or maybe he did want to hang out with his other friends, and nothing's wrong.

Ugh. This is why I don't date. Way too much trouble.

When Zach doesn't come to the next class, I wonder if he's avoiding me.

Portia chooses the workshop on diction, and without Zach, I'm the third wheel. To make things extra awkward, she leans so far over that she sits more in Devin's chair than her own. Their whispered conversation hums around me, emphasizing my unnecessary presence.

"Can I get a volunteer to run through tongue twisters?" The teacher's bland voice reminds me of dry wheat toast. It gets the job done with no extra pizzazz.

Slinking lower in my seat, I avoid eye contact with Mr. Boring. I hardly slept, someone with dirty magic is after me, and I have boy paranoia. No way I add tongue twisters to the mix.

Class ends, and I'm out of my seat before Mr. Boring finishes the phrase, "Thanks for coming." Portia and Devin don't move. Their noses touch as their conversation continues buzzing.

"Hey, Portia." I poke her in the shoulder. "Time for the next workshop."

It only takes twelve pokes before she climbs from Devin's seat. "Sorry. Did we decide where we're going next?"

My crumpled schedule proves how often I checked it during the diction seminar. "How to Steal a Scene."

"Ooh, grand theft drama. Let's get criminal." She rises, and as always, I feel less cute next to her. She wears shredded camouflage jeans, an A-line black tee, and green wedge sandals that make her tower over me.

I went for a black skirt and gray shirt that says *Let's taco 'bout it.* Plus, my Vans, of course. While Portia and I aren't quite Beauty and the Beast, we're at least Beauty and the Bland.

No wonder Zach walked by me like the less appealing window display.

Ugh, boy paranoia.

"Zach better meet us for this one." Devin takes out his phone and starts texting.

We head to the workshop, and my nervy stomach rolls, wondering if Zach will come. The class is a popular choice, and seats fill up. Portia marches to the empty front row, claiming a chair, Devin at her heels. Despite not wanting to sit in the front, I follow and save a spot next to me. Just in case.

I casually glance at the door, not checking for a cute boy or anything. Only some simple observations and people-watching. Julie Jolley comes into the room with the J-Crew in tow. Gag. And then he walks in. The cute boy I wasn't watching for.

Zach gives a head nod to Devin and makes his way toward us. He doesn't look at me. He doesn't sit by me, choosing the seat on the other side of Devin instead.

He's definitely avoiding me.

Fine then. I declare this The Moment CeCe Stops Being Distracted and Starts Focusing on Drama. But not boy drama. Theater drama. I take out my notebook, the pen in my hand a comfortable reminder I came here to learn.

After a few minutes, the teacher bustles through the door in a flurry of motion. His graying hair runs a little long, not necessarily a style choice. More like he forgot to cut it.

His jeans and button-up shirt are the quintessential professor wardrobe, with glasses perched on the edge of his nose. He carries a large stack of papers, rustling in the force of his fast walk.

"Welcome to class. I'm Mr. Olsen, and we have a lot to cover, so let's jump in." He sets the pages on a podium and takes a deep breath. A smile lights his expression as he scans the crowd.

He calls on people to come up front. Julie Jolley walks up, and her gaze finds me immediately, shifting to note Zach sits by Devin. Her beady little eyes (which are actually big and brown and beautiful) recognize the cold shoulder I'm getting from Zach, and her lips turn in a predatory grin.

Zach better keep his promise.

"Each of you will recite the same two sentences, putting your spin on it." Mr. Olsen instructs the fifteen people and hands them each a paper. Turning to the rest of us, he says, "We'll decide who steals the scene."

He points to the first person in the row, and she steps forward. "I came as soon as I heard. I hope I'm not too late."

The selected people recite the line, trying to make it distinct. Some choose funny. Some choose dramatic. Julie Jolley goes with a British accent. As soon as she speaks, I look at Zach and find him watching me. He lifts an eyebrow, and I respond in kind, the tiniest interaction.

At least he didn't show his dimples.

We vote for our favorite performer by applause, and the resounding winner is *not* Julie Jolley.

Mr. Olsen thanks the participants and sends them back to their seats. "Being a scene-stealer takes a level of charisma, yes. But the best embody a character, maybe even creating an entire backstory to present a fully realized person."

We go through a few more exercises as he teaches us how to relate to our characters. I take a lot of notes, and even Portia and Devin pay attention.

"Before we end, I have one more scene," he says. "I'd like two volunteers."

"We volunteer as tribute," Portia yells, her speedy hand raises, beating everyone else. Mr. Olsen grins at her earnest *pick me* expression.

"You and your seatmate have made googly eyes at each other all class. How about we choose your friends on either side instead?"

I laugh along until Mr. Olsen's words register. Your friends. On either side. Me, and the person avoiding me. I hear Zach say, "sure." He stands and walks to the front. Somehow, despite my nervy stomach making an encore performance, I join him.

Julie Jolley shifts forward in her seat, watching my every move. Waiting for me to mess up and embarrass myself.

Boy drama meets nemesis, playing out in a crowd near you.

Mr. Olsen gives Zach and me a paper and explains the scene. "This is a play called *Stuck*, by Donna Capshaw. We'll be meeting Beck and Allie, who find themselves trapped in the dorm elevator."

He takes a few steps back, leaving us front and center. "I'll be playing the important role of stage direction." This gets a laugh from the crowd. "While Beck and Allie read over their dialogue, we'll review scene-stealing strategies."

Scanning the paper, I meet my character, Allie. She seems pretty relatable, a diligent student striving for success. The last thing she needs or wants is to be stuck with some guy, too cute for his own good. A guy with beautiful eyes, as blue as crystalline water, and a smile that could melt a girl from the inside out. He probably has some hang-up, a reason to be standoffish. Maybe it's her magic? Although Allie doesn't have magic.

I might be personalizing the scene too much.

"And action," Mr. Olsen says, pausing a few seconds before he reads the stage direction. "Beck and Allie are alone in an elevator. It shudders, stopping with a jerk."

Zach mimes pressing the buttons on the panel, and shrugs, crossing his arms.

Beck: "Stuck."

Allie: "I should've taken the stairs."

I glare at Zach and clench my fists. No one forced him to be stuck with me. There's no Cotillion handbook rule about hanging with your best-friend's-make-out-partner's-best-friend.

Beck: "It's no big deal. This happens all the time."

He shakes his head, a "chill out" look in his expression. With the cold shoulder he's given me all morning, that should be easy.

Mr. Olsen reads the next direction. "The power flickers off, leaving the elevator dimly lit by the red glow of emergency lights."

Beck: "Well, *that* doesn't happen all the time."

Allie: "I have to get out of here. I'll be late for class."

Beck: "It's just class. No need to hyperventilate."

He lowers himself to a seated position on the floor. Facing me, the audience to his right, he meets my gaze and waits for my dialogue. And I'd love to say it. But his eyes distract me. A swirling ocean of sparkling blue depths. I look at the paper to refresh my line.

Allie: "Of course, you'd say *it's just class.* You don't care about anything, do you?"

Beck: "Judgey much? You don't even know me."

Allie: "I know all I want to, Beck."

Those words don't ring true about Zach. I want to know him better. I want to know why he's avoiding me. I want to know why my magic tingles every time we touch.

Beck: "Did we hook up or something? Sorry, I usually remember things like that."

Allie: "Are you insane? No."

Beck: "Did I date your roommate?"

He quirks a brow, and I read his humor as easily as I read the script. Zach and Portia...not happening. My amusement shows in the tiniest curve of my lips.

Allie: "Thus far, she's safe from your clutches." The direction tells me to sigh deeply, and turn my back on him, but it doesn't feel authentic. Instead, I laugh. "She dragged me to Alpha Beta Pi last night."

Beck: "Ah. Let me guess. Lip Smackers isn't your game? I do have a vague memory of a sexy librarian slapping me rather than kissing me."

Allie: "I'm not a librarian."

I'm not supposed to sit for a few more lines of dialogue. I do what feels natural. Lowering to the floor, I mirror his position, my knees up, hands by my sides on the ground.

Beck: "You are librarian-esque. And you're wrong about me. I care about a lot of things, Marian."

Allie: "Marian?"

Beck: "Yeah, it's a good librarian name. Since I don't know yours, I figured I'd give you one."

He stretches his left foot out, tapping the top of my Vans. I stay still, leaving our toes touching. It's the smallest contact, insignificant. I tell the butterflies having a party in my stomach to remember that.

Allie: "And Marian is the best you can come up with, Music Man?"

I lean forward and hug my legs. His foot gently brushes over mine. Are cold shoulders and warm toes a thing?

Allie: "Why won't this elevator start?" I say it in the same tone as if the words were, *why have you been acting weird today?*

Beck: "Relax." He skips a few lines of dialogue. The funny insult, the suggestion Allie could talk the elevator into working. "Worrying won't change anything."

I stare into his eyes, allowing myself to get lost in the rhythm of the blues. This is just a play filled with dialogue neither of us wrote. But I can't help the way my heart beats, or the way I sense these words mean something more.

Allie: "You're right. But I'm good at worrying."

I stretch my leg to touch our toes on the other foot. *Calm down, butterfly farm.*

Beck: "How about we start over? I'm Beck."

Scooting forward, he bends his knees and draws closer to me. He reaches out, his hand hovering. The similarity between this moment and when we first met hangs between us. I know how his magic affects me, the way it takes the chill out of my necromancy. Keeping my eyes on his, I stretch out and our palms meet.

Allie: "Allie."

A tingle runs from my fingertips and down my arm, making the butterflies flutter at triple speed. The first time we touched, he pulled away, wiping his hand off as if he handled something dirty. This time we hold. He smiles a dimpled dream drawing a return smile from me.

I'm not exactly sure what just happened, but it was good.

The audience applauds and Mr. Olsen stands next to us,

fanning himself with a sheaf of papers. "Wow. That is how you steal a scene. Well done, both of you."

Zach helps me up, and we take a quick bow. As he releases my hand, the magic fades.

"And with that, class is dismissed." Mr. Olsen sends everyone out. Everyone except Zach and me. "Can I chat with you two a second?"

"Of course," Zach answers, and I nod.

We walk to the podium, and he gives us each a packet. "This is the script for *Stuck*. My Exhibition piece. I was going to have auditions, but after watching you..." He pauses and takes a breath, confirming his decision. "I've marked the last scene in the play. I'd like you to perform it at the end of the week. If you're willing."

My mouth falls open. My eyes bulge. Every unattractive symptom of shock afflicts my body as I turn into an advertisement for surprised elation. *The Exhibition?* The very one I told Portia I would maim and bribe to perform in. Anyone who attends the Young Entertainers Conservatory dreams of taking part in The Exhibition.

This script might as well be gift-wrapped in scholarship money.

Zach shakes Mr. Olsen's hand, thanking him profusely.

"You'll have to find time to rehearse on your own. I'll only be able to work with you twice." He glances at his phone, scanning the calendar. "Let's plan tomorrow evening, after the last class. Be memorized and ready."

My feet hardly touch the ground as we leave. "Can you believe it? We're going to be in The Exhibition."

"I think I'm in shock." Zach shakes his head, and the weirdness from earlier vanishes.

Walking into the hallway, I almost run into Julie Jolley.

Gemma and Jaelynn take their regular positions, flanking her sides.

"You're a liar," Julie accuses.

His forehead crinkles, and he stares at the finger pointed at him. "I am?"

"You have a beautiful smile." Her posse echoes the sentiments, *such a beautiful smile, yeah Zach, beautiful.*

Julie Jolley saw his dimples. I want to throw up.

His shoulders sag, and he blows out a breath. "I never said I had a bad smile. Just that I was self-conscious. There's a big difference." He looks at me, his eyes full of apology.

It's okay, I mouth. He didn't break his promise. Julie Jolley was in the wrong place at the wrong time. As usual. The dimples were meant for me.

I take the opportunity to reinsert myself into the conversation. "Ladies, while I always love our chats, Zach and I have some practicing to do for The Exhibition."

He grabs my hand, the new urgency in our magic swirling. But this time he doesn't let go and instead, leads me from a sputtering Julie. The sound of disbelief echoes behind us, and a smile stretches across my face.

I rendered Julie Jolley speechless. I'm going to be in The Exhibition. And Zach Wren voluntarily held my hand.

This day just leveled up. Way up.

CHAPTER
EIGHT

DRAMA CAMP: DAY TWO – WEDNESDAY
AFTERNOON

Before meeting Devin and Portia in a movement class, I check my texts. Dad wants to know when he can bring the salt. Deciding to call and tell him about The Exhibition, I wave Zach ahead while I chat.

"How can I help you, CeCe?" A distinctly un-dad-like voice answers.

"Hey, Rivera. Is my dad around?" I ask, wondering why his partner answered his phone.

"He's in a meeting, but the real question is have you gotten into any trouble lately?" Ah, Rivera. He always asks me the same thing.

"Not too much, there's still hope, though."

He laughs. "What's up?"

I almost tell him about The Exhibition, but Dad should hear it first. "Will you let him know my lunch is at 12:30? He's dropping something off."

"At New Harmony?" He asks, referencing my high school.

"No, I'm at a drama camp at Tulane. Can you have him meet me in the courtyard?"

"12:30, Tulane, in the courtyard. Got it," he says.

"Thanks, Rivera," I hang up and head into class.

Everyone stands on the stage, legs close together, arms outstretched. The teacher yells, "Grow little tree limbs."

What did I walk in on?

I hop on the stage, adding to the forest, planting my tree between Zach and Portia. My arms sway to an imaginary wind. We shift to imitating beams of light, and then soda pop fizzing. The class is pretty weird, and I'm not sure what I learn about movement. Other than my limbs work.

We're in the middle of playing plastic sacks in the wind when I have the chance to talk to Portia. "Guess what Mr. Olsen wanted?"

"He could tell you and Zach are destined to be together and gave you the 'ship name ZeCe?" She scrunches her nose. "That's not a great name blend."

"At least ZeCe is better than Porvin." My fingers wave in the air. Fly, plastic bag, fly.

"Please don't ever refer to us as Porvin again," she laughs. "What did Mr. Olsen really want?"

"He asked us to be in The Exhibition."

"Shut up! That's amazing," she yells, and a few people look over, including the teacher, who shushes her. Plastic baggery is serious business.

"Right?" I grin so hard that my plastic bag develops a headache. "We're doing the same play, different scene."

"Just so you know, y'all were dynamite." She speaks in a softer tone to avoid another shushing. "Julie Jolley looked like she was going to self-combust from jealousy."

Not only did I render my nemesis speechless, she almost self-combusted. This is a good day.

We finish class, and Portia hooks her arm through Devin's. "I'm starving. I hope it's not sandwiches again."

"We're having bento boxes." Zach seems a little jittery, and as I move next to him, he puts space between us. Weird Zach is back.

"You have the inside track on lunch. What's your secret?" I smile at him, trying to bridge the weirdness gap, wanting the return of the guy who held my hand between classes.

"Zachy's got a connection," Devin says as we walk into the hall.

"Congratulations!" A loud voice startles me, and I look up to see Ms. Black. Her long blond hair hangs loosely, and she's in a flowing red and white striped skirt. Red toenails peek out from the top of her strappy sandals. "I got so excited about The Exhibition news I wanted to see you."

A tender smile lights her face and Zach's expression warms.

"Thanks." He hugs her, patting her on the back a few times before facing us. "This is my connection to the lunch menu. And my mom, Jennifer Wren. Although she goes by her maiden name when she teaches."

Ms. Black is Jennifer Wren. His mom. Freckles dot the bridge of her nose, a perfect copy of Zach's.

Devin gives her a hug. "Hey, Mama Wren."

"Hi, Devin." She seems especially petite between the two guys, barely coming to their shoulders. About the same height as me. "CeCe, congrats to you as well. The Exhibition is a big deal."

"It blew my mind when Mr. Olsen asked us." She knows

who I am? I'm both confused and flattered. "I was in your class yesterday. I loved it."

"Thank you. I noticed you there. Your pink hair is hard to miss." She tilts her head toward my bestie. "You were in my class too, right?"

"Yes, ma'am. I'm Portia Landry."

We chat for a few minutes, and I check my phone, noticing the time. 12:34. "I have to go meet my dad. I'm already late."

"Want me to come with you?" Portia asks.

No one wants a Hangry Portia. That girl needs some food. "No, I'm good. I'll see y'all at lunch. Save me a box."

"I'm glad I got to meet you." Mrs. Wren touches my arm, and a light flow of magic buzzes my skin. Similar to Zach's but not as strong. I've gone my whole life without meeting another person who uses magic, and now two in just as many days. "You know what? I'll walk with you. I was going out anyway."

"Everything okay?" Zach asks.

"Things are fine. Mason needs a little help, and asked me to come by," she says, and he nods in understanding.

After a quick farewell, we go our separate ways. Zach, Portia, and Devin head to the cafeteria, Mrs. Wren and I go outside. I squint in the sunlight, and my eyes adjust to the bright day.

"What kind of magic do you have? I've never felt anything like it."

My shoes screech on the sidewalk, and I stumble before regaining my balance. Obviously, she sensed my ability, but people don't bring it up in polite conversation. Do they?

I bite my lip, weighing what to say. My voice whispers out in a hesitant murmur. "Necromancy."

"Oh, interesting. I've never met a necromancer. That's a rare gift." She looks at me, and a soft smile creases her lips.

"How about you?" I guess we're doing this talking-about-magic-thing.

"Just your run-of-the-mill Voodoo," she says.

"Hmmm." My knowledge of Voodoo is limited to the trinkets and gris-gris bags sold at tourist traps. But there's nothing run-of-the-mill about the humming current of Mrs. Wren's touch.

The sun glints off her blond hair, and a slight breeze lifts the strands. "Does necromancy run in your family?"

"Not that I know of." Dad and I don't have any contact with Mom's side, so her guess is as good as mine.

"How did you discover your gift?" She asks. We round a corner toward the front where Dad's expecting me.

"It's kind of a funny story." Not really. Traumatic and awful describe the event better. I'd rather play it off as a humorous anecdote, though. "My dog died when I was six, and we were going to bury him in the yard. Dad dug the hole, Mom offered a few words, and I sensed I could bring him back. You can imagine their surprise when Max got up and tried to lick my face."

Her lips turn down, and she winces, not buying the funny. "That must have been a hard way to find out. How did your parents take it?"

"Mom left. She...couldn't really handle it." Those first few years nearly crushed me. No one knew how to guide me through figuring out my power.

"I'm so sorry," she says.

"It's okay. I had Dad and his mom, my Mawmaw. She found a book about necromancy. I still use it anytime I have a question."

Mawmaw. My person. She helped raise me. Taught me

all the important things like how to make perfectly fluffy biscuits and to never apologize for my magic. Pain hollows my lungs at the thought of her, grief piercing my heart. How long will the sorrow of losing her steal my breath? I push the image of her smiling face away so I can focus.

"I'm glad they helped you. We all need our special people." She squints against the golden light. "Is that your dad?"

He sits on a bench, his knee bouncing up and down. In his hands I see a big canister of salt and my magic bag. His slacks and suit jacket have the slightly wilted appearance that comes from the humidity.

"That's him." He's a good-looking guy, in my biased opinion. Tall, with a muscular build, dark hair, and green eyes matching mine. I wonder why he's never dated again.

"It was a pleasure talking to you CeCe." Mrs. Wren wraps me in a hug. "I'll see you later."

I sit by Dad on the bench, and the silence stretches between us. Not an uncomfortable quiet; the type bringing to mind long summer nights on the porch swing, listening to the wind and the cicadas. He's a New Orleanian by birth and can't be rushed. He'll talk when he's ready. Until then, I lean my head on his shoulder, and he pats my knee.

After a few minutes, just long enough for my skin to pink, a shade closer to my hair, he clears his throat. "Someone was at the morgue last night. Henry Guillory had been pulled out of the fridge. There was soot on the floor and candles left behind."

"So, it wasn't a dream." I tried to convince myself I imagined the whole thing. A super vivid nightmare brought on by worry and stress. And the loaded nachos I ate for dinner.

"Apparently not."

"Did you find any clues? Hair? Fingerprints?"

"Forensics is looking, but nothing so far. Rivera and I are going back, see if we missed anything." He nods toward the street, and I see a black SUV parked on the curb. Detective Rivera leans against the passenger door, his arms crossed, the sleeves of his blue dress shirt rolled up. With the sun glinting off his reflective glasses, and his casual pose, I sort of see why Portia once called him Detective Sexy Pants.

Dad gets up from the bench, and I do as well, taking the salt and magic bag. A deep grumble rattles in his throat, and he lifts my chin. "What happened to your neck?"

The makeup must have worn off where I covered the bruises. I touch the tender area. "It happened last night. The magic caster grabbed me by the throat."

"You need to come home."

"Dad." After getting into The Exhibition, a Taylor Swift sighting couldn't get me to leave. "That's what the salt is for."

"I don't like it, CeCe."

"I'll pour a protective circle. It'll be fine." I'm not above pleading, and I clasp my hands in prayer. "If things get worse, I'll let you know, but I have to stay. I'm going to be in The Exhibition, which is a huge—I can't overstate that—ginormous opportunity. This could mean scholarship money. You can't—"

"Okay, okay." He holds his hand out like a stop sign, and I follow directions, ceasing the babbles. "We'll see what happens tonight. But call me in the morning."

I start to thank him, and he talks over me. "I also reserve the right to pull you out if it gets dangerous."

"Deal." I'd agree to just about anything to compete in The Exhibition. "Thanks, Daddy."

With the magic bag and salt in my backpack, I walk to the cafeteria. Convincing him to let me stay means my focus needs to center on *Stuck*. That is, if Zach sets his weirdness aside to work on it. Rehearsing under the constant threat of mood changes doesn't fly.

Ugh. I have to talk to him.

Portia calls me over to where the three of them lounge at a table. Devin's arm rests around her, and Zach sits across. Taking a deep breath for courage, I aim for the chair next to Zach and slide in.

"How was Dad?" she asks.

"Good." I offer a distracted reply. In my mind, I practice what to say. *Can I talk to you? We need to chat. Did I do something wrong?*

Portia pushes the bento box closer. "We got you lunch."

"Thanks." I'm not good at confrontation. Or talking through problems. I prefer to ignore an issue and pretend everything is fine. Hence my ongoing passive-aggressive feud with Julie Jolley.

Pushing against the table, Zach gets to his feet. "I wanted to see..." he pauses, clearly making an excuse. "Whatever's next."

"Zach, wait." I stand, blocking his exit. I alternate between *can I talk to you?* and *what's wrong with you?*

"Can I wrong with you?"

All three people gape at me. Portia tips her head, her eyebrows raised.

"Babe." Devin pulls her closer. "For future reference, you don't have to ask. I'm always happy to wrong with you."

I drop to my seat, slapping my forehead. I should have just pretended everything was okay.

DRAMA CAMP: DAY TWO – WEDNESDAY
AFTERNOON (STILL)

My words betrayed me, and I shovel in food to keep my mouth busy. Devin laughs, his finger pointed at me. Portia bites her lip to keep quiet. Zach sits back down, so I accomplished something. Sort of. He watches me in all my awkward glory. My eyes remain on the bento box, white rice suddenly fascinating, and I continue to eat despite my stomach tying in knots.

"Pinky, you're hilarious! Does that line usually work for you?" Devin slaps his knee and wipes the moisture from his eyes.

Come on. It wasn't THAT funny.

Zach leans closer and coughs to cover his laughter. "Do you want to talk alone?"

I'd like to be alone right now, just me, replaying what I said over and over as a reminder I shouldn't interact with others when I'm stressed. But he means talking to him. And words and I are fighting.

"Nope. I'm good." I push a piece of carrot around, unable to get it on my fork.

"I'm pretty sure you wanted to ask me something." He smiles, fun and flirty Zach returning in force.

"We'll let you talk." Portia grabs Devin's arm, pulling him with her.

"What? No! I want to listen," he protests.

My thoughts are similar to his. But more like, *What? No! You need to protect me from being awkward.* "You can stay."

"Devin," Portia has the best warning voice, a touch of sassy mixed with drill sergeant. "We're leaving."

"Don't go. I'm done eating." I beg her with my eyes.

She ignores my pleading look and gives me a hug. "Drama camp double couple," she whispers in my ear. Seriously, shrimp on grits.

Her hips sway as she struts out of the cafeteria, and I watch her leave.

"So...CeCe," Zach says. "Was there something you wanted to say?"

First, I covered his mouth. Then, I asked him to wrong with me. What will come next? My conversation skills can't be trusted. But I need to resolve the boy drama. The Exhibition depends on it.

"Give me your number," I say quickly, tugging at my hair to hide behind the strands.

"What?"

"Your phone number." I set my cell on the table and unlock it, nudging it towards him. "I'll text you."

He stays still, making no move to pick it up. "I'm right here and you're going to text me?"

Well, when he says it like that, it sounds silly. "Absolutely."

Shaking his head, he laughs and grabs my phone. "Or we could write letters and mail them."

He passes my cell back with a new contact filled in. First name, Zach. Last name, Stuck.

Stuck. As in the play? Or that's how he feels?

Boy drama sucks.

I type, erase. Type again until I settle on what I want to say.

> ME: You've been weird, and we have The Exhibition coming. Are you trying to avoid me?

I hit send and immediately want to take it back. Someone needs to invent the do-over button for texting.

His phone buzzes, and he smirks as he reads.

Have I overreacted? He behaved strangely for half a day, and maybe it was a bad morning. But the evasion was there in his eyes.

Something is off. I feel it in my gut.

His thumbs move across the screen, and I clutch my phone. No need for nerves. It's only the future of our Exhibition performance hanging in the balance.

> ZACH: I was trying to dodge u. Pressure's on since our friends are dating.

His candor surprises me. I'm not sure what I expected, but not the truth. I start typing out a response, and he laughs.

"We can talk. Face to face."

"I'm already halfway through. Might as well finish." Besides, I express myself better in emoji.

> ME: Can we agree to be friends? No
> weirdness or guessing games.

I hit send and look up to find his deep blue eyes filled with humor. It takes him an excruciating amount of time to read the text. My life flashes before my eyes, and I almost solve global warming before he finally speaks.

"I really like your pink hair."

Wait, what? I told him we should be friends, and now he likes my hair? "Thanks. I, uh, like your hair too."

He smiles and runs a hand through his self-consciously. "And you make me laugh. A lot."

"I'm...sorry?" It comes out like a question because I have no idea where this is going.

"Laughter is a good thing. So, don't apologize." He shifts, and his leg brushes against mine. Some very un-friend-like feelings squirm in my chest. "You're so talented and sharing a stage with you felt magnetic."

Settle down, Heart. Don't get ahead of yourself.

"Thank you," I manage to say through the palpitations beating in my chest.

"You're welcome. The point is," he continues, leaning forward. "I like you. And it would be easy to start dating. Too easy."

Agree to agree. Wait, is that Optimism joining the conversation? *Get outta here, Optimism. There's a 'but' coming.*

"But..."

Called it.

"We can't date for two reasons. One, it's ridiculous to hook up at drama camp." He scrunches his nose, the freckles bunching adorably.

"I told Portia the same thing. But drama camp makes the heart grow fonder."

"Exactly." His dimples peek at me.

Point one is solid. "I acknowledge dating and drama camp don't go together."

I stick out my hand, and we shake, a business deal in the making. His warm touch thrums like the magic remembers me. The familiarity takes us both by surprise, and time ceases to exist to our tangled fingers. I try to think of something to say. Instead, I let his magic zip through my veins, telling Heart and Optimism to RSVP because we're having a party. A platonic, we-agreed-to-just-be-friends kind of a party, of course.

He draws away, and my hand falls in my lap, a useless thing. For a moment, I thought my hand was made to hold his. I flex my fingers a few times to get the blood pumping and remember it's a very handy (*ha ha, pun intended*) limb to have around.

"And that's the other thing."

A gut boulder forms, anxiety building at his words. "I have a compelling handshake?"

"You have magic." He turns away, folding his arms on the table. "I don't use it. And I definitely wouldn't date anyone with it."

The wind knocks out of me, and the gut boulder lodges in my solar plexus. My necromancy scares people. It keeps me emotionally isolated. My mom left because of it. *Your magic is too much,* she said.

But Zach has magic. If anyone grasps living on this lonely island, I assumed it would be him.

"I understand. It isn't for everyone."

"It's dangerous," he says, his fists clenching.

Dangerous? My experiences involve conversations with

dead people. Scary, maybe. Unusual, certainly. "I wouldn't say dangerous."

"Trust me. It is." His shoulders stoop, and he stares at the table. Dude's got deep trauma about the whole magic thing.

"We can still be friends, though, right?"

"CeCe, that's why I'm telling you. I want to be friends." The hardness leaves his expression, and a sparkle lights his eyes. "And no one, especially Julie Jolley, needs to know what's going on. Okay?"

"Okay. No cliché drama camp couple for us." I'll pretend his aversion to magic doesn't bother me because, yes, my acting skills are legit. "And we won't touch, so we keep our magic to ourselves."

He laughs, the sound echoing in the empty cafeteria. "Have you read the scene for *Stuck* yet?"

"No." Between movement class and meeting with Dad, I haven't pulled the pages from my backpack. "Why?"

"Let me know when you do." He picks up my empty bento box and throws it in the garbage. "We can catch the last few minutes of the workshop if you're interested."

"Sure. Let's learn how to connect with a co-star." The class held no interest to me before lunch. Now, I wish I'd gone.

The script sits in my bag, an inferno on my back fueling my curiosity. Why was he so amused? It must mean we have to touch again. Maybe hold hands, or even hug.

I'm not sure how I feel about that.

The pull between us quietly thrums, and his magic tries to draw me in. But what he said echoes in my head. He doesn't date anyone with magic.

I decide I don't find him attractive anymore.

Yep, just like that. His eyes are simply blue. Not the

color of Lake Pontchartrain on a perfect day, where the water appears translucent under the shimmering sunlight. And his hair is only hair. Not the perfect length, the strands always falling into place. And his dimples are tiny dents, not a masterpiece carved by Michelangelo to be adored by generations of fawning fangirls.

In fact, I hardly even realize he walks next to me, his tall, muscular frame easy to dismiss.

We attend the end of the connect with a co-star workshop, followed by a music theory class. For the first time at camp, I focus on music. Mr. Bellamy talks about chords and scales, asking for a few volunteers to come up and help demonstrate. My eyes fasten on an acoustic guitar, the pale wood highlighted by a cerulean neck and bridge, the color almost an exact match to Zach's eyes. Or ocean waves. I totally mean ocean waves.

It's a beautiful instrument, and I raise my hand, happy to strum out a few notes. I blink in surprise when I'm not the one called, but Zach makes his way to the stage. He picks up the guitar, pulling the strap over his head, and grabs a pick from a bowl. Holding my breath, I wait for him to play. Wait to see how his fingers move over the strings.

The notes ring out and show his obvious skill. The natural way he strums and tips his head slightly to the right mesmerizes me. Other volunteers join in, one on the piano, and one on the drums, and Mr. Bellamy directs the pick-up band to teach a lesson about rhythm.

"Did you know he plays?" Portia asks.

I shake my head. No. No, I didn't.

Dragging my attention from him (pffft, totally not drooling over his guitar skills), I distract myself by getting out the script for *Stuck*. I flip through and find the section Mr. Olsen marked. It's a few pages in length, and as I read, my imagination brings Allie to life. Her words and gestures connect, and I see myself becoming the character. The excitement grows. I'm going to perform this piece for The Exhibition.

And then I read the last page. Double take. Read again.

My head thumps, a pulse starting somewhere in my skull and traveling through my body. The drummer on stage has nothing on the pounding in my brain. I check it again, just to make sure I read it correctly the last three times.

Beck: "It's too late. I'm already stuck."

Beck pulls Allie close and kisses her.

Kisses her.

Zach is going to kiss me.

I snap the script shut and look at the stage. Zach must sense my gaze because he lifts his eyes, meeting mine. And then he does the absolute worst thing. He smiles. A full dimple-bearing blessing that automatically enrolls me in the fawning fangirl club.

May the drama camp gods have mercy on my soul.

CHAPTER
TEN

DRAMA CAMP: DAY TWO – WEDNESDAY NIGHT

Ancestor Night is a longstanding tradition of Tulane's Young Entertainers Conservatory, passed down from generations of drama camp participants. Famous actors and actresses attended during their time at camp. Musicians, directors, and anyone accomplished have taken part in the hoopla. Rumor has it, if you don't participate in Ancestor Night, you have no chance of winning any of the competitions during the week.

It's stupid.

People enact a *fake* séance to ask the ghosts of performers past for a blessing on their talents. If acquiring A-list talent was as easy as talking to the dead, I'd be Meryl Streep by now.

The rules are simple: sneak out of the dorm (although the teachers know and don't try to stop it, so "sneak" is generous), gather in a group, pick an ancestor, and perform the séance.

Portia and I dress appropriately in our "espionage special." I have on yoga pants and a shirt, both black, and a black backpack slung over my shoulders. She dressed similarly, but her shirt sparkles with glitter. I didn't even know black could bling.

We meet the boys outside, and they wear the same thing they did this morning, just jeans and t-shirts, not even bothering to play along.

Killjoys.

Hordes of people slink around, finding quiet spaces to séance. We hang back and duck under a cover of trees. A slight breeze rustles the branches and masks the ambient sound, giving us an illusion of privacy. Devin slings an arm around Portia's shoulders, kissing her on the cheek. I turn to Zach, giving him a half wave, half high-five attempt, which leaves me awkwardly dropping my hands and shoving them in my pockets. Except my yoga pants have no pockets.

Why me?

"I have an idea," Devin says.

Zach leans against the brick wall of the building, crossing his arms. "Those words usually get us in trouble."

I have a friend like that too.

"What's the idea?" Portia asks, a mischievous eyebrow raised. Sometimes I think she likes getting into trouble.

Devin's eyes dart around, before he drops his voice to a whisper. "Let's spend ancestor night with actual ancestors. I have a family tomb at Lafayette Cemetery."

"Lafayette's too far. It'll take an hour to walk there." I know my graveyards. Far better than most.

He slips a set of keys from his pocket. "I drove to drama camp."

"I like the way your brain works, Devin Gough." Portia hugs him tighter.

"That's not all you like about me." He winks as he leads us toward the parking lot.

Zach leans close to me, speaking in a hushed tone. "Why are we doing this?"

"Because we both have an eccentric yet loveable best friend?" I glance at his upturned lips, and warmth heats my cheeks. Are we really going to kiss on Saturday? My kissing experience is limited. Small encounters reserved for party games and dares. Nothing serious. And nothing with a cute boy who threatens to make my insides fuzzy.

"Did you read the script for *Stuck*?" He asks, and my face lights up like a neon billboard advertising my thoughts.

"Hey, Dimples!" The loud greeting stalls my steps as I recognize the voice.

Julie Jolley.

Did she really just call Zach Dimples? So gross. Gemma stands next to her, the J-Crew only two-thirds strong.

"Have we met?" Devin asks, stopping to converse with the intruders. "Obviously, you know Zach."

Yeah. His dimples are hard to miss.

"Julie Jolley." She points to her sidekick. "And Gemma."

"Where's Jaelynn?" I try to purge her label for Zach from my mind. Who does she think she is? The queen of cringey nicknames?

"Sick." She barely glances my way before ogling Zach. "Can we join you? The more the merrier for Ancestor Night. Am I right?"

"You want to come?" Zach sounds genuinely confused. And rightfully so. Julie wouldn't willingly join me for anything.

"We're actually driving somewhere. No extra room.

Sorry," Portia says, adding another notch on the gratitude post.

"I drive an old Suburban. Plenty of room." Devin throws my gratitude on the ground and stomps it to pieces. He's dead to me. "As long as y'all aren't afraid of a more *authentic* experience."

He misses my heated glare, the panicked headshaking from Portia, and the evil spark in Julie's eyes. We might as well stop for a hitchhiker with bloody clothes or pick up a stranded clown.

"I'm an actress," she says with a hint of offense. "Authentic is my middle name."

And all this time I thought it was Satan.

It takes less than three seconds to figure out Julie's motive for tagging along. She and Gemma surround Zach, each of them linking an arm with him. I follow behind. Nothing escapes her jealousy.

Portia whispers in Devin's ear, and floating pieces of his reply make their way to me. *It's fine. It'll be fun.* Zach glances over his shoulder, his eyes scrunched in apology. I step on the back of Julie's shoe, and the purple sneaker pops off her heel.

"Sorry." Yep, not sorry.

She tightens her grip on Zach's arm, ignoring me, and stutter-walks in an awkward shuffle, step, shuffle, step until the shoe sinks back on her foot. "Your smile is beautiful. You don't mind if I call you, Dimples, right?"

"I mind." He attempts to pull away. It encourages Julie to dig her claws in and leave him the option of linked arms or amputation.

"You're so funny," she laughs, and the moonlight glints on her nose ring like a sparkling wink.

Devin unlocks the car, and Zach rushes to open the door.

"Why don't you two ladies go in the back? You're both small and can easily fit." He layers on the southern boy charm. Mawmaw would approve.

Julie wants to argue but ends up getting into the back. Gemma climbs in and sits next to her. Which leaves the middle seat open for Zach and me. I win this round.

The radio plays, and the duet *Meant to Be* blasts through the speakers. Devin and Portia start singing at the same time, wearing wide smiles as they put on an impromptu concert. She sounds great, her rich tone adding depth to the song. And Devin is a real surprise. His voice blends with hers and creates a perfect harmony to her melody.

It's too cute. The synchronized singing. The way their eyes adore each other. Their fingers twining over the console. Even a good friend might be jealous over the carefree, non-magical ease of their relationship. Luckily, I'm a best friend.

"We should do a duet on Friday," Devin says when the song ends.

"I'm already doing a duet with CeCe." She glances at me and holds a fist in the air. "Girl power."

"Zach and I are signed up too." He shrugs his shoulders, making no move to hold up a fist and shout, *boy power.* "I wonder if you can do more than one?"

"You can sing as many as you want, but you can only compete with one." Julie offers from the back.

"Then let's do it. We can each compete with our originals and then sign up to perform together." He lifts their linked hands, kissing her fingers.

"I'd love to." Her shoulders squee, and she scoots as close to him as the bucket seats allow.

After a wonderful car ride, where Devin and Portia kiss at every traffic light and stop sign, we arrive at Lafayette Cemetery. Huge oak trees tower above, the trunks and roots large enough they invade the sidewalk. Pale plaster walls surround the graveyard and glow in the moonlight. The closed wrought iron gate blocks our entrance, the words *LAFAYETTE CEMETERY NO 1* arched above. I climb out of the Suburban and grab my backpack, slinging it over my shoulders.

"Why are we here?" Gemma hugs herself, and her eyes flit in every direction.

"Authenticity." Devin's bright smile glimmers in the twilight.

He gives Portia a boost, and she pulls herself over the gate. With a little teamwork, we all make it inside.

The cemetery is laid out like a mini city. Paved sidewalks cover the ground and mausoleums stand along the path like rows of tiny houses. Tree roots poke through the dirt and cement. The whispering leaves above preen in this neighborhood of the dead. Our cell phone flashlights bathe the darkness in bursts of white, and we follow Devin to his family tomb.

Hanging back, I trail my fingers along the family plaques lining the plaster-sealed stone. I come to Lafayette Cemetery often and speak to the residents. In New Orleans, bodies aren't buried, but laid to rest in tombs. The corpse stays inside their "home," waiting a year and a day for the Louisiana heat to scorch it to dust, before it's shoveled below ground. The spirit may linger, but the body is gone.

I come across a family plaque that reads Guillory. The engraved stone front lists name after name of the deceased, the family line dating back to the early 1800s. I think of Dad's latest case, Henry Guillory, and the strange dream visit to the morgue. This isn't his tomb, but I picture him as The Caster showed him to me. The red-tipped pins poked in his body, his chest, and in his eyes.

Touching my neck, I run my fingers along the still-tender bruises. Clouds roll in and cover the moon, diluting the luminous light. A chill rises on my skin, and I whip around, checking behind me to see an empty walkway. In all my years visiting graveyards and morgues, I have never been spooked.

Until now.

It's not the old tombs or the memories of the departed, but something else. An eerie foreboding whispering haunting words against my skin.

I arrive last to the cement structure at the edge of the sidewalk. The Gough tomb. Behind us are the wall vaults, stacked chambers built into the plaster. They have a similar setup to the morgue, but instead of metal tables gliding out, these are rows of stone.

A scraping noise echoes from the direction of the vaults, interrupting the hushed atmosphere. Goosebumps raise on my arms even as I excuse the sound. *Probably tree branches.* The wind picks up, blowing fallen leaves across the walking path, and the dread in my gut tightens.

Julie motions for us to sit, and against my better judgment, I join the séance. She faces the Gough tomb, her back to the wall vaults, with me directly across from her. Portia sits on my left, Zach to my right. Gemma and Devin sit to the right and left of Julie, completing our lopsided circle. My gaze volleys from Julie "evil personified" Jolley and the wall, trying to place the intermittent scraping behind her.

"Beloved ancestors." She adopts a British accent and projects her voice. "We humble attendees of drama camp have come to seek your blessing." I deserve an award for holding back my eyeroll. Participating in this fake ritual is silly when a real panic screams in my head to *get out!*

She tells us to hold hands, and as Zach's fingers wind with mine, our magic ignites. The cold of my necromancy mixes with the heat from his power. Everything magnifies, the touch of his skin, the smell of the earth. More than that, I clearly hear the abrasive grinding coming from *inside* the wall vaults.

His blue eyes go wide, and he swings his head toward me. He stays silent, but his expression asks if I can hear it.

Yep. I can.

"Ancestors, bless us with your talent." Julie raises her chin to the sky.

"Ancestors, bless us with your talent." Gemma's voice rings out, her exaggerated accent a poor copy of Julie's.

The scratching grows louder. *Maybe rats?* But that thought vanishes as a thick magic oozes in, seeping over my body like a dense fog. The last time I felt this oily sensation, I ended up spirit-kidnapped in a morgue. But it's here at Lafayette. Now.

Someone is using dirty magic.

It's Zach's turn in the fake seance. He stays quiet, releasing my hand to stand and stare at the wall vaults. From his pocket, he pulls out a gris-gris bag and rubs it between his fingers. I shouldn't be surprised by the token of protection because his mom practices Voodoo. Believers usually carry a talisman. But with his attitude of *I don't do magic,* I assumed he wouldn't.

His nerves have me on edge, and I get to my feet.

"Zach," Gemma glances over her shoulder, not seeing what keeps our attention. "You have to ask the ancestors for a blessing."

A thunderous crack splits the night as freshly mortared

bricks explode outward from the vaults. A horrible smell like rotten eggs hits my nose, and a half-decomposed arm creeps from the now gaping hole. Julie turns, her big, brown eyes bulging. The reaching hand grabs her hair, fleshy fingers clutching a section of her perfectly straightened brown locks. Her face pales, her shrill cry ringing out. Gemma scrambles, crab-walking to put distance between herself and the tomb. Devin lifts Portia in his arms and moves several feet away. I take short, panting breaths, horrified by the body attempting to crawl from the tomb.

Kneeling next to Julie, Zach tries to pull her from the rotting hand.

"Don't touch it," I yell, and use the bottom of my shirt to pry the fingers from Julie's hair. In our backward escape, we almost trip over Gemma, who curls on the ground.

"Hey, are you okay?" I ask.

"What's happening?" Fat tears roll from Gemma's eyes.

"It's going to be okay." My encouraging smile fades as an awareness trickles into my mind. I straighten and look around. A sludgy power makes the air heavy, and a whisper speaks to me.

CeCe Leblanc, I need your magic.

It's The Caster from the morgue.

Their power is cold like mine, but the similarities end there. Where my magic is clean, like swimming in freshwater, this dirty magic slumps on the bottom of a filthy pond, waxy silt leaving everything greasy.

A piercing crack thunders from the wall vaults, piles of stone and brick crumbling as more bodies fight their way from the tombs. The smell of decaying flesh hits the back of my throat and makes me gag. A body falls in a heap from the uppermost level, splatting on the pavement, and it stretches out a hand, the clacking fingers a unique music of the dead, the melody a warning, the harmony a cry of decomposing sound.

Fear threatens to control my actions, and I close my eyes, taking a deep breath. I won't allow the bodies to be defiled when I can do something to stop it. The Caster might have caught me off guard in the morgue, but I'm not powerless.

Clenching my fingers, I stand and let my necromancy build. The spirits of the dead speak to me, a collection of voices flashing through my consciousness, vying for my attention. I use that connection to push back, allowing Zach to usher Gemma and Julie further from the tomb.

He strides over to Devin and points to the others. "Get them to the Suburban."

"I'm not leaving without CeCe." Portia's panicked breath huffs out. I appreciate her fierce loyalty in the face of zombies, but I can't concentrate until I know she's safe.

"I'll be fine. Just go." I don't have breath to waste arguing. Energy pulses from me as I push my power at the wall vault, slowing the dozen or so corpses. I've never used necromancy like this before, and I feel the magic slipping.

"Run!" Zach yells, and Devin springs into action, herding Portia, Gemma, and an ashen Julie to the edge of the graveyard. He makes quick work boosting the girls over the gate before hopping to the top.

"Come on," he shouts from his perch.

"Get out of here. I'll meet you at the dorms." Zach's grip remains locked on the gris-gris bag.

"What about Pinky?" Devin points at me, and despite the seriousness of holding back a zombie horde, I wonder if he knows my actual name.

"I'm staying with Zach," I yell.

Devin disappears over the gate, and Zach moves to stand by me. "This isn't funny." His jaw clenches, accusation sizzling in his expression. "You have to stop."

CHAPTER
ELEVEN

DRAMA CAMP: DAY TWO – WEDNESDAY, LATE

"I know you don't like Julie Jolley, but this is extreme." Zach's eyes stay on the zombies as his voice lashes at me.

Is he serious? No doubt, the terror on Julie's face when the hand grabbed her will replay in my fondest memories, but I would never use my magic to hurt anyone.

And this magic isn't even necromancy. These are animated bones. No connection between the body and spirit. The Caster managed to make zombie puppets, nothing more. Fifteen corpses in all shamble from their small, cement tombs. Loose skin sloughs off, and the broken bits attempt to stay together against the strain of mobilizing.

"I didn't raise them. I'm keeping them back." I try not to be offended by his accusation. But...

I'm offended.

"Well, I didn't do it. And nobody else is here." He grits

his teeth and the gris-gris bag with equal enthusiasm. "Plus, I felt black magic in you. I know you're using it."

"Wait. What?" The oily residue. Being spirit kidnapped. The red-tipped pins and circle of ash. It could definitely be black magic. "You felt it in me?"

"Yeah." He runs a hand through his hair. "I tried to ignore it, to tell myself it didn't matter. But it does. I can't be around someone who uses it."

"Well, I don't." How is it even possible that he felt black magic in me? When Zach touched my arm this morning, I knew something was different. *What did The Caster do?*

My power slips, and I lose my grip slowing the dead.

Two corpses get to their feet. Zach and I both back away quickly, outpacing the zombies' slow shuffle.

"We have to get out of here," he says.

"I can't leave them out like this. But I don't have anything to help them." Then I remember stuffing the salt and necromancy gear in my backpack after Dad visited. I love that man. "Actually, I do. Keep an eye on the walkers and let me know if they get too close."

Dropping to one knee, I sling off my backpack and search the contents. The heavy canister sits at the bottom.

"Do you always carry salt?"

"Not usually. Weird things have been happening. There's a Caster, who apparently uses black magic, and knows I'm a necromancer. It's a long story." I shake my head and pour a large salt circle, encompassing us both. The white grains pile on the ground, a solid wall of protection against the dead; a necessary protection to keep their touch away.

"You're a necromancer?" he asks, a note of surprise in his voice.

"Yes. I can raise the dead. But this isn't necromancy.

More like an animation spell. This is The Caster's work."

"I can feel the black magic." Stuffing the crumpled gris-gris bag in his pocket, he hovers at the far edge of the circle. "I'm sorry for assuming it was you, but when the hand broke the plaster—"

"It freaked me out too." From my magic bag, I pull out a candle, lighting the wick. The tiny flame glows, filling the protective circle with yellow light. I sit cross-legged and wait for enough melted wax to make a moon token while the zombies slowly draw closer. Their shuffling steps shush along the ground. The putrid, decaying odor worms in my nostrils. My heart races as the candle heats. "Julie's lucky it only grabbed her hair and didn't touch skin."

Zach lowers to sit next to me. "Why?"

"Once, I raised a murdered homeless guy, and he touched my dad," I tell him, pouring the scarce melted wax into my palm. I barely have enough to shape a small moon token. "Dad was haunted for two days, wandering around the house as the dead guy's life blasted him. Then he woke up, back to normal."

A corpse slams against the protective circle, and I jump, fumbling the token. It almost bounces from the circle, but I clutch it in my fist. Skeletal zombie fingers twitch against the restraint of the magical wall. And worse than that, I feel The Caster's power swirling near, oozing around the salt. The thick and stewy magic pushes at the bounds, the press a building pressure in my head.

I rifle at the bottom of my bag, finding my pen knife. It has an infinity symbol on the black titanium blade and the words *Death is good for the soul* engraved on the handle. Steadying my breath, I poke my finger, allowing the blood to pool, and I drip it into the consecrated dirt of the graveyard.

A second corpse hits, and I vibrate like a metal tuning fork. Because of my connection to the wall, everything happening outside reflects a sensation back to me. The zombie fingers claw the invisible barrier, and it prickles up my spine, a full chill shaking my body.

"I'm going to call my mom. She'll help." His voice rises, and he keeps a wary eye on the dead.

"Or *you* could help."

"I can't. I mean, I won't." He tips his head, staring at the massive oaks blanketing the sky. "But my mom can come. We're surrounded by black magic and bodies. CeCe, we need backup."

"No, it's okay. I can do this. Death is kind of my thing." Scooping the blood and dirt off the ground, I put the mixture in the candle flame, turning the glow blue.

Power fills me. I close my eyes and direct the cold, moving it through my body as the death magic builds. I crackle with energy, the moon in my palm, my blood in the flame, and the graveyard soil grounding the magic.

Images of the dead collide, their lives jostling to the forefront of my mind. I push aside the dreams cut short, the missed family, and lost opportunities. With eyes tightly closed, I rise to my feet, and take control of the cemetery.

"Stop," I say, and the two zombies battling against the salt circle freeze. Their bony hands literally grind to a halt. Beyond the circle, the zombies pause, some in mid-stride, others falling apart, all ceasing movement at my command.

The greasy dregs of black magic vanish. The Caster's presence leaves, the dirty power disappearing like smoke fading in the air. I want to chase after; follow the dwindling trail and find out who's doing this.

But I'm left to clean up the mess.

Sorting the dead is tricky, especially with so many. The

eternal resting place is a sacred thing. Even though their spirits weren't raised with their bodies, whatever happens to the physical remains affects the soul. I need to arrange the right bodies in the correct family tombs.

The magic flows, a rushing stream of ice water in my blood, and I focus on the corpses. One-by-one, I put all the pieces together. Skin repairs, un-sloughing off, if there's such a thing. Bones reattach.

Clouds shift across the sky, pale light reflecting in the cemetery again. The moon token presses heavily in my hand. A runoff of my power rests in the wax and makes my arm shake under the hefty burden. The more I work, the more my muscles tire, and I worry about dropping the token. And then Zach is there to steady my elbow. His magic warms me from the inside and melts the ice, which confuses the dead. They slow and stall, cars running out of gas, or in this case, bodies running out of magic.

"Not your bare hands." It takes effort to speak, my lungs tight.

The support vanishes and I struggle again. I clench my jaw to fight the trembling. My palm sweats, the wax token slipping in my fingers. It must weigh a million pounds by now. I can't continue to hold it.

Zach returns, using my backpack to shield his bare hands and balance my arm. He might not be willing to use magic, but at least he's still here.

It doesn't take much longer to clean up the zombies. Bricks and stone litter the front of the wall vault, but at least the bodies are sorted.

Using my necromancy sapped every ounce of energy, and I'm exhausted. I wearily blow out the candle, gather my supplies, and toss the heavy moon token into my magic bag with the salt canister and the cooled candle.

"What happens to the..." Zach connects his finger and thumb at the tips, making a circle. "Wax thing?"

"I have to melt it and release the buildup of magic." I wrestle my backpack off the ground.

Without asking, he takes it from me and slings it on. "Wow. Feels like I'm giving a piggyback to a small pony."

I laugh and hobble to the edge of the graveyard. Zach has to help me over the gate. I grip the top, and after a boost from him, I strategically fall on the other side. By the time I meet the ground, my necro-shivers start. Ice engulfs me, and my body shakes.

"Are you okay?" He tilts his head, leaning closer. "Are you cold?"

"Y-y-y-y-y." That's pretty much all I can manage with chattering teeth.

He lifts his hand, testing the temperature. "Really?"

"N-n-n-n-n." I try to tell him necromancy is cold. Instead, I sound sarcastic, like, *no, I'm not* really *cold even though I'm shivering hard enough to drill a hole in the sidewalk.*

"C'mere." He drops the backpack and steps forward, opening his arms.

I should act like I don't want or need his warmth, especially after the crappy accusation he threw down—as if I'd waste good magic on Julie Jolley. Instead, I fully plow into him like LSU's entire offensive line. He stumbles back a step, nearly tripping over my bag he dropped. A chuckle sounds in his chest, which I can hear because my ear presses tightly against him in my attempt to absorb his warmth. And he is warm. Like a summer sunset. My personal human toaster.

His arms fold around me, and everywhere he touches heats up. His magic is lava, liquid fire spreading inside me. My interior ice melts, and his hands move to my back, rubbing out the trembling. I close my eyes and enjoy the sensation. More than I should.

Oh no. Optimism, you need to get outta here. Zach and I have an agreement to be just friends.

But it's okay for friends to revel in the contentment of a platonic hug. Right? This embrace may make cameo appearances in thoughts and daydreams for months to come.

"Are you okay?" His fingers brush small, slow circles. A hypnotic rhythm reminding me of Dad's record player at home. Spinning around and around, a consistent and constant motion.

At some point, I wrap my arms around Zach to clench his shirt. The chill alleviates, and I begin to notice other things. Like the way he smells, a soft, subtle scent. Possibly soap and a mild cologne, clean with a hint of citrus. His breath whispers a path from my ear to my neck, leaving behind a puff of warmth and cinnamon. The worn cotton of his tee bunches under my cheek, and I brush against the smooth fabric.

"CeCe?"

My name hangs in the air, and I stop moving, hoping he didn't recognize the way I nuzzled him like a cat needing affection. I also neglected to pay attention to anything he said. "Did you ask me something?"

"Do you always get this cold when you use magic?" His tone tells me he noticed the cat preening.

"Portia calls them necro-shivers." I weigh the merits of another nuzzle vs. backing away. Retreat wins out, and I put space between us, shoving my hands in my pockets.

Except these yoga pants STILL don't have pockets. Ugh.

Which, of course, his dimples notice because they wink at me. "I'll call my mom and ask for a ride."

"Sure. Whatever. I mean, I could call, you know, someone too...." I can't even talk. Why am I such an awkward human?

The smile remains on his lips as he makes the call. I only hear his side of the conversation, which is:

"Hey Mom, sorry it's late." He pauses, his eyes scrunching at the corners. "Nope." Another pause. "No ma'am. Absolutely not." (Insert laugh here).

"I actually need you to pick me up. Well, me and..." he glances at me, his blue eyes taking on the darker shades of the night, and I wonder for the millionth time why he has to be so attractive. "Me and CeCe." (Introducing a dimpled pause here). "Yes, THAT CeCe, as if you know any others." (Insert eye roll here).

"I'll tell you about it later, but can you grab us at Lafayette One?" He nods at whatever she says. "Yeah, you too. Bye."

"So, how's Mom?" I ask.

"She's on her way. Well, once she changes out of her pajamas." He puts his phone in his pocket, because his pants have functional pockets, and leans against a tree trunk. "CeCe, I'm sorry."

Mirroring his pose, I lean on the trunk of the next tree over and cross my arms. "Would that be an apology for thinking I use black magic? Or accusing me of sending zombies to attack Julie Jolley?"

"Both, actually."

I tap my lips, mulling it over. But who am I kidding? Life's too short to hold a grudge against a cute boy. Not to mention, he seems to know a lot about magic, and I have questions. "Apology accepted. What can you tell me about black magic?"

"It's bad. Worse than bad." Zach runs a hand through

his hair and blows out a breath, his words hesitant. "I have some personal experience with it."

"Oh." I waver on asking for more info. How personal are we talking? "That sounds interesting."

He moves closer, a breath away, where no trees stand between us, just Zach and CeCe leaning on the same tree. "If we're going to be Beck and Allie and get to the last page of the script...." *The last page being the K-I-S-S-I-N-G.* "You should understand where I'm coming from. With magic."

My blushing cheeks match my cherry-dipped-rose-gold hair. "Fair enough."

"My mom does Voodoo, but my dad's genetic line has life magic."

Life magic. No wonder his touch warms me. Death magic, by nature, is cold, and it would make sense for the opposite to be true.

"I've heard of it." In passing, as I read my necromancy book. "Doesn't it have something to do with the sun?"

"Yeah, every magic requires power from a source. The abilities of life magic come from the sun. Voodoo draws energy from ancestors."

"Necromancy uses the moon." I glance at my backpack on the ground, where a very heavy moon token proves the point.

"That's what makes black magic different. You're not born with it, it's a learned magic, and there's no natural source to draw from. Instead, it's fed by sacrifice. There's always a price to pay." His muscles clench tighter as he talks. "It's selfish, and the more you use it, the more you want to. Like an addiction."

Suddenly I know his *personal experience* means he's used it. "What happened?"

He sighs and rolls his shoulders to loosen the tension.

"Life magic usually passes down, like a strong genetic trait, and my parents assumed I'd get it. But not only did I inherit it, I got the Voodoo line as well. You probably know it's super rare for both lines to pass down."

I had no idea. My knowledge of inherited magic is pretty much nonexistent. I don't even know where my necromancy came from. "So, you're extra powerful?"

"Something like that." He averts his gaze, staring at the cracked sidewalk. "When my brother, Mason, was born, my parents assumed he'd be just as 'gifted.'" He air-quotes the word, saying it with a grimace. "He ended up with no magic."

Mason. His brother. Mrs. Wren left Tulane earlier to help him. "Were your parents disappointed?"

"They were fine, but as we got older, Mason wanted magic of his own, and it affected our relationship. I studied darker and darker magic, searching for ways to give him some of my ability."

"Black magic."

"Yeah." A sheen of pain glosses his tired eyes. "I tried a spell to strip magic from me and put it in his body. But the spell backfired. Instead of giving him magic, I cursed him with paralysis. Now, Mason will be in a wheelchair the rest of his life."

Breath stalls in my lungs, and a painful burst expands my chest. "I'm so sorry, Zach."

"This Caster who uses black magic? Stay as far away as you can."

"I plan to." I take his hand, and he looks down to where we touch. Our magic cuddles up, the life and death mingling together like old friends.

"Magic is dangerous." He winds his fingers with mine and holds tight.

TWELVE

DRAMA CAMP: DAY THREE – THURSDAY MORNING

My busy schedule overwhelms me, and while I normally love anything related to drama (the theatrical kind, not the real-life kind), today, I want to go back to bed. I need to be memorized for my rehearsal with Zach and Mr. Olsen tonight. Not to mention the dramatic monologue, the pop duo, the regular classes, and the crazy Caster causing commotion.

At least my alliteration is on point.

Zach and Devin stayed in their room, presumably to sleep in, and I'm jealous. But Portia wanted to come to the early class. Some people annihilate anxiety with exercise, punching bags, or Netflix. Portia uses drama as her personal stress ball, her ultimate therapy. So after our grisly night in the graveyard, I shouldn't be surprised to find myself seated in the auditorium with her.

While the teacher starts, I take the time to text Dad. I debate whether or not to mention the zombie attack and decide against it. He doesn't need another reason to worry, and I handled it. I mean, The Caster found me, used black magic, animated bones, desecrated a graveyard, all concerning details.

Yep, I really should say something.

> ME: I didn't have time to call, but this is me checking in. No dream snatching last night. The salt worked. All is well. Also, check out Lafayette 1. The Caster might have been there. Love you.

Truth with a hint of avoidance. Perfect.

Julie Jolley comes into the class and looks at me. Her eyes widen, and her face pales. She walks out at a quick pace. Apparently, I'm the bad guy from the graveyard. I accept. If it means she gives me a wide berth, then something good came out of ancestor night. Well, that and The Hug.

I reminisce on Zach's scent, closing my eyes and trying to recapture it, which makes me sound totally stalkerish. I've never been one to care about the way someone smells, as long as they practice general hygiene. But something about snuggling into his chest, his bright essence surrounding me, and I've become an obsessive fan girl.

"Why are you smiling?" Portia stretches and hides a yawn. Her hair is in a short ponytail and her only makeup is a swipe of tinted lip gloss. An understated, but still perfect beauty. Without her full armor of Maybelline and MAC, her vulnerable side pokes through. Not the unstoppable queen who could walk a runway while taking over the world, but my best friend, Portia. The loyal one who Ubers siblings and cleans vomit.

"I'm not smiling." My lips turn up even wider, and I mask it with my own yawn.

She lowers her head, giving me a lot of eyebrow. "Yes, you are. You have this look on your face. Dreamy. Very un-CeCe-like."

"Shhh." A person in front of us turns around and glares.

"Sorry," Portia whispers and gives me a look saying, *we'll talk about your dreamy imaginings later.*

After last night, she keeps a close watch on me. When I got back from Lafayette, she was awake, her bare feet wearing tracks on the carpet. She cried, hugged me, and haphazardly tossed clothes and shoes into her suitcase, insisting we had to leave. She finally calmed enough to sleep once I pointed to my safe bed, surrounded by a protective circle of salt, and added a promise to never get caught in a zombie attack again.

I sincerely hope it's a promise I can keep.

At the end of the lesson, I head out, guitar case in hand. I packed my personal guitar to camp and am excited to give her a workout.

"CeCe!" Gemma, one-third of the J-Crew, waits for me by the door. I've never seen her alone. It's like a sighting of Bigfoot or the Loch Ness Monster. She grabs my arm and digs her fingers in, dragging me to a corner of the hallway.

"What are you doing?" Portia, being a loyal and amazing friend, follows.

Gemma glances left and right, making exaggerated movements. Her coral hibiscus barrette bounces in her hair. "What happened last night? Is Zach okay? I didn't want to leave you behind."

Oh. She's worried about me. Something akin to tenderness blossoms, a little coral hibiscus of surprise. "I'm fine. Zach is too. Devin set it up. It was all an elaborate prank. Ridiculous, right?"

Mrs. Wren suggested we tell Julie Jolley and Gemma

this story, keeping them out of the magic loop. Zach and I readily agreed, and I told Portia about it last night over the melting of the moon token.

"Really? Doesn't that seem over the top?" Standing this close to Gemma, and without the distraction of Julie's evil glare, I notice her cute heart-shaped face and long eyelashes. A literal embodiment of a girl who sings to her pet rooster and glides on the backs of dolphins. So why does she hang around with the J-Crew, aka Satan's favorite minions?

"Devin called it authentic," Portia says. "You know these drama types."

"That's unreal." She laughs, the weight of the world lifted from her shoulders. "Well, I'm glad you're okay. Don't tell Julie I talked to you."

As if I'd willingly talk to Julie Jolley. "My lips are sealed."

"Thanks." She employs her over-the-top secret agent moves, scouring the hall before striding away.

"She actually bought it. And now she'll sell it to Julie. Two for the price of one." Portia's mouth curves, and she chuckles under her breath.

"I can check it off my to-do list." I lift my hand like I hold a small notebook. "Ah, there it is, right below *stay awake*, and above *don't kill Portia for dragging me to the early class.*"

"Look at you, flying through your list." She winks and heads down the hall.

For those singing or playing an instrument during the conservatory, a portion of the day is reserved to access the music room. It's set up with large, soundproof glass booths lining the walls, allowing people to practice in peace. A big stage sits in the middle, and several groups gather, some chatting, some playing instruments. We see Zach and Devin there, and Devin rushes to greet Portia.

"Hey, babe. I missed you this morning," Devin says.

Dodging around the gushy affection, I walk to Zach, who sits on the stage, strumming the same guitar he played yesterday. The blue neck offsets the bleached wood, the leather strap a darker blue matching the color of his eyes in the moonlight.

I have to stop measuring degrees of blue by the shade of Zach's irises.

"You okay?" He focuses on the placement of his fingers, and I don't realize he's talking to me until he looks up.

Blue, like a crystal, carefree sky.

I clear my throat. "Good. I mean, I didn't sleep much, but what's new?" Since the night at the morgue, I haven't gotten a decent eight hours. Or six, for that matter. At this point, I'd sell my soul for five.

"Yeah." He stuffs an abundance of sympathy in the syllable. "I had a hard time sleeping too."

"Dreaming of zombies?"

Laying the guitar in his lap, he gives me his full attention. A soft smile teases his lips. "Among other things."

My heart races, stupid organ. Heart and I have been down this road before, getting extra pumpy over a dreamy look and a turn of phrase. If falling for Zach was on my to-do list, it would be right below *the friend zone* and right above *heartbreak*.

"Did you memorize Beck's lines yet?" I change the subject, choosing not to ask what fills his head in the wee hours.

"Sort of. How about Allie?"

"I wish."

"Instead of rehearsing our duets, we should use this

time to work on *Stuck*." He lifts his chin, nodding towards Devin and Portia, who are with Mr. Bellamy, the music teacher. "Looks like our friends are going to duet, after all. They won't even realize we're busy."

"What if..." I pause, wondering about my nutty idea. Then I remember Zach and I are just friends, and it doesn't matter if he thinks I'm crazy. "What if we play guitar together, and sing the dialogue? Double up on our practice."

He taps his fingers on the body of the guitar "That's—"

"Stupid?"

"I was going to say brilliant." He laughs, shaking his head.

"Ah, yes, brilliant was my second guess." I survey the room and notice most of the private booths are full. "Where should we practice?"

"The stage is pretty empty. Let's just work here. If a booth opens up, we can move." He slings the strap over his head and lifts the guitar.

"Great idea." I lean down, unsnapping the latches on my case.

Not everyone chooses to name their instrument, and as I take Van HellSing: The Slayer of Music, from her case, I feel sorry for all the other nameless guitars. Van HellSing is black from her body to her headstock, all except for the pic guard and sides, which are white. She's beautiful.

Zach drags a music stand over and places the script where we can both see it. "Should we start in C?"

Beck speaks first, and we both strum the chord as Zach attempts to put some kind of rhythm to his line. Then he calls out "G," and we shift our fingers, hitting the strings as I sing my dialogue.

"D."

It's awkward, cringey, and hilarious as we create a new song to memorize the play. After a few takes, we get better and more in sync, to the point it actually sounds like music. Zach has a great voice. A rich tone with a hint of rasp, and I want to wrap the sound around me like my favorite sweatshirt.

Every time we finish, I read the glaring italicized words at the bottom of the script, *Beck pulls Allie close and kisses her.* And every time I read it, I look at Zach. He looks at me, and we have this...pause.

I've heard of giving pause, a pregnant pause, and pause buttons. But none of those phrases gives justice to the *Stuck* pause. It's a whole mood. The feeling of being the only people in a crowd, no matter the noise and chaos. Or being in a downpour and ignoring the soaking rain just to keep your eyes on each other one second longer.

And Zach thinks magic is dangerous.

"Wake up, CeCe!" Portia stands beside me, her hand on my shoulder. When did she get here? "You coming for lunch?"

"Lunch?" The clock on the wall lies. There's no way Zach and I practiced for ninety minutes.

"I can't believe how late it is," Zach says. "CeCe, that was brilliant."

"We nailed it. Tonight will be a piece of cake." I smile and lift my hand for a fist bump, and his knuckles meet mine.

"Time flies when you're making music." She waggles her eyebrows, innuendo all over her beautiful face.

"Ha ha." I give my best sarcastic laugh as I put Van Hell-Sing away. I'd like to leave her in the music room. Beats hauling her around or going back to the dorm.

I approach Mr. Bellamy to ask if Van Hellsing can stay.

He notices me and smiles. "CeCe, hi. What can I do for you?"

"Hi." I didn't realize he knew my name, and the surprise causes my brain to stop. Just a pause button moment, not a *Stuck* pause. "Could I leave Van HellSing, I mean, my guitar, here for the day?"

"You named your guitar Van Helsing? Like the monster hunter?" He leans back, crossing his arms over his pink plaid shirt.

"Well, she's a slayer of music that makes the very gates of Hell sing, but yep. Same idea."

"How could I deny such a worthy request?" His energetic belly laugh rumbles the rafters. The acoustics in the room are awesome.

"Thank you." I smile and turn to leave, but he stops me.

"Now I have a favor to ask."

"A favor?" I tip my head to study the music teacher. He's black with a bald head and stylish scruff. The kind of scruff that appears purposeful without being an actual beard.

"I'd like you and Zach to sign up for the pop duet. You could spruce up the song you wrote today. Add a chorus and a refrain." His fingers tap on an air piano, experimenting with the extra elements.

"We didn't write it. It's from a play."

"It has good bones. I could really make something of it." He gestures to Zach, calling him over and explaining his idea. "What do you say?"

Zach sticks his hands in the pockets of his navy-blue shorts. His denim button-up shirt and red Adidas complete the look. "Not to compete, right? Just for fun?"

"Competing *is* fun." Mr. Bellamy shakes the rafters again. "How about I put together an arrangement, and if y'all like it, you can sing it."

Zach and I glance at each other, and I must be completely insane because, despite the five thousand other things going on this week, I agree.

What is wrong with me?

At lunch, Portia and I sit across from Devin and Zach. I tell them what Mr. Bellamy wanted when my phone buzzes. It must be my dad since I never heard back from him this morning. My brow furrows as I see the text is from Zach.

> ZACH: Does it feel like drama camp keeps pulling us together? Our friends, the play, the graveyard, and now the duet?

The words light up my screen, and I stare at them, trying to figure out what he means. Does he feel pressured by Mr. Bellamy to sign up for the duet? Maybe he doesn't want to sing with me. I think about my response, going for playful banter over silly assumptions.

> ME: Magic eight ball says: signs point to yes.

The three typing dots appear, and I look at him. His elbows rest on the table, and his thumbs move across the screen. A swoop of hair shadows his eyes, and when he finally lifts his chin, I'm met with a piercing blue stare.

My phone buzzes.

> ZACH: I'm reconsidering my stance on magic.

THIRTEEN

DRAMA CAMP: DAY THREE – THURSDAY
AFTERNOON

With a slow blink, I clear my vision to make sure Zach's text says what I think it says. Reading it again, I see the words didn't morph into something less seismic.

> ZACH: I'm reconsidering my stance on magic.

Does that mean *using* magic, or—the big OR—*dating* someone who uses magic?

My gaze flits up to find Zach watching me. The corner of his mouth quirks the tiniest bit, and those deep blue eyes gauge my reaction. I lift my eyebrows, and he copies my expression. I tip my head to the right, unsurprised he tips his head to the left, mirroring my movement. We both hold our phones, our forearms resting on the table's edge, his words a glowing banner between us.

Portia talks about her duet with Devin, but I hear nothing as Zach's foot nudges me. And then more than a nudge, a caress, if feet do such a thing. His red Adidas rub against my black and white Vans, and he makes a pointed glance at my phone.

I resist the urge to wipe off my sweaty palms as I type.

ME: ~~Does that mean what I think it means?~~

ME: ~~Do you want to date?~~

ME: ~~You're really cute, and I've been talking myself out of thinking that way because you just want to be friends, but now...~~

ME: Reconsidering?

There. That sounds good. Not too presumptuous, and not too mouth vomit-y.

He reads the text and smiles, his dimples etched in amusement.

ZACH: My stance. On magic.

Super helpful.

His foot brushes over my toes, and there must be some connection between my feet and stomach because his movement causes flutters to swell. Big butterflies dance in my belly, and my mouth responds, a slow smile stretching wide.

"You're smiling. Again." Portia squints at me like I'm an interesting new specimen, then turns to Zach, back at me, her eyes bouncing. "Oh!" Her expression says, "*I see what's going on here.*"

And I laugh. Because if she knows what's going on, she's way ahead of me.

After lunch, we get through the rest of our classes in a

blur. I barely have time to run back to my dorm and change for the rehearsal with Mr. Olsen. Choosing my black jumper, my most confidence-boosting outfit, I slip on the one-piece ensemble, tying the stretchy belt at the waist. I step back from the small mirror on the wall, trying to see as much of my outfit as possible, which only shows my bare shoulders and the V-neck front.

"You look beautiful." Portia sits on the bed, watching me get ready. Her body practically vibrates, and I know her well enough to understand this is her practicing "restraint."

"Just spill it. What do you want to say?"

She bites her lip and waits all of three seconds before talking. "I thought you and Zach decided to be friends. Not part of my drama camp double couple dream."

"Sorry to crush your double couple fantasy, but nothing's happened with Zach." Nothing except some interesting texts and flirting in the form of footsie.

"Oh, it will. Zach said it all without saying anything. The smile meant only for you. The eyes full of longing. Classic drama camp hook-up material." She steps behind me, putting her arm around my shoulders, and squishing her face next to mine. Our reflections watch each other, her dark curls pressed against my straight, pink hair. "Y'all are really cute together."

"Don't get your hopes up," I say, but my smile takes any bite out of the words. "Do you have plans tonight?"

"Devin and I are meeting later. I'm not hiding my drama camp romance." Her reflection winks.

"You're hilarious." I shift to give Portia a hug. All teasing aside, I'm grateful she's my bestie. "I don't know what's going on with Zach. I'm trying to figure it out."

"Girl, he likes you. Trust me."

"Sure. You just want to be a double couple," I joke, and her laugh follows me out the door.

Stepping into the sunshine, I close my eyes and enjoy the warmth. Heat dapples my skin as the sun sinks lower in the sky. Shadows lengthen, and in the quiet, I think about him.

All day we've floated in the undefined zone, a place between friendship and more. I'm like the tall bayou reeds caught by the wind, but still fixed to the ground. I could cling to the soil, keeping things status quo between us. Or I could allow myself to be uprooted, the breeze carrying me somewhere new.

"Hey, CeCe." At the sound of Zach's voice, I open my eyes. Bright rays backlight him, the golden halo shrouding him in a dangerous cloak, the kind of dangerous that tugs at my roots.

He wears jeans and a tight gray tee. His damp hair flops onto his forehead, and he brushes it back, the sun picking up lighter shades in the brown strands. As Mawmaw would say, he looks gooder than grits.

Fire spreads in my chest, and it has nothing to do with the fading day. "Fancy meetin' you here."

"I was in the neighborhood." His intense gaze makes my cheeks blush. "Are you ready to go?"

"Depends." I shrug a shoulder. "Will you be able to speak your dialogue and not sing it?"

"I'll do my best. How about you?"

"I'm asking Mr. Olsen to change the whole play into a musical."

He laughs, reaching out a hand, and my roots tug a little more. *I'm reconsidering my stance on magic.* His words tease at the edges of my mind as I take his fingers in mine. His thumb rubs against my knuckles. The blaze of life magic floods my veins, and the light touch causes tingles to spread.

Will Mr. Olsen have us kiss at rehearsal? My heart beats faster at the thought.

We make it to the building where The Exhibition will be held, a smaller theater with no curtain across the stage, and moveable seats. Although it's not a grand auditorium, this place will be packed.

Mr. Olsen paces, a stack of papers in his hands. He looks up as we enter. "I'm glad you made it. Come on down."

A steep, carpeted stairway leads to the front, and I precede Zach down. His fingers pull at my stretchy black top, the slight tug keeping me from getting too far ahead.

"Hi, Mr. Olsen," I say once we reach the bottom.

"Beck and Allie." His perpetual motion stalls as he greets us. "We're working on blocking today, so hop on up, Beck stage right, Allie stage left."

Zach helps me get on the raised platform, and we move into position. I stop near the edge, my back to him. Allie's lines run through my head, and her anger at Beck builds. The things he said as a girl threw herself at him are unforgivable.

I imagine Zach flirting with Julie Jolley, which really helps me get into character.

Mr. Olsen calls for the first line.

"Allie, can we talk?" Zach approaches, his steps echoing on the wooden floor. My body stiffens, and I press my lips together. Looking over my right shoulder, keeping my face towards the audience, I give my best glare.

"I don't have anything to say, and you've already said enough."

I turn to the wall again, and Mr. Olsen stops me. "Allie, let's have you face Beck and step closer to center stage."

Following directions, we line up, and I shake out my arms, ready to pick up the dialogue. I actually have to go through the singing in my mind to get on track.

"Sugar, please." Hearing him call me "Sugar" makes my insides warm. But this is Beck, not Zach, and it takes skill to plaster the annoyed grimace on my face.

"I'm not your Sugar."

We continue through the blocking and dialogue. Mr. Olsen shifts us around the stage, and each line spoken, each action, brings us nearer to the kiss.

Suddenly, I worry about my breath, hoping it smells okay. Why was I more worried about brushing my hair than brushing my teeth? I want to check, a quick exhalation into my palm to make sure. Maybe a swipe of Chapstick as well. But Mr. Olsen watches closely, taking in every motion we make because this is The Exhibition, the most important event of the whole conservatory, and he's chosen us to represent him, and DOES MY BREATH SMELL OKAY?

"Allie, drop your head, and Beck, close the distance," Mr. Olsen calls out.

The last lines approach at freight train speed. I swallow down the anxiety, the worry about dry lips and halitosis. My stomach dances, the resident butterflies partying in anticipation. *Kiss, kiss, kiss,* they chant in my gut.

It's my turn to speak, to give my last line before his last line. Which will be followed by the last stage direction: *Beck pulls Allie close and kisses her.*

"You don't have to stick around anymore." I keep my eyes glued to the floor and force myself not to fidget. Or swipe my sweaty forehead. Or pass out.

Zach lightly touches my chin, lifting my gaze to meet his. The blue in his eyes has darkened to navy, a midnight sky full of dreams and promises. He bites his lip looking both confident and nervous.

"It's too late. I'm already stuck." He leans forward, his cinnamon whisper teasing my skin.

"And that's a wrap." Mr. Olsen claps, his solo applause jarring in the quiet room. "When you perform for the audience, you'll finish with the kiss, but we'll call end-scene for today."

A sigh whooshes from my tight lungs, and I swallow a giant lump of something I refuse to call disappointment.

"Fantastic job, both of you. I'm thrilled you were memorized and ready. I couldn't have picked a better Beck and Allie." He pauses and looks us over, a proud parent moment. "Practice in your spare time, and we'll have a few minutes to walk through it again before the performance."

"Thank you, sir." I take Zach's proffered hand, and together we jump off the stage. We could be more civilized and walk down the stairs on either side. But we're rebels like that.

Mr. Olsen gives a few more instructions before excusing us. Zach keeps our fingers twined as we go through the double doors leading outside.

The dark, pastel sky holds its breath between daylight and dusk. Balmy air washes over me, a pleasant warmth singing along my skin. The sound of crickets accompanies our walk, and our slow pace matches my mood.

"You were ready. I'd even say anticipating." Zach's odd statement breaks the silence.

"Anticipating what?"

"The kiss." His words take a second to sink in, and once they do, I gasp.

"Of course, I was ready. For the sake of the character. Not because...anything else. I'm a professional." A professional liar. I imagined the moment our lips met again and again, like an overplayed song on the radio.

"Mmm hmm." He gives my hand a squeeze. "So, you wouldn't want to throw in an extra practice tonight? Make sure Beck has the right moves?"

"If you need the practice, I can accommodate."

He laughs. "That's really nice of you."

The sweet perfume of honeysuckle drifts near, the vines announcing the end of our walk. We stop outside my dorm and face each other. Twilight paints him in a deepening shadow, hiding the freckles across his nose. I spent so much effort dodging my attraction and convincing myself we were just friends that I didn't enjoy the art of looking. And it is an art, taking in the beauty of Zach Wren. I reach out, softly running my fingers along his brow line and down his cheek.

He slowly exhales and presses his forehead to mine. "Thanks for practicing with me."

"I wouldn't want to practice with anyone else," I whisper and close my eyes.

The pressure of his forehead vanishes, and I watch him back away, hands tucked in his pockets. I try to hide my confusion, because, *isn't he going to kiss me?*

He smiles and rocks on his heels. "See you tomorrow."

I laugh. I can't help it. This boy knows exactly what he's doing. Building the suspense of the kiss. So, I give him my best *I anticipate nothing* smirk, and head into the dorms.

Portia lies on the bed, her face buried in the pillow. Dark curls spring out like overgrown ivy. I think she might be asleep until I notice the slight shaking of her shoulders and the sniffling.

"Are you okay?" I sit on the edge of the bed and pat her arm.

"No." Her muffled voice barely reaches me, and she shakes her head further into the pillow.

"Is there a problem at home?" I whisper the question, my daughter-of-a-detective brain working overtime.

"No."

Her answer eases my immediate worry, and I rub her back, letting her cry. The occasional sounds of snuffling and hiccupping pop our quiet bubble. Otherwise, I wait until she calms enough to talk.

Eventually, the shaking slows, and the silence lengthens. She rolls to her side, revealing puffy eyes and mascara smudges. Her chin trembles as she struggles to talk.

"Devin and I are over."

"What?" Shock leaves me unable to say more. She and Devin have been the "it" couple of drama camp. I lie on my side and use the other pillow, adjusting to face her.

"We planned to meet in the cafeteria, and I was running late because..." she pauses to swallow a sob. "I called home to check in."

"Everything was okay?"

"Mostly. Peter complained because he's in charge. Then Piper stole his phone and threatened to flush it down the toilet, all while I was on the line." She almost smiles, but it quickly fades. "I had to make my own threats to get the house back in order, and just like that, twenty minutes had passed."

"And Devin left before you got there?" Ending a relationship over an unwillingness to wait around seems extreme. But I support Portia's high standards.

She rubs her eyes, smearing the mascara even more. "No, he was there. A girl was sitting on his lap, and they were kissing."

"What?" I lurch to a sitting position. Forget high standards, this is insulting. Disrespectful. Abhorrent. "I will end him."

"I marched up, said "hi," slapped his face, and walked away."

"That's my girl. I hope you left a handprint." I give her a hug while plotting revenge schemes. No one messes with my bestie. "I'm so sorry."

I quickly change into my pajamas and lay back down next to her. Tonight, it's my turn to offer comfort. I don't even stop to think about my bed, the one surrounded by a protective circle of salt keeping me hidden from The Caster.

CHAPTER

FOURTEEN

DRAMA CAMP: SOMEWHERE BETWEEN THURSDAY
AND FRIDAY

"C*eCe LeBlanc.*"

Confusion fogs my brain, a hazy mist to navigate as I awake. My heavy eyelids survey the room, and I remember where I am. Portia's bed. The only light comes from a small window, and a pale glow alleviates the darkness. I rub my eyes and glance at the clock on the nightstand.

2:07 a.m.

"*CeCe LeBlanc*," a voice whispers, faint like a breeze. So faint, I wonder if I imagined it.

I try to get up, and something heavy presses on my chest. An invisible weight holds me down, and I bat at nothing, pushing to sit without any success. Panic adds to my confusion, and I double my efforts to move. From the corner of my eye, I see the salt circling my bed, and realize I've made a huge mistake.

I left myself unprotected.

The pressure gets heavier, crushing me until I think I'll break. Breathing becomes impossible, and I open my mouth, unable to make any sound. Twinkling lights glitter at the edges of my vision. I'm seconds away from passing out. Before I fall into oblivion, the weight disappears, and my spirit lifts from my body.

The strange incorporeal leash pulls me from my dorm to float along the grounds of Tulane. Brightness above illuminates the campus like a spotlight. It's a full moon.

Murky black magic saturates the air, growing heavier and thicker. It becomes so dense I drown in it. I have no desire for a meet-up with The Caster, and I call on my necromancy. It's like attempting to ignite a wet match. Everything's in place, the striking surface, the friction, but I can't get it to light. Digging my metaphysical heels in, *come on, necromancy,* I reach for the power and come up empty.

What happened to my magic?

My spirit travels to a little corner off the beaten path, a secluded spot among a grove of weeping willows. The branches tilt, almost touching the ground, the heaviness weighing the leafy limbs to the point of breaking.

I finally stop outside a circle of ash where The Caster sits, protecting their identity with magic. Two voodoo dolls lay on the ground outside the circle. One, a male doll, has dark yarn on top of the head and button eyes sewn onto burlap skin. The other doll makes me gasp; a girl dressed in black, green button eyes, and pink yarn. A CeCe doll. A rock rests on the chest, weighing it down, and I understand why I couldn't move when I woke up.

Beneath the rock, a strand of cherry-dipped rose gold hair—my hair—peeks out. It's freaky to know The Caster has been close enough to collect it.

"*CeCe Leblanc.*" They don't talk to me in the traditional,

person-to-person way. They speak to my mind, the whisper sounding like my own voice as if I conjured it.

A gloved hand reaches outside the circle to pick up the male doll. The covered arm gives me no helpful identifying information. My spirit floats near and watches the strange ritual, trying to pick up on something to give my dad.

The Caster dips a finger in ash and draws a dingy stripe across the forehead of the CeCe doll. My world spins, the moon rotates around me, and the leash drags my spirit again. The dizzying movement pulls me to a back alley. I recognize the brick building and the dumpster rolled against the wall. This is the same alley where Henry Guillory died.

It confirms my suspicions that this is our killer. The Caster murdered Henry Guillory.

I absorb the new scene, memorizing all the details. A different man in a dirty polo shirt slumps on the ground, possibly drunk, maybe homeless. His head leans against the dumpster, and his legs fold up to his chin. Clouds roll in and cover the bright moon in a thick, dark vapor. The alley fades to murkiness, casting the man in shadow. I know what comes next. I've seen this before through Henry Guillory's eyes. Trying to warn the new victim, I scream at him to run. But no sound leaves my lips. Spirit CeCe can't talk, can't move. Can't do anything more than observe.

The polo-shirt guy stands and glances up and down the alley. "Who's there?"

I look around as well, surprised The Caster stands next to me, veiled in magic and holding the male voodoo doll. They pull a loose seam on the side, and the doll opens, exposing the stuffing. The man screams, a tortured agony reverberating in the open air. He crumples to the pavement, holding his side, his polo shirt and hands covered in blood.

Dread and disgust ripple along my senses, and even though I'm not in my physical body, I feel my eyes tearing up. *Stop,* I think, hoping The Caster hears me. *Please!*

Unholy shrieking comes from the man huddled in the fetal position. The Caster reaches inside the doll and fishes through the stuffing. The muscles clench as they grip something in their fist, and the gloved hand slowly slides out. Blood drips from the burlap to puddle on the ground, and the man's screams stop, a shocking silence that leaves only the *plop, plop* of crimson rain.

I stare at the glove covered in blood, aware it holds something awful, not wanting to know but unable to turn away. The Caster shifts, fingers unfurling to reveal what he pulled from inside the male voodoo doll. It takes a few seconds to understand what I see.

It's a kidney. A human kidney.

The Caster tightens the doll's stitching, and the man's wounds seal. Dad told me Henry's wounds came from the inside, and I understand it now.

"I need your necromancy." The Caster speaks in that strange whisper that sounds like my voice.

No. Giving away magic doesn't work. Zach tried to transfer power to his brother, and it backfired. *You'll leave me crippled.*

Or worse.

I have to get out of here. The Caster moves closer, the CeCe doll in hand. They hold it to lay flat with the rock still pressed on the chest. Since I'd like to keep my kidneys, thank you very much, I fight harder to draw on my necromancy. It fizzles, barely more than a spark.

And then I remember the moon. The powerful full moon shining like a beacon.

Necromancy and the moon work hand in hand, the

peanut butter and jelly of magic. I've never tried to use the power for something other than raising the dead, but I need it now. The hum of energy surrounds me, and I grab at it.

Clouds clear, and the light beams above. Power pours in and fills me to bursting, the sensation bordering on painful. Guided by instinct, I focus on the moon's gravity, the push and pull like the sway of music, and I'm the conductor. I'm high tide CeCe, using the waves of energy to move the rock off the voodoo doll. The weight trembles, shifting to the side and falling to the ground.

Necromancy rushes through me, my essence trembling with the cold. I don't waste any time getting my spirit back to my body. Just the thought of my dorm room, and lying next to Portia, pulls me back.

FIFTEEN

DRAMA CAMP: FRIDAY BEFORE SUNRISE

I wake with a gasp, no longer floating in dream form.

"Portia," I glance at the protective circle around my bed. "We have to move."

She grumbles, rubbing her eyes. "Move where? It's still dark outside."

"Come on. Please." I tug her arm and must speak in an urgent enough tone because she switches beds.

"What happened?" she asks in a bleary voice.

"I watched The Caster kill someone. They took me again, like my dream from the other night." A ball of ice unfurls in my core and spreads, the necro-shivers attacking. The blanket is bunched beneath us, and we both struggle to wrap me like a burrito.

"You had to watch? That's awful." Her throat clears, and she blinks heavy eyelids. "My brain isn't awake yet, but we decided it wasn't a dream, right?"

"You're right, not a dream." I close my eyes and take a

breath. "I need to call my dad. He'll never let me stay for The Exhibition now."

I think of the long nights ahead, endlessly ticking by, where Dad works the case and I stay home alone. A knot forms in my throat as I imagine every sound making me jump, every blink filled with the fear of being taken.

Portia sits closest to the nightstand and grabs my phone from the charger, handing it to me. Dad answers on the second ring with a grunt.

"Hey." My body trembles and I pull the blanket tighter. Portia squeezes me and rubs my arm, taking some of the chill.

"Am I killing someone or burying a body?" Dad asks.

"Burying a body. Most likely," I say softly.

That gets his attention. "What do you mean?"

"There's another victim in the same alley where you found Henry Guillory. The Caster is the murderer." I shake my head, wanting to forget the things I saw. Wishing to erase the ear-piercing screams followed by the muffled sound of dripping blood.

"How do you know?" He doesn't doubt me. I can hear him shuffling around getting ready. He adds a grunt, really asking *how much danger were you in?*

"I wasn't in any danger." Liar, liar pants on fire. "And I know because The Caster took me on a ride along to watch."

"Like the last time?"

"Yes. I saw how the murders are being committed. The weapon is a voodoo doll. Really bad black magic stuff."

"That's...unexpected." Living in NOLA, Dad knows about magic. But this is our first experience with death by Voodoo. "Anything else that might give us a lead?"

The pink yarn hair and green button eyes come to mind.

But Dad doesn't need extra ammo to make me come home. I don't mention The Caster somehow collected my hair for the CeCe doll. At this rate, I won't have any pants left, all of them blazing with my lies. "The Caster was here at Tulane. I got pulled to a grove of willows on campus."

"I'll come check it out. Anything else you can tell me?"

"The new victim is missing a kidney." I explain about the stitching of the doll opening and The Caster pulling out the organ. Portia's face pales at my explanation.

"Henry Guillory was missing his lungs," he says.

The phone line goes quiet, both of us thinking. On his end, all I hear is breathing. On my end, I'm sure he hears my shivers.

He breaks the silence. "We have a suspect. Someone we're watching."

"A suspect? That's great." Relief chisels at the extra stress I've carried around, making me lighter.

"Another thing." He sighs, low and slow, letting the words simmer between us. "I need you to stay put. It's safer for you to be surrounded by people."

Wait, what? He wants me to stay? I try not to sound too excited. "I can do that. There's a teacher I can talk to who knows about Voodoo."

"Let me know how it goes. And be careful," he says. "You're all I've got."

"I will."

We say our goodbyes, and I hang up, tossing the phone aside. Portia bites her lip, her eyebrows scrunched in concern. I reach over to smooth out the crinkles in her forehead.

"Everything's going to be okay." I desperately hope I haven't charred another pair of pants. The Caster knows who I am and where to find me. A protective circle of salt won't stop everything. "Dad thinks it's better for me to stay here. Be around people."

Portia meets my eyes, and I'm surprised to see tears clinging to her lashes. "If it wasn't for me, this never would have happened. You would have been safe in your salt circle."

"Portia, this is not your fault." I fight to speak through the shivers, forcing my chin's trembling to a minimum. "Do you realize how amazing it is to have a best friend who loves me despite my necromancy? I'd rather be here with you than anywhere else. I'll just pour a circle around your bed."

"I can't lose you." A quivering tear escapes and trails down her cheek. Using the bedspread, I dab it away.

"I'd never die on your watch. I couldn't leave you with that kind of guilt."

She smiles, a tremulous effort at best. But still a smile. "That would be cruel."

"We're the Two Amigos," I say, sticking my hand in the middle like a team cheer.

"The Amigos," she repeats, putting her hand on top of mine. We lift our arms, hands pointed to the ceiling, and I scoot closer to give her a hug.

We both lie down, Portia curling on her side away from me. I end up staring at the wall. My brain runs on a hamster wheel of worry. Around and around. Caster. Voodoo Dolls. And the dramatic monologue. I need my rest. In the morning, I face off against Julie Jolley.

CHAPTER
SIXTEEN

DRAMA CAMP: DAY FOUR – FRIDAY MORNING

My bare feet pound the hot pavement, blisters forming on my soles as I run across the sizzling blacktop. The screeching of birds follows my path, their high-pitched whistles a constant reminder I slept through my alarm.

I can't believe I'm late.

Last night, the dark ceiling shifted from black, to gray, to horizontal stripes of sunshine reflecting through the slats of the blinds. Sometime after, I finally fell asleep. And stayed asleep when the rhythmic beeping tried to wake me. Portia's unconscious form hardly moved, her puffy post-cry eyes slitting open to wish me good luck as I ran out the door.

The long skirt of my Antigone costume bunches in my fingertips, the silky fabric swishing as I run. I have it on backwards, and I don't have time to change it. Tears fight to escape, but I won't let them out.

I can't let Julie Jolley win.

People linger in the main building, and I push through the crowd, not caring about the destruction left in my wake. I reach the classroom where the dramatic monologue competition is and take a second to catch my breath. A guy performs at the front, and five judges watch from the first row, leaving the other actors to fill in the seats behind.

Julie Jolley sits on the second row, confidence radiating off her as surely as stress radiates off me. Her hair piles on top of her head in a messy bun, and her costume looks like something picked up at Goodwill, the perfect outfit for an unhoused street-performing orphan from the wrong side of town.

Tears threaten again, and I bully them back into submission.

I wait until the guy takes a bow to walk in. The judges scribble notes, and I approach the desk, hands behind my back. None of them are in a hurry to acknowledge my presence. Everyone else stares critically at my backward skirt.

The complex costume has a whole underdress, a Grecian tunic with a cape attached, and a high-low skirt, the high part intended to be in front. A roped belt weaves through the top and bottom, connecting them, keeping me from simply twisting the skirt the right way. I was going to finish off the look with gold sandals that lace up my legs but ended up going barefoot to save time.

A male judge sporting a terrible comb-over gives my pink hair a glare of disapproval. "This is a closed event."

"I'm signed up." I self-consciously tuck a loose hair behind my ear. Portia had practiced an elaborate braid with ribbons woven through the strands, but instead, I wear it down. Stupid Caster and stupid sleepless night.

The bald denier stares at me, his lips pinched. "Name?"

"CeCe LeBlanc. I'm doing a scene from Antigone."

He checks a clipboard, and all the names are high-lighted except mine. I glare up in black and white shame, no bright yellow mark announcing my punctuality.

"There's a 10% deduction for being late. Sit down." He holds a red pen, writing a note, probably something like *shame on you, shame on your family.*

My embarrassing entrance makes me the bad kid no one wants to sit by, and each gaze shifts away as I look for a seat. Awkward silence follows my steps, and I choose the back of the room. Julie Jolley glances over her shoulder, her evil grin landing a direct hit. She knows I screwed up. I know it too. A 10% deduction puts the nail in my mono-logue coffin.

Comb-over calls the next competitor, and I only half watch, using the time to get into character. I close my eyes and picture Antigone fighting for the burial of her dead brother. She stands in front of the king, defiant and strong. But somehow, the scene shifts. Suddenly, she can't be heard over the screams trembling in the air. And the king veils himself with magic. Lifting his hand, he opens his palm to reveal a blood-soaked kidney.

My eyes shoot open, and my heart pumps wildly.

After a few more monologues, Julie Jolley is called. She makes her way to the front, flashing a shy smile to the judges. The same lips that said, *screw you, CeCe,* now ask the front row to believe in Julie Ann: the girl next door.

I'm not the only one with pants on fire.

Tipping her head down, she waits for the signal to begin.

"People who think money can buy anything obviously never lost their parents in a horrific, fiery car crash...." Julie slathers her words in a buttery southern accent. I control the urge to laugh. Or smile. Or show any facial expression at all. The last thing I need is another deduction.

At some point, I shift from amused to engaged. It's… good. Really good, although I'd rather swim in a pool of sharpened steak knives than tell her. The three-minute buzzer dings, and she finishes, curtsying and flashing the timid smile.

Performance after performance passes until the judge calls my name. Truthfully, I'm grateful to go last. The delay gave me time to center myself and prepare to blow the judges away.

I take my spot up front. All the thoughts about murder, black magic, and The Caster detour to the back of my brain, stored to worry about later. Right now, I have a brother to bury and a king to tell off.

"Begin," the judge says.

I slay the opening lines and keep going. The room quiets, a heavy kind of silence alive with anticipation. In the three-minute time limit, I give the best monologue of my life. Every line delivered perfectly, every emotion real. Tears fall in twin trails as I finish the final words. The timer buzzes, and I take a bow.

In my mind, my personal soundtrack plays the soulful sound of Alicia Keys singing *This Girl is on Fire*. Despite being late, and the 10% loss, I could still win. Walking back to my seat, I smirk at Julie Jolley, a confident smile that says, *what else you got?*

Comb-over stands and brushes a hand over his limited hair. "Thank you all for coming. The winner will be announced at the banquet tomorrow night. You are excused."

The high of my performance propels me, and I race to my room. An explosion of clothes greets me. The rainbow of colors and fabrics covers the floor, beds, desks, and chairs. Portia emptied everything from her suitcase to find the perfect revenge outfit.

She stands in front of me, looking like a woman ready for any club's VIP lounge, her world domination/super-model armor in place. Her hair is pinned in a fauxhawk, and her makeup expertly applied with lips painted in no-smudge blood red. The white button-up top is made from soft fabric, the sleeves belling out above the elbow in a sheer chiffon and cinching at the wrists. The black, feathered skirt dances above mid-thigh. The red wedge sandals on her feet add a splash of color.

She runs her fingers along the fluttery edge of the skirt. "Someone dropped this off at *Swapped* and I hid it in the backroom until the end of my shift." Her job at the clothing consignment store funds her love of fashion. And fuels her current plot of revenge-by-looking-extra.

"Wow." There are no other words. Just wow.

"I'm going to have a chat with Devin."

"Have a chat, or give him a heart attack?"

"To-may-toe, to-mah-toe." Her phone buzzes on the nightstand. The rattling cell dances near the edge, and she ignores the call. "He's been trying to get in touch."

It stops vibrating, and the display pops up, reading seventeen missed calls. "Are you going to put him out of his misery?"

She shrugs, emanating total diva vibes. Yeah, they've been the drama camp 'it' couple, but she won't allow anyone to see her as brokenhearted. "How'd the monologue go?"

"I killed it." The change in the subject makes me smile. "Julie Jolley looked like she swallowed swamp water after my performance."

"Then it must have been fire." She dodges around the shoes littering the floor to give me a hug. "I'm sure Julie's performance of Annie couldn't even compare."

"You know she didn't really do a scene from Annie, right?"

"I know. But it bugs her more when I pretend I don't."

I laugh and shake my head, glad to have Portia on my side. "Let me change and call my Dad. Then you can serve up Devin's regret."

Searching through my suitcase is meaningless. No matter what I wear, I'll look like her less fortunate sidekick. I pick out white cargo pants and a green wrap shirt. Grabbing my phone, I see a missed text from Zach.

> ZACH: Good luck. J-Shrew's got nothing on u.

J-Shrew might be my new favorite nickname for Julie Jolley. I laugh as I respond.

> ME: It went well.

Understatement.

> ME: What are you up to?

> ZACH: In the music room with Dev. U coming? Or is Portia plotting his death?

The diva in question leans close to the mirror, slicking a few stray hairs.

"Do you want to go to the music room?" I ask. "Zach and Devin are there."

She meets my gaze, her scheming eyebrows rising in devious determination. "If Devin is there, we're going."

She scares me sometimes.

ME: On our way.

I call Dad, and it goes straight to voicemail, which means he's working. I leave a message.

"Hey, it's me checking in. Nothing exciting to report, other than my monologue was lit. And no, I don't mean like a candle. Love you!" I hang up and slide my phone into my pocket.

"Ready?" I ask Portia.

"Don't I look ready?" She poses with a hand on her hip.

"To get everything you want and more."

"Excellent." She links her arm through mine, and we head out.

On the music room door hangs a list—the order of performances for the pop duet competition. Across the top, the words FINAL SCHEDULE: NO CHANGES stretch in bold print. At number five, it reads, "Meant to Be: Devin and Portia." And at number twenty-three, "Original Song: Zach and CeCe."

Portia freezes, staring at the list, her jaw tight. Zach and Devin's duet is missing. Not to mention our girl power song. I read the list again to make sure I didn't miss anything. Nope.

"Are you okay?" I put a hand on her arm. "Maybe we can talk to Mr. Bellamy about switching it up." Although, any changes would force our disqualification. Final means final.

"I can't believe it." The muscles in her arms flex, her fists clenching. "I got second billing."

I laugh, and the sound echoes down the hall. Of course, she's more worried about her name appearing after Devin's than our missing song. With a deep breath, she marches into the room, a woman on a mission.

A few people mill around, their attention drawn to her as soon as she walks in. Devin can't look away, his eyes locked on the beautiful revenge queen strutting like a model on the catwalk. His feet move two steps before she holds up a finger, silently ordering him to stop.

She approaches someone sitting at the piano, a cute red-haired guy with broad shoulders and a shiny, green earring. He startles at the spotlight she shines. "You. Do you have a girlfriend?"

He looks behind him, no one there, then faces Portia and places a hand on his chest. "Me? Umm, no."

"Good." She walks closer, and he stands, his curiosity and fear equally obvious. Without warning, she puts her arms around him and slams her lips against his. Just like that. She kisses him in front of God, country, and Devin.

Zach moves next to me, taking my hand. His scrunched forehead asks, *what is she doing?* And truthfully, I have no idea. This is Portia. Mere mortals aren't meant to understand her ways.

Piano guy responds in kind, his hands pressing Portia close. Before things progress to PG-13, she pulls away.

"If you had the opportunity to date all of this –" she poses, a game show hostess on display– "Would you be an idiot and cheat?"

"Definitely not." He ducks his head, a smile lighting his eyes. "So...no girlfriend. But I do have a boyfriend."

She smiles, reaching out to pat his cheek. "You're adorable."

"Happy to help make *your* boyfriend jealous, though." He looks her over with apparent appreciation. "That outfit is killer."

Devin growls, actually growls. "Portia, let me explain."

No one even pretends to give them privacy. This is drama camp. And a scene like this pours gasoline on the drama fire. One girl leans so far forward the back legs of her chair lift three inches off the floor. Another person sits frozen with his strumming hand halfway to his guitar.

"You get one chance. Don't blow it," Portia says, taking Devin by his shirt collar and leading him to a secluded corner. "Y'all can get back to work now," she calls out.

Everyone moves at once. The tipped chair falls completely forward, the girl landing in a heap. The strummer plays, the notes a jumbled mess. Motion restarts as the Devin and Portia soap opera moves off stage.

Portia and Devin, I mean. She deserves top billing.

"So, that was fun." Zach leads me to an open sound-proof booth where Van HellSing waits. I unsnap the case and take out my guitar while keeping an eye on Portia.

"Did Devin tell you what happened?" If I can't listen in to their conversation, at least I can get his side of the story.

Zach scooches his chair until our legs touch. "Kind of the same thing Portia did. Some girl walked up to him, sat in his lap, and kissed him. It was a dare."

"Seriously?" I roll my eyes, letting out a pent-up breath. "A girl walked up and slathered her lips on him like butter on pancakes?"

"Yeah, she did." He smirks with more than agreement. His smile says personal experience.

"Has that happened to you?"

"Girls have tried. I'm more agile than Devin."

My mouth drops open. How dare some theater hussy attempt a lip assault on my...Co-star? Friend? Boyfriend? This drama camp has truly lived up to its reputation.

I glance at Portia, and she leans into Devin's embrace.

Her head tucks under his chin, and his eyes pinch closed. One of his hands presses against her hair, the other squeezes her waist. Looks like they made up.

"We should practice." Zach picks up the guitar by its cerulean neck.

"Apparently we need it. I saw our name on the list. For an original song." I run a finger along one of Van HellSing's strings.

"Yeah, Mr. Bellamy gave me the music before you got here." He drops his head, shaking it back and forth. "He's pretty stoked for us to sing it."

"Oh." An original song that we have to—not just perform in front of an audience—but compete. With only a few hours to prepare. "Fantastic."

CHAPTER
SEVENTEEN

DRAMA CAMP: DAY FOUR – FRIDAY AFTERNOON

Zach and I practice our duet, and ninety minutes in, my cell vibrates. I wonder if it's Portia calling to request my help burying Devin's body since they left over an hour ago and haven't been back. Awkwardly juggling Van HellSing and digging my phone from my pocket, I see the words "Chief Daddio" flash on the screen.

"Hold on a sec," I tell Zach, swiping my finger to answer. "Hello?"

"There was another murder." Dad jumps right in, skipping the *hey* and *how's it going*? "You were right."

"Was there a, umm," I cup my hand around my mouth and turn to the side. "Kidney missing?"

By the way Zach's eyes widen, I didn't accomplish the art of subtle phone conversation.

"We won't know until the autopsy." Dad covers the mouthpiece, and mumbling comes from his end. Then the line clears. "Have you seen that teacher? The one that can help you?"

"No. I'll go after we hang up." However long *after* might be. The pop duet competition is two hours away, so I could probably fit in a trip to Mrs. Wren's classroom.

"Let me know how it goes." More noises in the background. "I gotta run. Call me later."

"Love you, Dad," I say as he hangs up.

Zach places the guitar on the stand next to his chair. "Missing kidney? That sounds freaky."

"You weren't supposed to hear that."

"But I did. So spill." He lowers his head, serious discussion mode activated.

Laying Van HellSing down, I keep my attention on the guitar case and slowly close her in. The last thing I want to do is drag Zach into this Caster mess and involve him in my magical problems. I take a deep breath and slowly let it out. "Remember at Lafayette I told you weird things have been happening?"

"Vaguely. That night was a lot to process."

"To sum up." I chew on my lower lip as I think of what to say. "Turns out The Caster is a murderer who can somehow kidnap my spirit and wants to steal my necromancy."

"Steal your..." He doesn't finish but stands and reaches out a hand, helping me up. His fingers clutch mine with a little added oomph. The magic flows between us, the flooding warmth better than a mug of hot chocolate. "We need to talk to my mom."

"I was going to. Later."

"We're going now." He pushes the door with an extra serving of bicep, and it swings wide.

I struggle to match his pace because I wore my black ankle boots with a chunky heel. Curse Portia and her cute-ness today, making me feel like my Vans were too understated.

"You should have told me." His voice bristles with an annoyed edge.

"Are you mad?"

He stops, running a hand through his hair. "I'm not mad. I'm worried."

The empty hallway extends in either direction, leaving the two of us alone. I move in front of him and put my hands on his shoulders. He wears a short-sleeved button-up shirt with pineapples arranged in a pattern. Seeing the staggered fruit makes me smile, and I wait until he meets my eyes. He doesn't smile back.

"Why are you worried?"

"Are you serious?" He says he's not mad, but the way he asks the question makes me think otherwise. "You just told me a murderer is after your magic."

His declaration makes something fuzzy swell in my chest. He cares. "Oh."

Before I realize what's happening, he pulls me close, his arms solid around my back. It's a hug. A tight hug. And I am not immune to the power of his embrace. I wrap around him, my cheek burrowing in that perfect space between his neck and shoulder. The snug zone.

When we hugged in the graveyard, my shivers kept me from fully appreciating the sensation. If I thought holding hands caused our magic to mingle, this makes it sing. Hot and cold in harmony, conducting a full-scale symphony. The music makes my heart thump wildly, and I wonder if he can feel it.

"CeCe." His breath floats along my hair, the whisper blending in the strands.

"I didn't mean to worry you." I keep my voice soft, huddling in the snug zone where his pulse trembles under my skin.

A door opens, and several people file out, a sudden burst of chatter filling the hall. The noise intrudes and forces us to draw back. I take a deep breath, missing the scent of him.

"Let's go," he says, the harshness gone. Taking my hand, he leads the way through the crowded hallway.

We peek into his mom's classroom, and she's alone. He opens the door. "Hey, Mom."

Mrs. Wren is at the front, and we walk down the aisle. Zach still holds my hand, and she notices, her eyes practically a fire hazard. A big smile lights her face. Her long blond hair is braided, the plait running halfway down her back, and her vibrant skirt is a copy of the painting Starry Night.

"What a nice surprise!"

"Do you have a minute? We need to talk to you," he says.

"Of course. Is everything okay?"

She gestures to the front row, and we sit, with Zach pulling his chair around, so we form a triangle. Her gaze bounces between us, and I cross and uncross my legs, trying to figure out where to put my hands. *On the arms of the chair? Hanging to the side?* Totally awkward.

"CeCe, tell her what's going on." He scoots closer, nudging my knee with his.

The smile melts from her face, her sparkle dimming. My intestines feel like they're going through a pasta roller. Shifting in my seat, I decide on hands in lap, and clear my throat. "It started the first night I got here." Words dry up, and fear steals along my nerves, thoughts of the bloody kidney fresh in my mind.

"What started?" Kindness radiates from her eyes, and tiny crinkles form at the edges. This close, I can smell the soothing lavender and vanilla of her perfume.

Taking a breath, I tell her about the first morgue visit, the graveyard, the CeCe voodoo doll, and the murders.

"The Caster knows who I am and wants my necromancy."

A crease etches her forehead, getting deeper and deeper the longer I speak. Her lips stretch in a tight line, and she shakes her head. "When Zach told me about the graveyard, I thought someone was after him."

She stops, looking unsure if she should continue, but he picks up where she left off. "I told you about my brother, Mason. I got deep into black magic and fell into the wrong crowd. When I turned my back on them, they made it clear I'm a traitor. Mom assumed they targeted me."

Nope, not him. I'm the lucky one with a target on my back. Or spirit. Or whatever. "Can we stop The Caster from taking my magic?"

"Maybe." She clutches a pendant around her neck, rubbing it distractedly. "First, we have to know what spell they're using so we can counter it."

"How?" I ask.

"Research. Zach, can you grab my bag?" She points to a large black and gold floral carpet bag. "When you were pulled from your body, could your spirit speak?"

"Not really. At least, not out loud. I wondered if The Caster could hear my thoughts, though."

"Interesting." She takes the oversized tote from him and reaches in, pulling out a thick book.

How does she lug that thing around? It's probably twice the size of a dictionary in length and width. The dark gray faded cover frays on the edges, and no title adorns the front. A musty smell overtakes the lavender, the ancient dust hitting my nostrils.

Relaxing in his seat, Zach takes my hand. The simple gesture melts my insides, the hard ball of tension becoming less solid. He watches me with eyes a lighter shade of blue. The sky on a clear day rather than the murky ocean.

You okay? He mouths. And I nod, enjoying the warmth of his gaze and touch.

"Could your physical body feel anything?" She asks, her nose pressed close to the book.

"The Caster grabbed my neck, and I had some bruises the next morning." I rub my skin where the faded marks are no longer visible.

"How did I miss that?" Zach asks.

"You were ignoring me." I nudge him with my foot.

"I'm sorry, it wasn't you. The traces of black magic scared me." He bumps the top of my foot with his. Then he sits up straighter, his eyes widening. "Mom, it could be a puppetry spell."

A surge of heat spikes through our connected hands as a sizzle of excitement pulses along his skin. I don't know what a puppetry spell is, but Zach's magic hums in anticipation at the words.

"You might be right." Mrs. Wren flips a few more pages, her eyebrows raising. "I don't have many black magic spells, but I think I found it: Fetter of the Spirit Puppet."

"Fetter of the...what?" I try to follow along, but the thrill tap dancing in Zach's veins distracts me.

I realize he's drawn to black magic like a mosquito to a warm body. No wonder it scares him.

"Fetter of the Spirit Puppet," she continues. "It's pretty complex. Essentially, the spell binds a spirit to the caster. They could have used it to track you and force a connection."

Ice prickles along my spine, and an involuntary chill catches me. Maybe it's my imagination, but the sludgy feel of The Caster's magic slides through my mind.

"How did The Caster find me? Only Portia and Dad know about my magic."

"And now us." Zach clutches my fingers, his grip melting the tendrils of cold.

"Maybe The Caster felt your necromancy in the morgue and decided to use it." His mom looks up from the book, squinting in thought. "The magical elements needed for the spell would be similar to constructing a voodoo doll. Didn't you say there was pink hair on the CeCe doll?"

"Yes, but I don't know where they got it." I think back to the morgue, working with Dad, racing through the ritual before getting home to pack. Necromancy has become so routine, and I've been sloppy. Maybe even careless. I left traces of myself and my magic behind.

"Why would The Caster be there in the first place?" Zach turns to me as if I have the answer. I don't.

"It has to be connected to the first murder," I say, remembering the red-tipped pins sticking from Henry Guillory.

"There's no way to know, but we can do some things on our end to protect you." Her contagious confidence settles the churning in my stomach.

"She'll need a protective talisman. Maybe set into a pendant." Zach wriggles his leg, bouncing it up and down.

"Fantastic idea." She closes the book and shoves it into her bag. "It would be more powerful with your help, Zach."

"I can't." He wants to. Or at least his magic does, if the surge of excitement is any indication. He shakes his head.

Forget mosquitos. This temptation is more like a drug addiction. Does he realize the way his magic celebrates beneath his skin?

"I have class soon, but I should be able to pull something together by this evening." She stands, lugging the heavy bag over her shoulder. "In the meantime, stick close to Zach. You need to be careful. The more the binding spell is used, the harder it will be to free you from it."

"Thank you, Mrs. Wren." My grip slips from Zach's as I stand.

"Call me Jennifer. We're way past the whole 'Mrs. Wren' thing." She pulls me into a hug.

Zach and I leave the classroom, and he takes my hand again. I'm not sure when we became chronic hand-holders, but I like it. I like it a lot. The way his fingers curl against mine, his skin calloused from playing the guitar.

"I'm sorry," he says, breaking through my thoughts.

"For what?"

A low grunt of frustration echoes in his throat. "I'm sure it's hard to need protection and know your boyfriend won't help."

Did he just...? My brain replays the last few words, and yep. He said it. Boyfriend. Spoken super casually, like the weather's good. Saints are playing this weekend. You're my girlfriend.

I can't wait to tell Portia.

Measuring my tone, I make sure not to squee under the new label. "I understand why you said magic is dangerous."

"Do you?" The blue in his eyes has changed again. From murky water to clear sky, to now the shadowed navy of a dark horizon.

"Zach, I promise I will never make you use black magic." The darkness calls to him, moving in his veins, and I wonder how he keeps resisting the desire to use it. But this girlfriend isn't going to let it win. Even if that means forfeiting his protection.

CHAPTER
EIGHTEEN

DRAMA CAMP: DAY FOUR – FRIDAY NIGHT

"Listen for it." Portia bumps me with her elbow, her lips tipped in amusement.

Devin rolls his eyes, but his grin is all for her. From what I understand, they spent a lot of time making up. I asked her to leave out the details. Begged, really. Hearing about the three-hour apology session didn't win a spot on my to-do list.

"Thank you, Daniel and Marci," the emcee calls out. From my spot backstage, I catch sight of his blingy jacket sparkling in the light. "Next up, put your hands together for *Meant to Be* sung by Portia and Devin."

"Top billing," she gloats, and Devin takes her hand. They walk on stage together, restoring humanity's faith in the drama camp dream couple.

Portia wears the same thing she had on earlier and looks amazing. Devin changed into a red shirt and black jeans to match. Zach and I sort of match, if you take the crowns from the pineapples on his shirt, which is a similar green to my shirt. Basically, we didn't have time to change after talking to his mom.

The pre-recorded music starts, and I wonder what Zach and I were thinking by choosing to play our guitars. Most of the performers are using a track. Not us. Original song. Live music.

Disaster is inevitable.

Devin sings, his baritone smooth, and his stage presence fun to watch. He tackles the first verse by himself, and when Portia joins in on the chorus, the crowd goes wild. She's a star. Everyone knows it. The end.

"*Baby, if it's meant to be,*" they finish, in sync. Before the final pre-recorded note plays, he leans her back in a dramatic dip and kisses her. Applause and hollers resonate in the audience. The emcee chuckles, taking the stage, his mic hot as he says, "Ooh la la. Too bad we don't have an award for best couple."

"How'd we do?" Portia runs backstage, her smile so wide my cheeks have sympathy pains.

"You were incredible. Seriously. They should end the competition now."

She laughs, the sunny sound brighter than the spotlight. "You and Zach are going to give us a run for our money."

"Uh-huh. Sure." I add a heaping spoonful of sarcasm to my voice.

"Your song's amazing." She squeals as Devin picks her up and swings her around, saving me from coming up with a response.

Zach and I watch the duets from the wings. Number after number performs, and a few of them are even good. Very few. If I hear one more rendition of *Shallow*, the vomits might make an appearance. Lady GaGa is my idol, but every other song features a couple making googly eyes and singing about diving in the deep end.

Overdone.

Or maybe I'm being a little harsh. Between singing an original song and my sleepless nights worrying about The Caster, my mood is like unsweetened tea. I don't usually think about my magic. But lately, it seems to be a constant distraction.

"You're on deck. Break a leg."

I startle at the voice behind me and turn to see Mr. Bellamy. Anxiety has me jumping at the guy who wears pink neon sneakers. They practically glow in the dark. Portia would love them.

"Hi, Mr. Bellamy." I shake off the tension.

"Are you ready?" He asks.

"As I'll ever be." Which isn't true. I could use a few more practices and a few more days to get this song down.

"We'll try to do your arrangement justice." Zach leans around the music teacher to pick up his cerulean guitar.

"I'll be watching from the audience." He walks backward, tucking his hands in his pockets. "Make me proud."

"Yes, sir," Zach laughs.

I look at the singers finishing their song. The hot spotlight glares down, and the excitement builds in me because I go out next. In my heart, I am a performer. The stage calls, an echo of actors sharing the same space, displaying their talents. And now the stage is mine. I grab Van HellSing, running my hand down her neck.

Zach gently taps the top of my shoe with his. "We've got this."

A strange sensation tingles in my fingertips. The music fades, the room quieting like I put on sound-canceling headphones. The world slows as an oily shimmer coats the air.

"It's The Caster." I'm not sure if Zach hears me. My words come from underwater, trying to surface from my lungs. Invisible greasy hands caress my skin, and the touch seeps into my veins. Slithery magic wriggles, a snake traveling the same path as my necromancy.

Zach stands in front of me, and the harder I focus, the fuzzier he becomes. I blink to clear my vision, but darkness creeps at the edges.

"CeCe, fight it. Use your magic to drive The Caster out."

I grit my teeth, ready for a power tussle, and the black magic leaves. Gone. The sudden change disorients me, and Van HellSing slips from my grip, the strings screeching as she hits the wooden floor.

"No!" I pick her up, rubbing along the body, relieved there's no damage. I can't believe I dropped her.

"What happened?" He asks.

"I don't know. The Caster was in my head," and licking my veins like a hungry leech. Remnants of the slimy touch still linger under my skin. "And then vanished."

"This is bad. The more The Caster connects, the more attached your magic will become."

"Like our magic is becoming BFFs?" I say it as a joke, but Zach nods.

"Exactly like that."

The duo on stage bows, and the emcee walks out. The audience cheers, and normally it would send happy vibes pumping. But after The Caster's strange here-and-gone visit, the loud applause pounds in an ominous rhythm. I feel nervous. Watched.

"Zach, I think The Caster is here. In the audience."

The emcee talks about how great all the performances

have been. Then he introduces us. "Our only original song of the night is next. Let's welcome Zach and CeCe with *Stuck*."

"We don't have to do this." His chin tips towards the stage. "We can leave right now and see if Mom's got anything ready."

What good will running do? If we perform, I can search the audience, scanning for the murderer who wants my magic and is ruining my drama camp. "We've got this."

Planting a smile on my face, I walk on stage with Zach. My gaze skims the crowd, and I see several familiar faces. Portia and Devin found seats near the front, and her loud whistle carries over the applause. The J-Crew sits near the middle, and all three of them stare at their phones. Some of the teachers watch, including Mrs. Wren, Mr. Olsen, and Mr. Bellamy. He looks particularly excited as we set up to play his arrangement.

A man in the back draws my attention. There's something familiar about him, although I can't place it. A ball cap casts his face in shadow, and he wears a bulky jacket. In New Orleans. In May. Not to mention I haven't seen him once this entire week.

Super suspicious.

We sit, adjusting our guitars, and Zach reaches for the stand holding our sheet music. The chords are printed in bold, the words big for distance reading. I should focus on the paper and get ready to play. But I watch the mystery man, wanting him to look up from the shadows.

The houselights dim, and a spotlight shines over us, blinding me to anything off the stage.

"Ready?" Zach taps the floor, his foot close to mine, and I catch the beat. "Five, six, seven, eight."

The first chords ring out, our guitars selling the duet

before we even open our mouths. After a two-bar intro, he sings the lyrics, which have morphed into something very different from the scene in The Exhibition.

My attention splits between the song and thinking of the man hiding in the shadows. Could he be The Caster? The question plucks at my mind like my fingers pluck on Van HellSing's strings.

I join Zach, singing the harmony, and my anxiety calms. His voice soothes me, the song pulling me in. Thoughts of The Caster fade. The way Zach strums his guitar is super sexy, and the beat of his foot matches mine, our rhythm in sync. His blue eyes flash between the music and me, and every time he looks up, his lips quirk, my own private smile, and my insides swoon.

Until the last words of the song. They take on a sinister meaning as I sing them out.

It's too late, too late.
I'm already stuck.
Stuck with you.

Not the sentiment I want to express to The Caster.

Applause erupts, and the houselights raise. I can see the audience again, an audience that gets to their feet in a standing ovation. Even the J-Crew displays surprising enthusiasm. Zach takes my hand and leads us in a deep bow. Portia sticks her fingers in her mouth, eliciting a piercing whistle, and Mr. Bellamy cheers excitedly. We bow again, and I'm proud of us. This is an amazing accomplishment, tackling an original song and playing it live. We did it.

My grin freezes when I catch sight of the mystery man. He tucks his head, his shoulders hunched as he works through the crowd, heading to the door. If we hurry, we can chase him down. I run backstage, dragging Zach with me, both of us carrying our guitars.

"What's the rush?" He's laughing, high on our performance.

"I think I found him." I throw my guitar in her case— *sorry Van HellSing*— and kick it closed.

"What are you talking about?" He puts his guitar away, moving in slow motion compared to my urgency.

"The Caster."

"Let's go." The carefree expression evaporates from his face, and we run out the door.

Blinking against the bright lights, my eyes adjust from the darkness backstage. I direct us around the corner where the man would exit. A few people linger in the hall, but the bulky navy jacket and dark ball cap stand out. The man is tall, about the same height as Zach, and he walks at a brisk pace.

I point at him, and Zach nods. We both stay quiet, careful not to alert him that we're following. Adrenaline pushes me forward, and we move through the chattering people. A base beat rumbles from the auditorium, where the pop duos continue, and the floor vibrates as we pass. A group of girls walks out, opening the door and making the music audible enough to hear it's another version of *Shallow*. One of them laughs loudly, the noise attracting the attention of the mystery man. He looks over his shoulder, and I drop, pretending to tie my boot.

When he faces forward, Zach and I continue our pursuit. Mystery Man rounds the corner, and this part of the school is empty, which forces us to hang back or get caught.

"Should we look around the wall?" I whisper so softly Zach needs to read my lips.

"I'll do it." He crouches low and sneaks a peek. "He's heading toward the doors."

I join Zach, my eyes barely clearing the sheetrock to see the man shrug out of his jacket. The hat comes off next, and he shakes out his short, dark hair. Bells of recognition ring in my periphery, but who is he? He pulls a phone from his pocket, his strides not even slowing as he taps on the screen.

We wait until he pushes the doors open and heads outside before we rush to catch up. We watch him through the glass, the streetlamps in the parking lot lighting his path. When he climbs into a black Ford Explorer, I finally realize who he is.

"He's a cop." Detective Rivera. The last time I saw him, I'd brought Dad dinner at the station. Rivera kept me company, asked me how school was going. Stole one of the brownies packed in a baggie. Nothing unusual. Nothing about him dabbling in black magic.

"You think The Caster is a cop?"

The headlights flash across the pavement, and Rivera drives away.

"It doesn't make sense. Detective Rivera is my dad's partner." I stare out at the parking lot, confused. Frustrated. A headache builds, and I rub my temples. "What was he doing here? I need to call my dad."

Slipping the phone from my pocket, I hit "Chief Daddio" and listen to it ring. Four times, five times, and his voicemail picks up.

"Dad, we really need to talk. Nothing's wrong," I add, worried he'll think something happened with The Caster. "Rivera was here and... are you having me followed? Call me back."

Why didn't Rivera talk to me? He just drove away. Something strange is going on.

"Would your dad actually have someone follow you?"

"If he thought I was in danger, absolutely."

"Hey, it's going to be okay. Let's go see my mom." Zach puts his arm around me, and his fingers brush my shoulder. I close my eyes, savoring the sensation of his gentle touch. I shift the half hug into a full one and cuddle in the snug zone.

That's better.

He wraps me up, and I breathe his clean citrus scent. I want to bask in the feels, not worry about Rivera and the stupid Caster. And for the briefest second, I allow myself to enjoy the embrace.

But just like roller coasters and the Gilmore Girls, all good things come to an end, and Zach pulls back, leading me down the hall to see his mom.

CHAPTER
NINETEEN

DRAMA CAMP: DAY FIVE – SATURDAY MORNING

Last night, Portia and Devin came with Zach and me to visit Mrs. Wren. As we talked about The Caster and how to protect myself, Devin's eyes widened. He leaned forward, hands on his thighs, looking like a man ready to bolt.

"Are you saying CeCe has magic too?"

"Yes," I answered and waited for his reaction.

He nodded, sitting up and throwing an arm around Portia. "Cool."

That was it. Just *cool*.

We stayed late and raced to make curfew. But this morning I hoped to spend a little one-on-one time with Zach to practice for The Exhibition. I don't want our first kiss to be in front of an audience. For a performance. Which starts in less than an hour. And we'll be kissing!

I'm totally not freaking out.

"Almost done." Portia runs the flat iron over the last section of my hair. Everything else has been straightened to perfection, my shoulder-length strands not daring to defy her ministrations. She's also done my makeup, because, in her words, I don't know the difference between a blusher and a bronzer.

She's not wrong.

Leaning closer to the mirror, I study the pendant around my neck. Mrs. Wren, I mean *Jennifer*, did a great job making it not only a protective shield, but pretty. At the center is a small mirror, blessed to reflect bad magic. Black obsidian, a powerful blocker of negative psychic energy, surrounds the mirror in a beautiful sunburst pattern. She warned me the protective elements would fade over time, only providing temporary safety from The Caster. Who may or may not be Detective Rivera.

I wish Dad would call me back.

My eyes flick to the blank screen on my phone. I sent him a text this morning to check in, and he never responded. I'm not sure if I should be worried or frustrated.

Portia notices me staring at the quiet cell. "Still nothing from Pops?"

"No." I blow out a breath. "But he should know why Rivera was here last night."

"There's probably a reason for it." She sets the flat iron down and unplugs it.

"Like maybe Dad sent him as my bodyguard. Or he's working the case. But then why wouldn't he say hi?" I pick up my phone even though I know Dad didn't text back in the ten seconds since I last checked. "Or he's a crazy black magic user stalking me."

"Well, that *is* a reason." She pinches her lips together. "Do you think he's The Caster?"

"Not really." I picture how he always greets me with a

smile. The friendly way he asks if I've gotten into any trouble lately. "I don't want him to be."

"Because I have a crush on him?"

"Portia, gross!" I don't understand her insistence that Rivera is cute. When he and Dad partnered up six months ago, she actually told me, *if I ever get arrested, I hope it's by him.*

Double gross.

"Come on," she says. "The dark hair, deep brown eyes, his sexy accent. Not to mention he's tall and knows how to wear a suit."

"Can we never talk about this again?" I mean, it's Rivera. The closest person to an uncle I have.

"You're too easy to tease." She tips her head, engaging her "thinking face," which includes a scrunched forehead and faraway gaze. "What do we really know about him?"

What do *I know?* My brain sorts through the files of interactions and conversations between us. "He has a sweet tooth."

"Then it definitely can't be him. Dark magic and Snickers don't mix."

"Ha ha." I roll my eyes, acknowledging that, yes, his penchant to steal cookies and candy offers no insight into his drama-camp-skulking tendencies. "He's young for a detective, so everyone at the precinct calls him 'kid.' Dad invited him to Thanksgiving because his family lives outside of San Antonio."

It was just Dad and me, trying to take down a whole turkey and all the fixings. Then Rivera showed up, his smile shy as he shuffled his feet on our doorstep. *"I don't want to be a bother,"* he said, making Dad laugh. *"Kid, the only bother would be leaving me and CeCe to eat all this food."* So he joined us. Eating his fill and then some. Telling us stories about the less traditional Thanksgiving foods he grew up with, like Turkey empanadas, street corn, and pumpkin flan.

"Anything else? Is he married? Girlfriend?" Portia sprays my hair to set it. No flyaways on her watch.

"I don't know. But he's....nice. Funny." The opposite of a psycho caster killer.

"And cute." She laughs.

"I'm not setting you up with him."

"So you've mentioned." She moves back, crossing her arms. "Now, stand up and give me a twirl."

I shake my head but do what she asks, spinning in a circle. The protection pendant perfectly accessorizes my "costume," lying flat above the V-neck front of my black jumper. Eyeshadow, a shade called raisin, highlights my eyes, and a shimmery plum color paints my lips.

She assures me the lipstick is one that won't kiss off, and my cheeks blush a deep pink to match my hair. Maybe I know the difference between a blusher and a bronzer after all.

"Do I pass?"

"A solid B+." Her eyebrows waggle, and I know she's kidding. Her mouth says B, but her smile says I am exempt from the final. "This is just a day look. We'll be doing darker makeup and different hair before the banquet, so be ready for that."

"Seriously?" Spending the last day of drama camp getting prettified strikes me as wrong. "Shouldn't we be making memories and causing mischief?"

"My dear child." She clasps her hands and turns her nose down like a true authoritarian. "Do not doubt my ability to cause mischief. Even on a time constraint."

"You're right. What was I thinking?" My smile feels

more like a grimace, nerves about The Exhibition kicking in. I clutch my stomach and groan. "Gut boulder!"

The Exhibition is a huge opportunity. Most events at the Conservatory have limited or optional attendance. But not The Exhibition. Everyone comes, both teachers and students. University scouts also show up, and many scholarships have been awarded based on the students' performances.

Portia rubs my shoulder. "Gut boulder about Rivera or The Exhibition?"

"The kiss," I slap a hand over my mouth and try again. "I don't know why I said that. I meant The Exhibition."

"You're an actress, CeCe. You've starred in plays before." She demonstrates surprising restraint, ignoring my misspeak.

"I know." Including last year's major coup when I beat out Julie Jolley for the lead. Despite being the recipient of J-Crew glares for months, that play solidified my love of drama. Strangely, the memory calms my anxiety, changing my gut boulder to a gut pebble.

"This play might be more attractive. And have softer lips. But a play is still a play. You just pucker up and perform." She winks at me.

"What if the kiss is blah, and the audience witnesses it, and Zach hates me, and no one wants to act with me again, and one day I wake up an old lady who only has memories of puckering up." Each word manages to grow my gut pebble back to boulder size.

"Umm, you lost me there. Just calm down." Portia laughs and gives me a hug. "You're going to be great. If your stage chemistry has anything to say about it, the kiss will be legendary. Don't sweat it."

I close my eyes and take a deep breath. It's time. "Wish me luck."

"Girl, luck is for lotteries and girls in short shorts scooting off their leather seats in summer." She pulls back, her eyes meeting mine. "You don't need luck when you have talent. Break a leg."

"Thanks." I straighten my shoulders. "I just need to brush my teeth. Then I'll head out."

Her laughter follows me through the bathroom door.

Sunshine gleams as I exit the dorm, my eyes squinting against the onslaught. I blink and notice Zach waiting for me. He wears the same outfit from our rehearsal, a tight gray tee and jeans.

"Morning." His happy gaze travels over me, pausing at the necklace. "It looks good on you."

"Well, it is custom-made. Probably worth a fortune." I slide the pendant along the chain, the black obsidian already heating in the sun.

"A fortune, huh?"

"Valued at millions. Maybe billions."

"I can tell. One of a kind." He reaches out, running his fingers along the chain before taking my hand. "And the necklace is nice too." The pleasant hum of magic tingles.

"Thanks," I mumble, basking in his compliment and his magic.

"I thought we could go through our dialogue as we walked."

We're able to recite the scene twice on our way to the theater. Unlike the first trip here, when it was just me, Zach, and Mr. Olsen, now there's motion everywhere. Stage crews unload scenery and props, technicians carry microphones and soundboards, actors practice dialogue and blocking. This is game day for drama types.

At the entrance, playbills fan out across a table. I pick one up and scan the program, searching for our play. Fifteen scenes are set to perform, and *Stuck* is number eight. The Exhibition run time is listed at just over two hours, so there should be plenty of opportunity for my nerves to get in a warmup.

"Beck and Allie." Mr. Olsen calls from the front of the stage.

We make our way to him, barely getting out a hello before he starts giving instructions. He shows us the simple set design, a carpet runner (representing the dorm hall), and a framed door that opens and closes.

"Let's do a run through, and when we're done, you'll sit over there." He points to a roped-off section to the left of the stage, reserved for the performers.

After our short rehearsal, where we do *not* practice the kiss, we take our seats and watch the audience enter. The judges take their places up front. Portia and Devin come in together, and her eyes search until she finds me. She waves and gives me a thumbs up.

I've got this.

Zach holds my hand, and his knee bounces, sending tiny shakes up my arm.

"Are you okay?" I ask.

He smiles, his adorable dimples making a cameo appearance. "I always have this excess energy before a performance."

"I get nervous. Like a giant rock lodges right here, kind of nervous." I smooth a hand over my belly.

"How about this," he turns in his seat to face me, "If I stop wiggling, and you stop worrying, we'll win The Exhibition. Deal?"

Humor lurks in his eyes, the promise not really one he can make. But we shake on it anyway.

"Deal."

I think about suggesting a practice kiss, something to take the edge of my nerves. But the lights dim off and on, a signal to get seated and settled. No time for canoodling.

The Exhibition begins, and my stress fades as we watch amazing scene after amazing scene. This event is the crown jewel of drama camp. The creamed corn of the crop. I feel like someone at an awards show, numbered among the greats, saying, "it was an honor just being nominated."

As the seventh number performs, Zach and I take our position on deck, standing in the wings. He sticks to our deal, holding still, no extra jostling. My end of the bargain is less discernible, but I focus on my dialogue, the actors on stage, the way his hand holds mine, anything to keep the anxiety at bay.

The three performers bow, and the audience applauds. There's no emcee to announce us, and we wait until the stage crew rolls out our set and the lights dim. Zach's fingers tighten, a squeeze for luck, and we let go to take our positions.

I face the door, holding the knob, ready to walk into my "dorm room." Zach takes his position on stage right, and when the lights raise, his steps echo on the wooden floor.

"Allie, can we talk?"

My back stiffens, and I think of Beck's betrayal. "I don't have anything to say, and you've already said enough."

"Sugar, please." His soft voice swells with tenderness, and my heart responds, busting out a few extra pumps. *Calm down, Heart. The endearment isn't for you.*

"I'm not your Sugar." I spin around and look up to meet his gaze.

"I made a mistake—"

"No, a mistake is simple. Flip the pencil over and erase a line or two." Taking a few steps closer, I jab him in the chest. "You hurt me."

"I know."

We deliver our lines, wringing every drop of emotion from a sopping rag. The ache is so real, tears fill my eyes. Allie's pain and Beck's pleading rain on the stage, leaving a typhoon of passion blasting through the theater.

My nerves disappear. I'm calm. Ready. Like Zach and I have been building up to this moment all of drama camp. As inevitable as the sun rising or Taco Tuesday, we are meant to share our first kiss on this stage.

"You don't have to stick around anymore," I say. Our toes almost touch, and I drop my head, staring at my boots.

The gentle brush of his fingers lifts my chin. His eyes sparkle, a cerulean blue sky of endless possibilities. For a minute, we're Zach and CeCe, not Beck and Allie, bonded together under the hot lights of the stage.

"You're so beautiful," he whispers.

His off-script line causes a little laugh to puff from my mouth, and I don't even care. Because he isn't speaking as Beck. This is Zach talking to me.

"Thank you," my words barely float out on a sigh.

The silent auditorium refuses to make a sound to break the spell. Zach cups my cheek, his fingers sliding in my hair. The contact engulfs all my senses, and I hold my breath. His other arm wraps around me, pulling me closer.

"It's too late. I'm already stuck."

His hand trembles against my skin. My eyes flutter closed, and I feel his exhale a moment before his lips meet mine. And then Zach is kissing me. Finally.

Fireworks...

Stars...

Walking away from an explosion in slow motion...

His heat soothes the cold inside me, melting my inhibitions. I wrap my arms around him, one at his shoulders and one at his back, the kiss deepening. Flattened against him, I feel his heart beating wildly. Or maybe it's mine.

I can't believe I worried this would be blah.

Our power ignites. An injection of fire to my veins. Life magic and death magic weave in a dizzying rush until I can't figure out where his ends and mine begins. It bursts inside, the intensity sending sparks tingling through my body.

Kissing Zach might become an addiction.

He pulls back, less than a millimeter, our breath still touching. I feel the smile against his lips. "Whoa," he whispers.

'Whoa' might be an understatement.

Rooted on stage, locked in an embrace, the sound of applause interrupts our moment. And then I remember, the audience is supposed to applaud.

I bite my lip, laughing as I turn to face the clapping and whistling crowd. With clasped hands, we bow. Then again. And a third time as we wait for the applause to die down. The lights dim, our cue to leave the stage, and we walk back to our seats.

"Whoa," Zach says, and we settle in for the rest of The Exhibition.

CHAPTER
TWENTY

DRAMA CAMP: DAY FIVE – SATURDAY NIGHT

"It's too short," I mutter, pulling at my hem.

"It's not too short." Portia rolls her eyes at the tugging.

"It's too tight."

"It's not too tight." She pauses at the door to the banquet room and takes a breath. She insisted we make a grand entrance, which means we're fifteen minutes late. Zach and Devin saved our seats, and we plan to slip in, aka swagger like fashionistas at a photoshoot, and sit with them.

"How do I look?" she asks.

"Incredible," I say on a sigh. She's Portia Landry. *Average* need not apply.

She chose a dandelion yellow, one-shouldered dress. Despite the relaxed fit and length to the knee, it screams sexy. She flat ironed her hair, the dark strands sleek and shiny, and a deep purple gloss colors her lips.

My hair is half up/half down, thanks to Portia, and I

have on a mauve lipstick, also thanks to Portia. To top it off, I wear "The Dress." The only thing left in my mom's closet after she deserted Dad and me. I honestly don't know why I held onto it for so long, but I did. And here I am, wearing it to the banquet.

The long-sleeved ombre white-to-aqua sheath fits like a latex glove, stretchy but snug. The short length and deep V in back show more skin than my usual shorts and tee. Goosebumps rise every time the air conditioning breezes over the normally hidden surface area. My pendant lays against the high front, the black and mirrored necklace a great compliment to the shimmery fabric.

"Let's go make our boys drool." Portia walks into the room, adding a dose of sass to her step.

The catering staff sets out appetizers, and we wind our way through the busyness. As soon as Zach spots me approaching, he stands, his eyes not so subtly running down my tight (but not too tight), short (but not too short) dress. The appreciation in his gaze makes me happy I gave in and wore it. He has on black jeans, a white shirt and tie, and a gray sports coat. The sleeves are pushed halfway up his forearms, and suddenly I'm not sure who's making who drool.

Devin's on his feet, too, and he whistles, causing people nearby to turn and stare. He steps around the table to reach Portia, pulling her into his arms.

Zach waits for me, his dimples making every other smile dull in comparison. "You look amazing."

I don't even have a chance to reply. He lowers his head, meeting my lips in a soft kiss. Heat crawls along my body, leaving a trail of fire behind. I'm getting into it, ready to kick the kiss up to an eleven, when he draws back, taking his warmth with him.

"Should we eat?" he asks.

"I'm not sure I can remember my own name right now."

He laughs and runs a hand through his hair. "Yeah, it has that effect on me too."

We sit at a table for four, and Zach's hand rests on my knee. He brushes small circles on my skin, and my focus narrows on the slight touch. I think the food tastes good. I stick forkfuls of stuff into my mouth, hardly paying attention to anything but Zach.

The teachers prep the front, bringing in plaques for the awards portion. The dress code must be pink because they all wear something in that shade. Jennifer sets up awards near the podium. Her long pink skirt almost brushes the floor, and her white top is light and flowy, like something purchased at Angels R Us. From the corner of my eye, I notice a person hanging off to the side.

Detective Rivera.

The same hat rests on his head, hiding his face. The same bulky jacket covers his torso. He leans against the wall, directly in my line of sight, and I wonder if he placed himself there to keep an eye on me.

My muscles clench, and the food I shoveled down sours in my stomach. I clutch the pendant, the black obsidian smooth in my fingers.

"What's wrong?" Zach angles close to my ear, whispering the question.

"Detective Rivera is here again."

He searches the room, his gaze landing on the policeman. "What is he doing?"

"Watching." I recognize the stillness; the same way Dad gets when he really pays attention.

"Did you talk to your dad?"

"No." Something is off. His lack of response is about more than being busy.

"Welcome, thespians. We hope you've enjoyed our annual Young Entertainers Conservatory." A woman with a blond bob stands at the podium. Her bright Pepto Bismol pink pantsuit is a bold choice. Bold in a nausea, heartburn, indigestion, upset stomach, diarrhea kind of way. "Tonight, we celebrate your achievements and honor our award winners."

Everyone cheers, and she lists the competition categories. I only half pay attention, my eyes locked on Rivera. He stays motionless, his statue-like pose disconcerting in the energetic drama crowd. His presence doesn't fit—a piece to the wrong puzzle—and I wonder why no one questions his being here.

"First up, our music awards," she says. "Let's welcome Mr. Bellamy."

He wears a maroon bowtie and the neon-pink sneakers. Portia mouths, *I love his kicks.* I knew she would. I realize he always wears pink and wonder if he coordinated the teacher's dress code. He steps up to the podium, and I give a distracted clap. "It was a close competition, but after much deliberation, I have our winners."

I tick through reasons Rivera could legitimately be here. Maybe Dad asked him to watch me. Maybe he's a security detail for someone, a famous person coming tonight as a surprise speaker. Or maybe the camp organizers wanted a police presence.

It doesn't have to be because he's The Caster.

"The winner of the pop duet competition is...." Mr. Bellamy reads from the list in his hand. "Portia Landry and Devin Gough."

I stand, cheering wildly for my BFF and her BF. Devin

takes Portia's hand, guiding her to the front, where they pick up their winner plaques. Attempting a Portia-like whistle, I stick my fingers in my mouth and emit a wet sputter. At least I tried.

Portia and Devin pose, and the camera snaps several shots, a mini paparazzi session. I add to the picture taking, and my phone flashes to capture their win. As they head back to the table, I glance at Detective Rivera.

But he's gone.

I survey the room, scanning the tables and doorways. "Where did he go?"

"I don't see him," Zach says.

The awards continue, Mr. Bellamy finishes up the music category, and another teacher reads the group competition winners.

My head hurts, the tension moving from my eyes to my neck to my shoulders. I'm letting my worry ruin the last night here. After the dance, we'll pack up and go home. The buses chauffeur people like Portia and me, who didn't drive ourselves. And those who brought cars will disappear into the night, leaving the cloud of drama camp behind.

I want to enjoy every second I have left before real life invades. The day-to-day of school, homework, and the morgue. Not laughter with Portia, playing plastic bags, and Zach. What will tomorrow look like? The day after? How do relationships even work outside of drama camp?

I shake out the high-alert muscles and let the stress go.

Zach's eyes still search the room and the spattering of freckles along the bridge of his nose scrunch. He really is handsome. And I'm done wasting time. I decide to be bold. Not pink pantsuit bold. Good bold.

"Kiss me," I say, my voice squeaking in a nervous whisper. A blush heats my cheeks, but I remind myself that I'm the new and improved bold CeCe. Pink hair, not pink pantsuit.

"What?" He turns to me, his eyes the color of a darkening sky.

"Let's stop stressing. This is our last night." I tap his foot with mine. "Just...kiss me."

I don't have to say it again.

He cups my cheek and dips his head, meeting my lips. The butterfly farm in my stomach goes wild, wings dancing. I clutch his arms, needing to hold on to something, to ground myself in a world gone dizzy.

"Get a room," Devin shouts from across the table, his loud laugh killing my butterflies.

"Give them a break." Portia throws an elbow in his side. "They're in the honeymoon phase of drama camp. It took them a minute to catch up."

"We're overachievers." He bends down, wiggling his nose against hers and pecking her lips.

"We've endured way worse from you two." Zach's hand returns to my knee. "Unless my skill makes you jealous."

I expect the taunt to rile Devin and make him prove his lip incubus-ing. But he shakes his head and laughs.

Another woman steps to the podium, her rose-colored dress a marked improvement from Pepto Lady. "Next, we have the winners of the individual competitions."

Meaning the dramatic monologue.

Like the fires of Hell turned up the thermostat, I feel the heated glare of Julie Jolley. Her dark hair twists up in a complicated do, and her devil-red lips send a hate-filled sneer. As Mawmaw would say, *you can put lipstick on a pig, but it's still a pig.*

If she wins, I'll never hear the end of it.

A nagging voice in the back of my mind reminds me I

took a ten percent penalty for being late. But forget that voice. I did good. No, great.

One by one, people accept their plaque, a little engraved metal plate on a piece of wood announcing the accomplishment. I listen to each winner, occasionally sharing fake smiles with Julie "evil incarnate" Jolley.

"And for the dramatic monologue..." the woman reading the names loses her place. She uses her finger to trace down the page. Silence stretches, and she takes forever, her forehead bunching as she brings the paper closer to her face.

How long is this list?

"Sorry," she laughs. "Dramatic monologue. The winner is...Julie Jolley."

The applause sounds hollow in my ears. Julie won. For a play about an unhoused street-performing orphan from the wrong side of town.

She squeals and jumps up, her hand flying to cover her mouth. Her fingers tremble, and she swipes under her eyes, whispering *thank you, thank you,* as she walks on shaky legs to the front.

Talk about a dramatic performance.

Zach's hand tightens on my knee, and he frowns. "I'm sorry."

"She's so precious," Portia mutters, her applause slow enough she could stretch taffy between the claps.

I look at Portia and Zach, my best friend and my boyfriend. Just like finding a new show on Netflix or the first Cadbury Cream Egg of the season, they make me feel better. Shaking my head, I smile. "She can have the win. I've got you."

"Are you saying I'm a prize?" His foot rubs the side of mine, a pinky toe caress. *Monologue what?*

"You're definitely better than a plaque," I say.

Pepto Lady gets up to the podium again. "After this final award, we'll clear the tables for dancing." Everyone screams, the drama crowd ready to party. "But first, the winners of The Exhibition."

She holds a big envelope, and a pink wax seal adorns the flap. None of the other categories came packaged. It's the grandest of all awards, one so lofty and important someone took the extra time to melt wax, pour it, and press it with a decorative emblem.

The Exhibition award!

Do Zach and I have a chance? While our performance dazzled, the kiss broke all forms of measurement. The Richter scale; shaken apart. A barometer; too much pressure. Rotten Tomatoes; certified so fresh it's barely a seedling.

I'd say we have a chance.

Taking her time, Pepto Lady rubs a finger along the seal, her nail digging underneath the wax and popping the envelope open. She slides the paper out, and her eyes move across the page.

"The final prize of the night, the winners of The Exhibition are—" she pauses for dramatic effect—"Zach Wren and CeCe LeBlanc with *Stuck*."

What? Forget Netflix and Cadbury Eggs. I only need this moment for the rest of my life.

"We did it." Zach stands and pulls me up, lifting me from the ground. My feet come off the floor, and he buries his nose in my hair.

We float to the front on clouds of victory. I'm so happy I barely notice Julie Jolley, her mouth dropped open, eyes scowling, and fingers clenching the table like she wants to rip a chunk from it. Okay, maybe I do notice her a little.

Zach and I take our plaques and pose together for the picture. His arm goes around my shoulders, and I lean into him. Other cameras flash, more than just the photographer, and I imagine Portia and Devin snapping away to memorialize us. This win means everything. Not because of the scholarship opportunities or the scent of Julie's freshly baked jealousy coming straight from the oven, although it doesn't hurt. But because Zach and I accomplished this together.

Oh no! Portia was right. I met a boy who made drama camp coupledom a happy reality.

I sneak a peek at the leading man in question. A bright expression exposes his dimples, a masterclass in how a smile should look. His azure eyes twinkle, teaching stars the right way to sparkle. Freckles dot the bridge of his nose, and I imagine kissing every single one.

I've done it. I've fallen completely in like with Zach Wren.

And the way his flushed gaze rakes over me tells me he shares in the fall.

In a matter of minutes, the caterers clear the chairs and tables away. The overhead speakers pump out music on high volume, the bass beat rumbling the floor. Portia takes Devin by the hand and starts dancing.

Zach turns to me. "Do you want to dance?"

Are beignets God's gift to donuts? "Yes."

He wraps me up right where we stand, and his hands run along my back. Along that deep V where clothes usually cover, but tonight is open space. I shiver.

"Are you cold?" He asks, pulling me closer to share his warmth.

Cold? No. Definitely not. I've just never had hands touch my skin there, maybe not even my own. I'd give my flexibility a solid 6 out of 10, which means when I have an itch in the middle of my back, I find a backscratcher, pencil, or in the most desperate of circumstances, rub against the wall like a disgruntled bear.

"I'm not cold. I'm..." I pause as I watch two men walk into the auditorium. "Detective Rivera is back. With my dad."

Zach turns, following my line of sight. "Your dad's the guy in the gray suit?"

"Yep. That's him."

Foreboding looms like a cloud heavy with unshed rain. My internal narrator shows up, reading the scene like a page of stage direction. *Things were going well for CeCe, too well, and the drama gods decided it was time to cook up toil and trouble.*

Dad flashes his badge, talking to Pepto Lady. He ignored my calls, and now he's here?

I drag Zach through the crowd, the music and dancing a chaotic background as I force my way to Dad. Confusion stutters my thoughts, my mind on a loop of the same questions. What is he doing? Why is he here?

He walks toward the group of teachers, his badge still out. I bump into a dancing couple, and the girl yells at me. I ignore her. My heeled shoes click on the hard floor, and I move faster. I'm only a few feet away when I hear him.

"Mrs. Wren, could you please step into the hall?"

My stomach sinks, a Titanic level of dread forming a gut boulder at record speed. There's no reason for Dad to see Zach's mom. No reason for him to take her into the hall. The open, double-wide doors make it easy to watch their progress. He, Detective Rivera, and Jennifer are only a few steps ahead of Zach and me. Two plainclothes officers approach from the opposite side, entering through the doors leading to the parking lot.

Dad reaches behind his back and pulls his handcuffs loose. "Jennifer Black Wren. You're under arrest for the murders of Henry Guillory and Marcus Eagan."

And just like that, the heavens open and drench CeCe's victory in a tempest.

CHAPTER TWENTY-ONE

DRAMA CAMP: END SCENE – SATURDAY NIGHT

"Dad, what are you doing?" I grab his sleeve to stop him from slapping the cuffs on Zach's mom.

"Stay back." He glances at me, and does a double take, giving me a solid up and down. "CeCe Marie, what in the Sam Hill are you wearing?"

He hands Rivera the cuffs and takes off his suit jacket, throwing it over my shoulders. I told Portia this dress was too short.

Rivera looks at me and then away, shaking his head. The obvious disapproval stings. But not as much as watching him reach for Jennifer with the cuffs. Zach puts himself between them, and one of the plainclothes officers approaches, ready to step in.

"You don't want to do this." Rivera's voice adopts a hard edge, his accent more pronounced.

"Zach, it's okay," Jennifer says, moving around him. "Let the police do their job."

"Mom, no. You haven't done anything wrong."

"Call your Dad. Tell him what's going on." She holds out her wrists. Rivera snaps the handcuffs closed with surprising gentleness considering his harsh expression.

"She didn't do it," I shout at Dad. "You can't arrest my boyfriend's mom."

"Your what?" He shoots a glare at Zach and then slowly shifts back to me. "We'll talk about this later."

Dad reads Jennifer her rights, and Zach's fists clench. People gather at the open doors, and a murmur of gossip topples through the crowd like a line of dominoes. Everyone stares, and I know this will go down as the most climactic finish in the history of drama camp.

Dad, Rivera, and the other policemen flank Jennifer, leading her out. I follow, unwilling to let this go. The large suit jacket threatens to fall off my shoulder, and I slip my arms through the sleeves. Zach walks behind, and I glance at him. The same lips that kissed mine now turn down in a fierce scowl. I wrap my arms around myself, fighting to hold my composure. Moisture prickles my eyes, and a frustrated scream builds in my throat.

We step outside, away from the gaping witnesses, and I grab Dad's arm. "Wait, she's not a murderer. This is the teacher who helped me."

He stops, giving me his full attention while Rivera keeps moving to the patrol car. "I'm sorry, baby girl. You know how this works. We followed the lead you gave us."

"What lead? This doesn't make sense. Why would she help me if she's The Caster? She made this necklace for my protection." I grab the black obsidian between my fingers, and stand on tippy toes to show him.

"Mrs. Wren made that necklace?"

"Yes, and it works." I stare into his green eyes, so much

like mine, begging him to understand how non-murdery she is. "I can't feel The Caster anymore. Not since I put this on."

"Give it to me, CeCe." He holds out his hand, palm up.

"What? No." I cover the pendant as if hiding it will make him forget.

"It's evidence." He lowers his head, his voice a whisper. "And what if she's guilty? You don't know what that necklace might be doing to you."

"It's protecting me."

Dad holds out his hand with a grunt that says, *don't fight me on this.*

I yank the pendant off, dropping it in his hand. "Fine. But you're wrong."

My words give him pause; the conflict etched in his wrinkled forehead. His fingers curl around the necklace. "Be careful," he says with a sigh.

He joins Rivera at the patrol car and they both stare at me while they talk. The streetlamps illuminate the scene like a spotlight aimed at a stage. Jennifer sits in the back, her chin held high, her long blond hair swept behind her shoulders. Now she's the piece to the wrong puzzle, an angel under arrest. I hope they cleaned the seat before they put her in there.

I wait until Dad and Rivera get in the car and drive away before I face Zach. His jaw clenches so tight I worry he might break his dimples.

"You led the cops to my mom?" Hurt ekes from his tone.

"No, I didn't. That's not—"

"She only wanted to help. What did you say?" His voice raises, each word growing louder. He doesn't give me time to answer but grabs his cell. "Never mind. I have to call my dad."

"Please let me explain."

The phone presses against his ear, and he walks down the sidewalk, the conversation fading with him. "Yeah, that's what I said. Arrested. For murder."

He doesn't look back.

Everything blurs around me, like I'm on the Tilt-a-Whirl, spinning faster and faster, the pressure immense enough to break me apart. My brain fumbles for something to make sense. Emotions flit in the air, millions of dust particles, and I can't grab hold of one.

An arm winds through mine. Portia. Devin stands on the other side of her, a few steps behind us.

"Did you see what happened?" My dazed question comes from lips that hardly move.

"Everyone saw, sweetie," Portia says.

"It's a joke. They made a huge scene." The moonlight darkens Devin's frown, and he puts more distance between us. "I'm gonna find Zach. Make sure he's okay."

"Should I come with you?" I ask.

He laughs, but the sound is harsh and ugly. "No. Your dad arrested his mom. I don't think he'll want to see you, no matter how good you kiss."

Ouch.

"Don't be a jerk," Portia calls at his retreating back, and I appreciate her defense. But Devin's right. Zach won't want to see me. He probably hates me right now.

Rumbling music plays inside, the *thump, thump, thump,* a faint echo. Gossip floats through the open doors, every overheard word feeling like an accusation against me.

Ms. Black was taken by the police.

They said she murdered someone.

No—two people.

The dust particles solidify, and a giant ball of hurt

settles in my chest. I struggle to draw air. *Hey Lungs, I need you.* Lungs ignore me, and I press a hand over my heart to ease the ache.

"How do I fix this?" I whisper.

"I don't know." Portia adjusts, and I realize she holds our plaques under her arm. Those little slats of wood seemed so important less than an hour ago. "Let's go to our room and pack. We'll take things one step at a time."

Nodding, I fight the tears pricking my eyes. I concentrate on two things: moving my feet and not crying. The running dialogue in my head says, *step, step, don't cry, don't cry,* and I try to ignore thoughts of Zach, and the look on his face as Dad led Jennifer out in handcuffs.

What if he really does hate me? He already blames me for putting Jennifer in the crosshairs of Dad's investigation. Hate seems like the natural progression.

My heart aches, a buzzing pressure merging with my ball of hurt, making it bigger.

Portia leads me to the dorms, and even the humid outdoor air refuses its warmth. Shivers start in my core and spread outward. Not necro-shivers. Those I can handle, a temporary chill from being in the death magic too long. Nothing a warm blanket and hot chocolate won't fix. These are different; emotional quivers shaking me apart from the inside.

She opens the door to our room, and I go straight to my bed, flopping down. The best thing I can do for Jennifer is figure out who The Caster really is. I've been an honorary detective and solved murders for years. I need to analyze what I know and narrow down the possibilities. But all I can think about is Zach.

I already miss the snug zone.

"I'm a stupid girl," I say, mostly to the ceiling, but Portia eavesdrops.

"Stupid girls don't take AP Biology." Her suitcase lays open on the bed, and she fills it with clothes scattered on the floor.

"I'm a stupid girl who ruined something really good."

"Girl, we've all been there." She holds one red wedge sandal, searching for its mate. "But it's not as bad as you think."

"It's exactly as bad as I think. My dad arrested my boyfriend's mom." I sit up, emphasizing each word in case she missed the severity of the situation.

The red sandal lands on the floor with a thump, and she sits next to me on the bed. "Did you give your dad evidence against Jennifer?"

"No."

"Did you tell him she was The Caster?"

"I told him The Caster was here. That's why they investigated at Tulane." It never crossed my mind that Rivera secretly watched Jennifer. Gathering whatever evidence to justify her arrest.

"It's not your fault." She puts her arm around me, and I lean on her shoulder. "If Zach's too stubborn to see that, he isn't worth your time."

"But I really like him, Portia. A lot." I bite my lip, and tears collect on my lashes.

She leans her head to rest against mine. "And we both like beignets. A lot. We'll just eat more now."

I laugh, a wet sound that shifts into a sob. Ugly, wet streaks dampen my cheeks, and I let the tears go. "I don't want him to be stubborn."

"No matter what happens with Zach, you've always got me. The Two Amigos." She pats my shoulder and gets up from the bed. "Change out of your dress and pack your bags. The buses will be here by nine. I'll help you make a voodoo doll of him when we get home."

"Okay." I smile, but her mention of voodoo makes me think of the CeCe doll. My problems are a lot bigger than being a stupid girl. The Caster is still free. I no longer have the necklace. And with Jennifer in jail, I'm not sure how to protect myself. "I need to convince Dad he arrested the wrong person."

"That'll go down like a bucket of rocks in the bayou." She goes back to searching for the missing red sandal, scooping clothes and tossing them on the bed. How could she make such a big mess in five days?

Opening my luggage, which is still mostly packed, I dig to find a change of clothes. "He's a good cop. There's no way he wants an innocent person in jail."

"How do we convince him she's innocent?"

She said *we*. I love my best friend. "I guess we find The *real* Caster."

"Now you're talking." Her muffled voice echoes from under her bed. "But if we're going to Scooby Doo this thing, I get to be Fred, the fearless leader."

"You don't want to be the pretty girl, Daphne?"

"Danger-prone-Daphne? No thanks. The damsel in distress look doesn't suit me. Aha!" She slides from her spot under the bed, wielding the other red sandal triumphantly, like pulling the sword from the stone, then tosses it in her suitcase.

I laugh, my mood already a little brighter. "If you're the fearless leader, you come up with the plan. What's our first step?"

She taps her bottom lip, her long nail making small

indentations. "The Caster probably framed Zach's mom, right? It must be someone who knows about her voodoo."

"Or someone noticed she taught all the magic classes and figured she was a good scapegoat." Slipping out of The Dress, I put on my most comfortable clothes—blue and pink flannel pajama shorts and a pink tee that says, *if sleeping, do not disturb.* The other bus riders will have to endure my current fashion mood. I can't clothes anymore. A bra is the only concession I'm willing to make.

"Right. Someone who has access to the campus and knows the teachers. Where does that leave us?" she asks.

"Maybe another teacher?" I pause my packing, thinking about the possibility. The always-in-motion Mr. Olsen, who picked me for The Exhibition. The pink-shoed Mr. Bellamy, who somehow knew my name and wrote an original song Zach and I performed. Both possibilities seem ridiculous. "I don't know. We need more clues, Fred."

"We need to set a trap." She purses her purple lips, her thinking face engaged, fully embracing her role in the Scooby gang.

My phone buzzes, and I look at the screen.

> ZACH: We need to talk.

Just like that, I'm on the Tilt-a-Whirl again, my stomach swooping. Seeing his name makes a sheen of sweat break out on my forehead. Gripping the phone far tighter than necessary, I call in Portia for backup.

"Zach wants to talk. What do I say?" I bounce from foot to foot and tip my cell for her to see. She hovers next to me as I try to type the right words.

ME: *I'm so sorry.*

"No, don't apologize." She shakes her head in disapproval. "You didn't do anything wrong."

"Right." I know better than to debate her glower. I delete and start over.

ME: ~~*I'm so sorry.*~~

I type, *Are you mad at me?*

"Nope. Try again."

Trying again. *Please don't hate me.*

"Seriously?" She takes the phone from my hands and types.

> ME: Ok. When?

Well, less is more, I guess. She hands the cell back, and we both watch the screen until it illuminates with another text.

> ZACH: Can I give u a ride home?

> ME: Driving me to the middle of a swamp to leave me for the gators?

> ZACH: Depends on how the conversation goes.

My heart picks up speed, not because I worry about the gators. Because I want our chat to go well. If we could rewind to The Exhibition and live in that kiss, I'd stay there until the swamp dries up. My lips tingle at the memory.

> ZACH: JK. I promise to get u home, limbs intact.

I wish he could make the same promise about my heart.

CHAPTER
TWENTY-TWO

GOING HOME: SATURDAY NIGHT

"Nice outfit," Zach says, opening the trunk of a blue Subaru Forrester.

I glance down at my pink shirt, flannel shorts, and black flip-flops, wondering why I chose pajamas instead of something cute. But I fell into a spiral, wanting only ice cream and comfort, and no one needs to be cute for that.

"Thanks." I quirk an eyebrow. "I guess."

"I like it. Matches your hair." He takes my suitcase and lifts it into the trunk. I try to gauge his mood and come up blank. Despite his casual words, the expression on his face is serious.

He opens my door, and I climb in, fastening my seatbelt. By the time he enters on the driver's side, my worry has buckled in too. It's like the first day of drama camp, meeting by the toxic waste dump. Nerves crashing our lunch date.

Portia decided to catch a ride with Devin. Forget the fact I begged her to ride with me. I had a whole plan. We'd sit in the back, and I'd whisper my thoughts to her. She'd interpret in a more Portia-like, less CeCe-like way. Zach would gain instant understanding. When I told her my idea, she laughed and patted my head, insisting I'd be fine.

She was wrong.

The car starts, and the engine idles. I keep my gaze locked on the passenger window. Everything is so interesting, the trees, the gray stone building, the crack in the sidewalk. The darkness outside makes it hard to see clearly, but if I squint, I can make out shapes beyond the light of the streetlamps.

"How much longer before you're ready to look at me?" He asks.

My eyes stay glued to the window. "Just another minute."

"CeCe." He blows out a breath, sounding more tired than irritated. "I don't know where you live."

"Oh." I finally turn, and a glow from the dash illuminates him. His hair stands on end, his eyes fatigued. He's gorgeous. "I'm kind of nervous. I'm really sorry about your mom. I feel sick and—"

"It's okay. Let's start with directions. Then we can chat." A gentle touch brushes my arm, his fingers running slowly from shoulder to elbow. Warmth spreads, and I curl my hand into a fist, wanting to hold onto the sensation.

"Sorry." I clear my throat. "Head to Bayou St. John, near Broad Street."

He drives out of the parking lot, the headlights brightening our path. The silence holds for a full ten seconds until I feel obligated to fill it. "I don't know what evidence my dad has. When he showed up, I was just as surprised as you, and I *never* told him anything about your mom."

My defense is just getting warmed up, and he responds with, "I know."

"You know?"

"Yeah." He chuckles. A tired, beautiful sound. "More importantly, I know you. You're a great actress, but you wouldn't play nice with my mom and then set her up."

His words help me take my first deep breath since Dad and Rivera crashed drama camp. My muscles uncoil, and nerves stop hijacking this ride.

"Is your dad okay?" I ask.

"He couldn't believe Mom got arrested. I had to repeat myself a dozen times. And then a dozen more for Mason." This time, his smile looks real. The dimples even make an appearance. "But he knows a good lawyer. He'll get her out."

"Good."

He glances at me before switching his attention back to the road. The smile holds. "You told your dad I was your boyfriend."

"I did." More like yelled it out in a moment of extreme stress. "Is that okay?"

Reaching over, he takes my hand. "It's against the rules of the Cotillion Handbook for a gentleman to disagree with a lady. So, I guess I'm officially your boyfriend."

CeCe suddenly realizes there is no escaping this deep like of Zach Wren. Her heart pumps like it's throwing a party in her chest cavity. Lungs open like their only job is to breathe his scent.

I shake my head. *Shut up, internal narrator.*

"I haven't been a very good girlfriend yet, but I'll fix that. Portia and I are going to find The Caster." We approach the turn, and I point it out. "Take the next left."

The signal ticks and he moves into the middle lane. "If

that's the plan, you'll need another necklace. Good thing your boyfriend can get you one."

"You can't do magic for me. I promised."

"Your promise was about black magic, which isn't required for a protection pendant. Besides, I know someone else who'll make it." He hangs a left, and the blinker clicks off. "And I want to help you track The Caster."

If he's joining the investigation, who will he be in our Scooby gang? Smarty-pants Velma?

"Track The Caster. What does that mean?" As soon as I ask the question, I have the sinking thought that I might be Danger-prone-Daphne. The damsel in distress. I shift in my seat and lean on the armrest, tightening my grip on his hand.

"We need to reverse the spell they used on you." A trickle of excitement runs through his veins, and his power dances against my fingertips.

"The black magic spell?" I ask hesitantly.

"Yes." Another grin. He finds amusement in my concern. "But don't worry. The Caster used black magic to create the spell. You just need to manipulate it."

"Okay. It's important I keep my word. Mawmaw says a person who breaks a promise is as useful as sunscreen in a hurricane."

He smiles. "I get it. I have a Mawmaw too."

The wood siding of my house comes into view, the bright shade of periwinkle dimmed by the night. White porch rails gleam in the moonlight from the fresh coat Dad and I painted a few months back. Grass covers the ground, the weather still mild enough to keep it green instead of the dried-out beige of late summer.

"This is me," I say, pointing at the cottage-style house.

"The blue one?"

Periwinkle, really, but the darkness makes the exact shade indistinguishable. "Yep."

Pulling over, he parks along the curb and hops out to get my door. We collect my bags, and he hauls my suitcase, the wheels grinding against the sidewalk. I carry Van Hell-Sing and adjust the case as we walk up the path.

This is it. The official end of drama camp. Real life awaits; back to school, being at home, and late-night trips to the morgue. Ugh.

I lead the way up the steps, setting aside my guitar, and he pushes the suitcase right by the front door. The roof extends over the porch, and under cover of gable and night, he takes my hand.

I draw in a breath, restraining the unruly desire to become a lip incubus. "Thanks for the ride."

"Of course." He tugs me closer, and our toes touch. I wriggle in my flip-flops, grazing against his shoes. "Can I see you tomorrow?"

There are so many complications. My dad arrested his mom. His family might hate me on principle. Not to mention Dad's feelings about the whole boyfriend thing.

"I'd like that." My voice sounds heavy, slower. Like dark molasses. "We're good, right? You and me?"

The soft radiance of the porch light glimmers in his eyes, giving them a twinkling effect. I stare into his endless sky, the dark blue stippled in the reflective glow. "We're good. We're definitely good."

He cups my cheek, and I close my eyes. His scent fills my senses, the citrus and cinnamon making me want to snuggle in. My body leans closer, and he wraps his arms around me.

"I'm going to kiss you," he says, and I can't decide if he's telling me or asking permission.

But either way, the answer is, "yes."

By slow degrees, his head lowers. My heels lift from the flip-flops and I rise to my toes. As his lips meet mine, the first thing I feel, besides the touch of his mouth (*ahhhhmazing!*), is our magic. It's light. Sunshine. Brightening everything dark and cold. He stops to look at me, searching for...I don't care because he's back to my lips, the kiss deepening.

His fingers grip my shirt, and I tremble at the intensity, overwhelmed by his touch and his magic. Our power clings. A force of gravity. Dizziness engulfs me, and the only solution is holding onto Zach.

"You taste like black magic," he whispers against my lips.

Wait, what?

My body chills, and I jump back, shoving him away. "I'm sorry."

"I didn't say it was a bad thing." He attempts to pull me in his arms. I stay out of reach, exiling myself from his warmth.

"Obviously, it's a bad thing. Black magic probably tastes worse than garlic breath."

"No, it doesn't." He laughs. "It's more like dark chocolate. Sweet, rich, and smooth."

I ignore the way his eyes get all lusty. "That's weird. Because every time I feel black magic, it's like sewer sludge."

"You're really hung up on this." He bites his lip, trying to look serious and failing.

"Is it because of The Caster?" Stupid question. Why else would I taste like chocolatey evil?

"Probably. I felt it after the puppetry spell." He reaches for me again, and I take another step back. His foot taps the ground, and he fidgets, tucking hands in his pockets.

"But you said it's like an addiction." Nerves make bail, and I fight through them, asking the not-stupid question, the one I don't want an answer to. "Does kissing me make it worse?"

We stare at each other. I hold completely still, afraid of what he might say. And Zach jiggles like unrestrained Jell-o. Every time we kiss, every time he touches me, his magic chases away the cold of The Caster. But I taste like black magic.

"Kissing you makes everything better." He closes the distance and puts his hands on my shoulders. Even that small gesture turns up the heat. "We're going to figure this out, CeCe Marie."

He remembered my middle name. "Okay."

"Let me help you with your bags," he says.

I open the front door, and he hauls both my suitcase and guitar inside. Without hesitation, he pulls me in his arms and gives me another hug. Dipping my head in the snug zone, the crevice a perfect fit, I nestle in. Forget oxygen. This is all I need.

"I have to get home, but I don't like leaving you alone. When will your dad be back?"

"I'm sure he'll be home soon, and your family needs you."

"Don't forget to pour salt. Stay safe," he whispers, his soft voice revering the sacred snug. "I'll see you tomorrow."

He leaves, and the door clicks shut behind him. I stay in the living room, listening as his car starts, then drives away. I take my luggage down the hall.

My flip-flops suck against the floor, the rubber soles sticking to the tile. I walk to my room, lifting Van HellSing out of her carrying case and setting her on my guitar stand. The black and white veneer matches the black and white décor of my room. White stripes break up the otherwise black bedspread, and pink throw pillows add a splash of color.

I start unpacking by hanging The Dress in my closet. My fingers trail over the sleeve, the sparkling fabric crisp under my touch. My stomach rolls as I think of Dad's face when he saw it. Did he remember it belonged to Mom?

My plaque gains a spot of honor on my desk. The engraved metal plate reads: *Achievement in The Exhibition. First Place, Zach Wren and CeCe LeBlanc; "Stuck."* I'm so glad Portia grabbed it for me.

Thinking of her, I call and fill her in on the conversation with Zach. She asks a few questions, but she's still with Devin, so I keep it short and to the point.

After hanging up, I dig into my nightstand to pull out a candle and a canister of salt. I drag the bed away from the wall and walk around the perimeter, dumping a generous trail as I go. Forming a tight circle, I take another lap, pouring a second, larger circle. The white grains pile up. Small hills of protection surrounding me. Then I light the candle.

I intend to wait up for Dad, but my busy week catches up with me, and I doze. Eyelids droop, breathing deepens, and visions of drama camp dance in my head. It doesn't take long before I give up the battle and sleep. At some point, Dad comes to my room. He talks, and I try to respond. Fatigue buries me, and the conversation goes nowhere.

In the middle of the night, I startle awake. Gasping, I scramble to turn on my lamp, and the dim glow casts a soft light. My heart pounds, and I scan the room, wondering what caused the sudden alarm. Cold sweat glistens on my skin, and I clasp my blanket with clammy hands.

A curtain of dirty magic hovers, distorting the air like a heat wave. It lingers near the bed, stalling at the pile of salt. The candle burned out who knows how long ago. *Or maybe Dad blew it out?* I want to reach over and light it. But I'm frozen, scared to look away.

The Caster is here, and the connection has a stronger pull than before.

The magic droops to the ground, the curtain falling and shifting to oil. It oozes across the floor, fading into the salt. I watch in horror as the grains of white slowly dissolve in the murky liquid magic.

Opening my mouth, I nearly call out for my dad, but hesitate, worried about the effect the magic might have on him. If he enters my room, unprotected, would it hurt him? Haunt him like a zombie's touch?

I scoot against the headboard, pulling my knees to my chest. The oil seeps through the first layer of protection, bleeding to the second circle. A wave of cold mildew blasts me at the dwindling salt. I'm afraid to reach my arm outside the protective barrier, but I take the chance, grabbing my cell. I hit the phone icon and look up as the second circle dissolves.

My thumb hovers over Zach's name, but I go limp before I make the call, my spirit stretching away from my physical form. The incorporeal leash pulls me, and I have no ability or power to stop it. My vision is blocked, and different from the previous spirit kidnappings, I can't see where I'm going. The high-speed, blurry vision disorients me, but I can hear The Caster clearly in my mind, sounding like my own voice.

"CeCe LeBlanc. I've got you."

CHAPTER
TWENTY-THREE

TAKEN: SUNDAY, EARLY A.M.

My spirit floats in an unfamiliar place, overlooking a room with white plaster walls and no windows. The angled ceiling makes me wonder if this is an attic, the sloping wooden beams creating a sense of claustrophobia. A thick, metal door is the only exit, with a heavy, horizontal locking bar bolted across it, ensuring no one will accidentally stumble in.

The Caster is here, shrouded in magic, their features obscured. Height, weight, gender...I've got nothing. They stand in a circle burned into the wooden floor. Three smaller circles are etched on the inside of that, and in each of those, a large, glass container sits. In one is a kidney, which I assume came from the voodoo doll murder. Another jar contains something squishy and gross, probably the lungs from Henry Guillory. The third remains blessedly empty. In the exact middle, surrounded by a circle of ash, lies the CeCe doll, a rock crushing the chest.

I try to awaken my necromancy to no avail. I call on

moon magic, searching for the gravitational pull. Nada. Something blocks my ability and keeps my magic tank solidly on E.

A beating drum sounds, and I look around, unsure where the noise comes from. The ritual pound echoes in my ears, the rhythm strengthening the black magic. It rises, a tsunami of filth crashing through my spirit.

"Life magic has tainted you. We have to purge it."

Life magic. Zach.

The Caster holds a vial, dumping thick oil over the CeCe doll. Grime coats it, and sludge drips off the edges. The slimy invasion devours my link to Zach, the snake-like specter poisoning the life magic and leaving me cold. I clutch at the remnants of Zach's warmth, fighting to keep it with me, and the drums grow louder. The deep thumps vibrate, hammering my spirit. A slithering chill accompanies the beat, winding an icy melody of darkness through me.

It's all too much, and my spirit shrieks, the intangible pain unlike anything I've ever felt.

"Let me in." The Caster speaks in my voice.

I continue to resist, but I can't keep them out, and the greasy power eclipses me. Each beat of the drum brings me closer to The Caster until I float inside the circle with them. The last traces of life magic disappear in the onslaught.

Darkness.

The pain is gone. The drums go silent. Then oil. Thick, black oil filling me to bursting. Cramming my essence, spoiling in my gut. The heaviness brims over, the agonizing pressure erupting.

The Caster is with me, in my head, surrounding my spirit. I sense them, their mind, and their emotions. I don't know how we connected, but I see The Caster's thoughts.

"*Look*," they say.

Grief knocks me back. A crushing devastation. The misery I experienced earlier, fearing Zach might hate me, can't compare to this level of despair. It's consuming. Paralyzing.

It's loss.

In our minds, I see the remains of a car accident. Smoke rises from the twisted, hot steel. Two cars merge into one, the black and blue a tangled mass of machinery. There's blood too. Painting the blacktop in a ruddy stain. Police work to block the road, and paramedics wield the heavy Jaws of Life. Sparks fly as they cut away pieces of the mess.

But they're too late.

The Caster lost someone close to them. Someone they loved. More than that. The other part of their soul. They make me feel the overwhelming loneliness. Every night, staring at the ceiling. Every morning, a pit sinking at the sight of the empty half of the bed.

"*Have you felt this grief?*" they ask.

I think of my mom. The days, weeks, and months after she left, wondering if she was coming back. The anticipation as I got home from school, thinking she might be there.

But the real pain came a year ago when I lost Mawmaw. I miss her. Her home-cooked meals, somehow always ready when I stopped over. Her advice, spoken with a deep-south accent and a slice of opinion. Even her penchant for stubbornness and strong perfume. After she passed, I wrote in my journal. Pages and pages of everything I loved about her, so I'd never forget. I haven't read that journal entry again, and I haven't looked at a picture of Mawmaw since.

I understand loss.

"*Yes,*" The Caster says, seeing my experience as clearly as I saw theirs.

They relish my grief—believing my sympathy will convince me to help with their plan. Which opens to me.

I see spells. Dozens of them. Hundreds. The Caster, searching for relief from the pain. The fall into black magic, delving deeper and deeper, drowning before the answer finally surfaces. A dark and heinous spell.

Shroud of Reawakening.

The plan hatches. Targeting the criminals and drunks, the lowlifes who won't be missed. Those who can lose a lung, a kidney, and a heart—each part needed from a separate body for the spell to work properly. Collect the organs, preserve them with magic, and then comes the reawakening. Something that can only be completed by a true necromancer. The power can't be stolen. The spell only works when a person born with resurrection magic performs it.

"My necromancer." The possessive words drift around me, the declaration cold and rancid.

The Caster will get the body parts. A.K.A murder people. All I have to do is perform the spell.

"We can bring them back. First, my love, and then your Mawmaw. You don't have to live your life without her," The Caster whispers.

The image of the bloody kidney comes to my mind. *How many people will die?*

"Does it really matter?"

A spiral of disgust twists, making me sick. I understand the plan now and my role in it. To bring back loved ones who deserve a full life. A new life possible through killing a few scumbags and using an evil resurrection spell. The Caster thinks Mawmaw is the reason I'll help. What they don't realize is she's the reason I won't.

She taught me better.

I'm not going to do it, I think the words, knowing The Caster hears me.

"You will. One way or another."

The plan expands, showing me how—if I refuse—they'll force our magic to grow jointly, like old tree roots winding together to survive the gusting storms. Stronger and stronger until one can't be divided from the other without chopping both down. Until The Caster can control me and my magic, forcing me to perform whatever spell they want.

"Why should a good person stay dead when so many horrible people live?" The memory of the car accident plays in our minds again. The flashing emergency lights reflect off nearby houses. Metal cuts and a shower of fireworks blast from the saw, shooting too close to the dried-out grass bordering the sidewalk. The hot sun descends, the pink sky a backdrop to the devastation on the street.

Against my will, The Caster draws a memory from me. We see Mawmaw, close to the end, when she spent most of her time in the recliner. Her veiny hands clutch the armrests, and her hair thins out more and more. I sit next to her, cramming a lifetime into one visit. We watch *Downton Abbey*, her choice. Tears brim in her eyes at the death of her favorite character. Not bothering to swipe at the dampness on her cheeks, she allows the emotion to drain from her, and I realize I'm crying too. But I'm not even watching the TV. I'm watching her.

"We can bring her back."

She asked me not to raise her. She said, "Death is good for the soul." I nodded, and she wrapped me in a hug, her body trembling. At that point, just lifting her arms was difficult.

No, I respond, unwilling to defile her memory.

The drums return, starting quietly, then louder. And louder. The percussive banging surrounds me, coming from inside me. The black magic gathers into a swarm of rotten water, cresting into a swell. Each drumbeat sends a stabbing twinge through my spirit. I'm trapped, unable to call on magic, held in place by the strange leash. The silty liquid surges, and the flood smashes over me.

I'm in the water, treading the magic. Dad taught me to swim before I knew how to walk, and I stretch my arms, splashing the filth. I get exactly nowhere, swallowed in the murkiness. Panic grips me, and I fight to get out.

Let me go, I think. *Please let me go.*

The drums pick up speed, the beats pounding one on top of another. Darkness impossibly deepens, confusing my senses and spinning me in circles. The Caster presses in like a compactor, squeezing my resistance.

Until I can't fight anymore.

The black magic ravages my spirit, a thick sludge pouring into me. But it's not just silty liquid. Mucusy chunks swirl in the mix, fat, oozing gobs that encase me like sucking mud. I feel it everywhere, slick and cold. I open my mouth in a silent scream.

I come awake in my room, shivering in my twisted blankets. My cell buzzes on my nightstand, and I reach for it. I have three missed texts from Zach.

> ZACH: U okay? Felt something weird, can't explain it.

> ZACH: U sleeping?

> ZACH: Freaking out here. Call me.

The clock reads 3:09, and I debate whether to respond. A voice whispers to put my phone down and sleep. *Just sleep.* My eyelids droop in a long blink, and I force them open again.

I hold my cell, the front gone dark. Shaking my head, I flick the screen and type out a response.

ME: Still up?

The phone vibrates in my hand with an incoming call, and I slide to answer.

"Hi, Zach."

"Hey. Are you okay?" Concern sharpens his tone, and he sounds wide awake despite the hour. "I had a weird feeling. Like something snapped. It woke me up."

"I felt it too." Snapped. My magical tree roots wind with The Caster's now, my connection with Zach like a broken, barely attached branch. I open my mouth to tell him about it, but a thick sludge slides in my throat, choking my words. *Just sleep. You don't need him.*

"Do you know what it was?" His voice clears the whispers from my head.

"The Caster was here. The black magic seeped through the salt circle. Did you know that was possible?"

"They must be getting more powerful. Add some graveyard soil to your salt. Can you do that now?"

"Yes." Exhaustion begs me to cuddle into the mattress, but I struggle from my bed and dig in my magic bag.

"CeCe, are you there?"

"Just pouring a new circle."

"Good." The worry in his voice dials down a notch. "What happened with The Caster?"

"I was pulled, well my spirit was, and..." my words trail off as the black magic coils in my veins. Mixing with my blood. Drums beat, a distant rhythm, and my hand trembles as I clutch the phone.

"And what?"

"And now I'm back. It's all a little fuzzy." Fatigue fills me. Stronger than before. The weight of my head becomes unsustainable on my raised neck, and I drop to my bed, flopping on my pillow. Describing what I saw, The Caster's plan, the typhoon of dirty magic, and the oily CeCe doll all seems too exhausting. "I'll tell you about it tomorrow. I'm really tired."

"CeCe, talk to me." He uses the same inflection when he played Beck and said, "Allie can we talk." I picture him, the way his freckles splash across his nose, and I mentally trace each one.

"I'm fine. Don't worry." The distant drums soothe me, and I snuggle deeper into my covers. My cheek presses against the phone screen.

"You got the graveyard soil poured?"

"Yep. Shields up," I murmur, half asleep already.

"Okay." He sighs. "Get some sleep, Sugar. I'll have a necklace ready for you tomorrow."

"G'night." I allow the gentle beating drums to lull me into slumber.

CHAPTER
TWENTY-FOUR

THE AFTERMATH: SUNDAY MORNING

The first thing I notice when I wake up is I don't feel better. Far from it. The Caster's shadowy presence slides through me, spitting venom in my blood. It makes me angry. An agitated iciness putting me on edge. My skin itches, and I scratch my arms, leaving red trails behind.

The second thing I notice is the time. Dad usually forces me out of bed by 9:00, telling me only lazy people sleep the morning away. The clock says 11:42 a.m.

The smell of freshly brewed coffee gives the house a bitter perfume, and Dad shuffles around the kitchen. I hurry into the bathroom, not ready to face other humans. Opting for a shower, because my spirit spent the night swimming in filth, I turn on the water. The clean spray washes over me, but it's cold. Even turning the knob to boiling-off-skin temperature doesn't help. Goosebumps rise as I rinse the shampoo. I swipe the suds away from my face and check the spigot, making sure it's in the extra-hot

192

position. Soap slides from my hair, and bubbly trails go in my ears and down my jaw. All night I struggled to stay warm, fighting the black magic swirling inside me, and I just want a hot shower. The Caster's presence makes it impossible, the cold lingering.

Anger pulses below the surface, a constant ache in the back of my head. An itch in my throat I can't quite clear. My jaw hurts from the clenching, and as I get dressed, I open and close my mouth to loosen the grit. I barely make it to my room, lying on the bed, when Dad knocks. He comes in wearing a suit and tie. He's dressed in his Sunday best, but I know he isn't going to church when there's a murder to solve. He's going to the precinct. Which means our conversation will be short.

I try not to let the relief show.

"There are some things I need to do at the station," he says.

"I can tell." I eye his tidy navy suit and striped tie.

He sits at the bottom of my bed, feet planted, forearms resting on his thighs. His foot taps the floor, Dad's version of unsettled, and I prepare for what he's waiting to tell me. Pretty sure I won't like it. Drums sound distantly, a staccato *thump* matching the pounding in my head. I clench my fists as my temper builds.

"I'm going to interrogate Jennifer Wren." He tugs at the button on his collar. "Is there anything I should know about her magic?"

"Now you're asking? You refused to listen before." A sudden flash of anger coils, immediate and cold. I pull myself to a sitting position, crossing my legs on the bed.

"It was during an arrest. You shouldn't have—"

"She was just trying to help me. She's innocent." I cut him off, and The Caster heightens my irritation. *He doesn't believe you,* the voice whispers. If he hadn't taken the pendant. If he hadn't arrested Jennifer. *It's all his fault.* The aggravation threatens to overtake me.

I recognize The Caster's influence, and I try to relax. Rubbing at my temples, I push against the budding headache.

Dad stays calm. Steady. It makes me angrier.

"This is what we do," he says. "I handle the policework, you help navigate the magic."

"I'm done helping you." *Why did I say that?* The words coming out of my mouth shock me. We're supposed to be Sherlock and Watson.

It's all his fault.

"What's that supposed to mean?" His lips pinch into a frown.

You have a plan, The Caster reminds me. "Portia and I will find The Caster," I say.

"Give me your phone." He holds out his hand palm up, just like he did when he took the necklace.

"What?"

"This is dangerous. Do not investigate on your own."

"You can't stop me." *He doesn't believe in you.* Maybe he never did. He's always been the great detective, and I'm a poor substitute for a partner.

Enough! I cover my ears, wishing I could block the thoughts assaulting my mind.

"I don't know what's going on with you, but you're pushing it." He wriggles his outstretched fingers. "Phone, CeCe."

"Fine," I hand him my cell.

"No car, no phone, no Portia shenanigans." He slides my cell into his pocket. *My precious!*

"We have a landline," I say.

"And what's Portia's number?"

I open my mouth to recite it and freeze. Her number? It's #1 on my favorites.

He's right, and I'm embarrassed to admit it. And angry. And frustrated. And annoyed. Really, all the negative emotions fight, and it's hard to choose one. The black magic slithers, and my headache strengthens. An unrelenting pain.

"Stay put. I'll be back later." He gets up and pauses at the door, his shoulder resting on the wood. "Are you feeling alright?"

"Fine." My new favorite word.

He grunts. "If you need anything, call me from the landline. I'll write the number to the station by the phone."

And then he's gone. *Finally.* Wait, no. I love Dad. I hate it when he works and I get stuck home alone. Right?

Confusion fogs my brain, and I head to the kitchen. Thoughts flutter like hummingbirds buzzing around and never landing. Flying from flower to flower for a tiny drink and moving on. It's so frustrating, and the more I concentrate, the cloudier my mind becomes.

There was a plan to protect myself. Or maybe someone was going to help...gone. The thought skips to the next sip of pollen.

"Focus, focus, focus," I repeat, over and over, my eyes squinting as I dig through the cupboards.

I find a yellow candle and light it. Yellow represents clarity, and I sit at the table to meditate. Deep breaths in and out. Eyes closed. Mind centered. I relax my shoulders and push away the anger and irritation.

A pinpoint of yellow light pierces the dingy haze of black magic, and I remember Zach is going to help me. How did that slip my mind? I'm nervous to open my eyes and lose the smidgen of clarity I found, and I breathe, keeping his image in my head.

Without my cell, I have no way to get in touch. So, I think of him. Little by little, my memories open, our time together over the last week. Meeting by the retention pond, The Exhibition, and his kiss. Even the embarrassing things, covering his mouth, and asking him to "wrong with me."

I lose track of time. It's just me, the candle, and my reminiscing.

The phone rings, disrupting my meditation, and it takes me a minute to orient myself before I answer.

"Hello?"

"Girl, it only took a dozen calls and twice as many texts before your dad told me he took your cell."

"Portia!" Tears fill my eyes. "How did you get the number for this archaic device? Did Dad give it to you?"

"Nah. My mom still has it written down from a million years ago. Before we got cells. Hurray for hoarders."

My laugh sounds suspiciously like a sob. "I'm glad. Really glad."

"You don't think I'd let a little phone confiscation stop me from talking to my bestie." She speaks in a *you should know me better* tone. "Why'd Detective Dad take your cell anyway?"

"Because..." I hear drums. A slow beating. It draws on the confusion, fogging my brain like hot breath on glass. I shake my head. What did Portia ask?

She talks over the drums and my hesitation. "Was he mad about Zach? His eyes absolutely flared when you called him your boyfriend."

Zach. I look to the yellow candle, keeping it in my line of sight. *I need to see Zach.* My mouth opens, ready to ask for

Portia's help, but the black magic wriggles up my esophagus. The tightness stretches my throat and clogs my words.

"Yes." The affirmation slips between my breath and the sludge. That's not what I wanted to say.

You don't need her, a voice whispers.

"Yeah, I figured." A door closes on her end, which I assume means she's in her bedroom. "Okay, I've been working on our plan to catch The Caster, and the only trap idea I thought of is to use you as bait, dangle your magic out there. But that's a bad idea....right?"

A thrill of excitement tingles, and I realize it comes from my connection to The Caster. They like Portia's idea. Black magic chokes me, a snake in my throat, slithering against my tongue. The word, "No" slides from my mouth.

"Seriously? It's a terrible plan. I'll keep brainstorming." Something crashes on the line, followed by her yelling at someone to get out of her room. Loud stomping. A door slamming. "The little punks drive me crazy, but the truth is I missed them. Oh, wanna hear something hilarious?"

I make a noise, the equivalent of a Dad grunt, and she takes it as affirmation.

"Mom was making breakfast, and Peter was tossing the baseball around. Peter knocks down a picture, and Mom gets mad and throws off her apron, and runs to yell at him, not stopping to think about the gas burner that's flaming."

She laughs, and I try to follow her story. I close my eyes, and her words run together. Without my focus on the candlelight, the other voice hisses in my mind. *She's beautiful and confident. You're just her sidekick.*

Haven't I thought the exact same thing dozens, maybe hundreds of times?

"Within a few seconds, the whole apron's blazing, and

Presley comes in screaming and crying, because she's in that dramatic middle school phase, you know?"

"Portia," I squeak out too softly to carry. A shiver passes over me. My blood runs icy, and I shake harder than necro-shivers, my entire body adopting the cold.

"She worries it's a grease fire and screams that she can't get to the baking soda." Portia giggles and snorts through the phone.

She's too good for you, the voice tells me.

"Mom runs in and takes control like a boss. She's yelling at Pres and grabs the sprayer from the sink to hose down the whole stove, the cabinets, and the countertops. Every-thing was dripping. Oh man, I'm crying." She sniffles and takes a breath. "Hey, are you still there?"

"Yes," another affirmation forced from my lips. And then a laugh. It sounds genuine. Real. Just enjoying the conversation and not suffocating on evil.

"You seem off. What's up?"

Help me, Portia, I think. "Nothing. I'm good."

"You sure? Presley, what are you doing?" She shouts as her door crashes open. "*You need to take me to the store so I can get stuff for my book report,*" her younger sibling yells. "*I have to work,*" comes Portia's response. A small argument ensues all while The Caster whispers in my head.

She's too self-absorbed to notice your pain. You're the pathetic sidekick.

"CeCe, I gotta go. Apparently, I have to chauffeur Princess Pres which will probably make me late to work."

"Have fun," is what I say. "I'll see you tomorrow."

"We'll talk later. Call me when you get your phone back."

"Okay, bye." The Caster forces my conversation, the

words dragged from my mouth. I don't want to send Portia to work, I want her to help me.

To help me...

What do I need her help with?

I can't remember, and I pull my hair, tugging hard enough to feel pain. A scream builds inside me, barely eking out in a hiss of frustration. If The Caster stops me from talking, I'll just have to do something else.

Marching to my room, I throw on my Vans and head to the front door. Portia's house is a decent walk from mine, and the temperature outside has already hit 90, but I need to go. I swing the door open and find myself back in my bedroom. *What?* I try again, keeping my eye on the front door. It looms ahead, and the hallway elongates like a haunted mirror maze. Closing my eyes, I walk forward with outstretched arms and feel my way to the door. Only to end up in my bedroom again.

"Let me go!"

I run, my legs weighted, my feet buried in quicksand. Every step becomes harder, and I move uphill, my lungs on fire. I can't draw a deep breath with the sludge twisting in my throat. The front door moves further and further away.

Until I'm back in my bedroom.

The drums pound, growing in intensity and demanding my attention. A sound comes from right behind me, and I spin to find it. But nothing is there. The Caster speaks in my head, my own voice saying things I don't want to hear.

You don't need perfect Portia. Your dad doesn't believe you.

"That's not true." I clamp my hands over my ears and slide to the floor. The words chase me no matter how hard I shut them out.

The only one who understands you is me. You miss Mawmaw so much it hurts.

"Stop it!" Tears leak from my eyes to stain my cheeks.

We can work together, the voice says. *We don't have to be alone. Just let go and I'll make everything better.*

The drums slow, the rhythm changing. It soothes my frazzled nerves, and I lean into the beat, letting it calm me. It's like a lullaby. Peaceful. The smooth tones alleviate the anger and are a balm to my frustration.

I know how you feel. Perfect Portia doesn't understand. Neither does your dad. Let me help you.

I slip into a haze, a comfortable place between waking and dreaming. A place where I don't have to feel. I don't have to think. Just exist. It's nice. Easy.

We can be whole again.

The Caster helps me change into pajamas, my motions in their control. I crawl beneath my covers.

Just sleep. Everything will work out.

I'm falling. My mind descending into Dreamland. I sit with Mawmaw at the kitchen table, the one where the yellow candle still burns. Her thinning white hair surrounds a face gone wrinkled. Wire-rimmed glasses perch on the bridge of her nose, and her callused hands fold in her lap. She's the most beautiful sight.

"Things would be so much easier if you were alive," I say. A hard ball of emotion clumps in my chest.

"Sha, that's hogwash, and you know it. You'd keep everythin' all bottled up, afraid to worry me."

The clump stretches, making my heart ache. "But you'd be here."

"I'm still around. You just need to look." She pats my knee, and warmth radiates from her touch. "The whisper of wind, the twinklin' star, the rain on your face, it's all me."

I smile. How like Mawmaw to take credit for nature.

She continues. "And 'sides, you have Portia."

"Perfect Portia?" I ask. "It's so hard to be her friend."

"Yes. Someone loyal who loves you. Must be a challenge." She mmm hmm's, putting her arm around me, and I rest on her shoulder. I smell her Gardenia perfume, the same floral aroma she's worn for years.

"You don't understand. She's so beautiful and perfect. She stands out in a crowd. I'm her sidekick."

"Honey, Portia's a peach. Don't you listen to that snake in the grass," she says.

A blast of cold makes me shiver, and I snuggle closer. "What do you mean?"

"A trustworthy friend is hard to find. You hold onto that. Just wait. It'll all be okay. You're stronger than you think."

The dream cuts abruptly, and I wake in my bed. Darkness peers through my window, the sunset a memory. My phone charges on the nightstand. Dad must have brought it in. I reach out, but my arm falls, too weak to grab it. The blankets are insufficient against the cold sweeping through me, and I bundle deeper under the covers. The faint drumming lullaby echoes in the air and sleep beckons, barely outpacing me.

Things would be so much better if Mawmaw were here.

As I drift into slumber, I can't tell if the thought comes from me or The Caster.

TWENTY-FIVE

THE CASTER: MONDAY, EARLY A.M.

The dim bar lights cast shadows among the early a.m. crowd. I nurse the amber liquid in front of me, only taking small sips to make it last. From my dark corner, I survey the patrons, from the barely legal-drinking college students, to the quiet older gentleman who stares into his glass.

I need to find one more low life. One more organ donor.

Looking at my watch, impatience ripples, and I decide to head home. Shoving the glass away, I toss a few dollars on the counter. With a last glance around the bar, I almost walk away. Until the old man shifts in his chair, and I catch sight of the haunted expression in his eyes. His shoulders stoop, and he holds his phone where a picture of a woman lights the screen. Immediately, I understand he struggles with loss. Grief recognizes grief. Maybe I don't need another scumbag. Maybe I need someone who doesn't want to live anymore.

Sliding into the seat next to him, I glance at the mirror

across the bar top. Pink shoulder-length hair, green eyes, and high cheekbones stare at me, and I startle at the sight. *Am I dreaming?* No. But I know it's not actually me in the bar. I'm with The Caster, and somehow my image superimposes over theirs. They whip our gaze away from the reflection.

No, CeCe. You're not allowed here.

Drums beat, the peaceful tones emitting a calm hush. Tranquility calls, and the need to drift back into oblivion entices me. The bar disappears, replaced by my room. The soft mattress cushions my body, and the blanket wraps around me. The Caster pushes me back and our connection thins. My head clears, and I focus better than I have since the black magic invaded.

I can't pass up the opportunity to learn more. If The Caster doesn't want me there, it's exactly where I need to be.

Closing my eyes, I search for the link, grasping for the greasy string joining us. I imagine myself pulling along the leash to get back to the bar. Voices murmur in my mind, and I see the old man again, far away, like tunnel vision. But I drag myself closer until I'm with The Caster.

"*I'm sorry for your loss, Ben,*" The Caster says.

"*We were married 37 years. Most of them happy.*" The old man, Ben, smiles sadly, the corners of his mouth trembling. "*She's been gone almost two years. People say it gets better, but it's a lie.*"

The Caster understands no one should live with that kind of pain, and the decision is made. This will be the final organ. "*I lost someone too. I'd love to meet up again and tell you about it. Because you're right, it doesn't get better. But talking helps.*"

"*I'm here every night,*" Ben says.

The Caster gets Ben's number, and a spark of excitement lights. It'll be so easy to perform the magic to steal his heart. *Tuesday,* they think. Time to prepare the spell and ready everything for the Shroud of Reawakening.

They reach out to pat Ben's arm, a comforting gesture, but my silver nails gleam against the blue sleeve. The Caster's gaze shifts to the mirror to see me looking back. My green eyes narrow, and my lips turn down

Get out!

The drums pound, changing from the soft lull of sleep to a harder, more staccato rhythm. This beat demands compliance. A force pushes my essence and knocks me back. Mawmaw told me I'm stronger than I think, and I stand my metaphysical ground. I envision crisp, clean water attacking the filth, a power washer blasting oil stains on concrete. My magic *is* stronger. Their ability relies on deception. Tricking me into believing they have control. Freezing me out with the merging of our cold magics.

But they can't stop me.

I pierce the veil surrounding The Caster. The comforting grip on Ben's arm changes, my silver nails receding to leave tan skin and dark hair peppering the back of a hand. A man's hand.

Snap.

Our connection breaks, and I gasp, sitting up in bed. The slimy tendrils sluice from my veins, a biting tingle like acupuncture gone wrong. Pins and needles poke all over my skin as my magic chases out the filth. Burying my face in the pillow, I clench my fingers and breathe through the pain.

I did it. I beat The Caster with my magic.

The oily residue vanishes and the drums are gone. The missing pieces of my life float back in my mind. All the forgotten details from the brain fog. And Zach. I slap my forehead, shocked I forgot about going to his house.

As another test against The Caster's influence, I reach for my cell. No cloudy mind power stops me, no haunted effects. Just the phone in my hand. The display says 2:08 a.m., along with dozens of missed calls and texts from Portia and Zach. I check hers first, saving his messages for last.

The majority are from the morning to ask why I'm not answering. She got worried. Threatened to call the police. Typical Portia. That's probably when Dad finally let her know about my confiscated phone. Then: *Z's been trying to track you down. Told Dev you got grounded.* And finally: *Pick you up in the a.m. Back to school if you can believe it. Feels a world away from drama camp.*

Thinking of Portia makes a bright sun rise in my chest, and I smile. Mawmaw's right. She's a peach.

I click on Zach's name and read through what he sent.

> ZACH: Your necklace is ready.
>
> ZACH: Should I come to u?
>
> ZACH: U wanna meet @ my house?
>
> ZACH: U ok?
>
> ZACH: Getting worried. Especially after our last conversation.
>
> ZACH: NVM....heard u got grounded. Sorry.
>
> ZACH: Call me when u can, Sugar.

He called me Sugar. I melt a little, like a chocolate chip in a warm cookie. I feel gooey inside, thinking of the way his touch makes me glow. The way our lips meet and magic spins. The way we snug zone.

Definitely the snug zone.

I type out a quick response even though he's probably asleep.

> ME: You make me feel like a chocolate chip cookie.

Before I talk myself out of it, I let the feels in and hit send.

Setting my phone down, I take a breath, ready for the biggest test of my freedom from The Caster. Talking to Dad. I go to his room, knocking on the door and waiting for his grunt before I walk in. He sits up and turns on his bedside lamp, scooting to rest his back against the headboard.

"The Caster is a man," I say calmly. "Dark hair. Olive skin. Old enough to be out drinking at two a.m."

"Are you sure?" He reaches for the notepad and pen on his nightstand.

"One hundred percent." I sit down on the bottom of the bed. "The Caster did something to connect us."

"Connect? Like he did at drama camp?"

"Yes," I say. "And I saw his hand. Jennifer is innocent."

"I know." He rubs his jaw, his fingers scratching the scruff. "I knew as soon as you told me. But we need to do this the right way. Someone did a good job setting her up."

"That's not all I saw. There was a car accident." I fill him in on the vision, how The Caster lost someone. How they want to bring back their loved one.

"When was the accident? Where was it? If there was a fatality, it's traceable."

"I don't know." *He does believe me. I'm not alone.* "But what do we do?"

"We follow the evidence to find the real Caster," he says.

"He picked his next victim." I summarize the overheard conversation at the bar and how The Caster plans to take Ben's heart. "He's going to do it Tuesday night."

"Do you know what bar? Did you get Ben's last name?" He writes on his notepad.

"No and no. But I can describe them both."

"Baby girl," he stops me. "Do you know how many bars there are in New Orleans? And how many men named Ben? Even with a description, it'd be like finding a specific grain of sand on the beach."

"We can't give up."

He grunts and shakes his head, which obviously means, *of course not.* "Maybe I can have you work with a sketch artist. We can put his picture out there and see what pops."

"Okay." Sitting with him and discussing the case brings back our Sherlock and Watson vibe. I almost let The Caster ruin it. I clear my throat and fold my hands in my lap. "Dad, I'm sorry about how I acted. But you should know there was some magical influence there."

"What do you mean?"

"Without the right protection, I'm vulnerable to The Caster. He can get in my head, put thoughts in there." An image of tangled tree roots comes to mind. The Caster's whispered words that *one way or another* I will do what he needs.

"Do you need the necklace back? I don't know how else to protect you." He drags a hand across his face.

"I'm doing better now. Promise." Whatever snapped with The Caster left me feeling more like myself. "And Zach has a new one for me."

"Will that be enough?" he asks.

"Yes." At least I hope so.

"Good." He stretches, and a yawn catches him. "Let's

get some sleep. Meet me at the station after school, and we'll see if we can find Ben."

"Night, Daddy," I say.

I go back to my room and lay on the bed, staring at the ceiling. Thoughts crash through my mind, distracting me from sleep. *Grief recognizes grief.* The Caster picked Ben because of his despair. Holding onto the heartache, living with the burden of sadness, makes him a victim. And it makes The Caster a predator.

He's preying on my grief too.

I tiptoe from the bed and take out my journal, moving to the window where the bright moon provides enough light. My fingers tremble as I open the pages, and a tightness constricts my chest. I've avoided reading my journal, afraid that when I do, she'll really be gone.

Even though Mawmaw's already been gone for a year.

Pinching my eyes closed, I resist the urge to stuff the journal back into my drawer. To ignore the scooping in my chest that hollows out my happiness, and maybe put this off to face it another day. But it's time to give my grief room to heal. Because that wound is a weakness The Caster will continue to exploit.

TWENTY-SIX

LETTING GO: MONDAY, 2:30 A.M.

Spending a day being lulled to sleep and forced to stay in my room, brought me to the undeniable conclusion that I need to let go of my grief. Zach told me black magic, as the only magic without a natural source, requires a price. A sacrifice. After seeing The Caster's plan and his descent into the shadows, I understand what Zach means. I witnessed the way the dirty magic attached to The Caster, a parasite draining every ounce of hope and happiness. Drawing on his anguish to feed the darkness. If my sorrow feels like a melon baller, scooping out pieces of joy, his has become an excavator, leaving nothing behind.

And the black magic loves the offering.

Grief recognizes grief. The words from The Caster hover in my mind, making me aware of my part in this. I left myself susceptible, an easy target for him as I struggled through mourning the loss of Mawmaw.

I lift my journal, and my eyes move across the words I wrote.

We lost Mawmaw. My chest feels like a gaping hole, and every time I suck in a breath, it stalls in my lungs. Grief is a thief, stealing my air. Stealing my thoughts. Stealing my happiness. Nothing will ever be the same again.

I miss her. How she always listened. I'll miss her stories and her advice, how she saw things a little differently than anyone else. I'll never feel her arms wrap around me, and her whisper in my ear saying, just wait, it'll all be okay...

Tears rain from my eyes, cleansing the sorrow, allowing the memories to heal. I'm grateful I had something special enough that it makes saying goodbye so hard. The festering despair changes into a tenderness, dulling the hard edges of pain. It still hurts, and I still miss her, but I let go of the poisonous despair.

I stay by the window, reading, crying. Remembering. The pre-dawn hours shift, painting the sky in shades of orange sherbet. The ice cream horizon stretches in a sweet promise of hope for a new day.

"I love you, Mawmaw," I whisper to the faded moon.

Eventually, my eyes become too heavy, and I get back in bed. But first, I pull a picture from my nightstand, the one of Mawmaw and me, and I set it out. I eventually drift off to soft memories of Downton Abbey and Gardenia perfume.

MY ALARM BLARES after I've been asleep for thirty seconds max. The sun shines through the windows, and grit lines my eyelids. I grumble and swat at my beeping phone. Rolling out of bed, I grab a pair of tastefully ripped jeans and a green tee with the words "beignet, done that." Luckily, my shower is hot. No black magic juju keeping me cold today. Confidence swells, warming me more than the steaming spray.

As I reach for the spigot, the water turns cold. A normal chill, I tell myself, like I've been in the shower too long, and it's time to get out.

I go to my room and quickly dress, throwing my hair in a ponytail. To keep the shorter flyaways off my neck, I slip in a bobby pin and smooth the strands.

"CeCe, Portia just pulled up," Dad shouts from the kitchen.

Reaching for my backpack, I realize I'm holding the picture of Mawmaw. I don't even remember picking it up. Weird. I don't feel The Caster's presence snaking through me, and the chill accompanying his black magic is gone. So...I'm fine. Definitely. Just a normal day.

Dad sits at the table, drinking coffee. "Going to school?"

"You know me. Late nights solving crime, then business as usual."

He runs a hand down his freshly shaved cheek and sighs. "This one's different, baby girl. I don't like the way his magic connects to you."

"Everything's fine. I can handle the magic," I tell him, mostly confident. "It's better to be around people. I'll meet you at the station later."

His lips pinch, but he nods. "Call me if you need anything."

"Deal," I yell as I walk out the door.

Portia sits in her red Fiat 500, an older model she worked ridiculously hard to buy. And I'm grateful, because without her willingness to pick me up every morning, I'd be a bus rider. *Shudder*. One day soon I'll hopefully have my own car and take turns driving. Once Dad switches off his cop brain long enough to believe I won't leave a wake of fiery destruction in the glow of my taillights.

She leans close to the rearview mirror, finishing her makeup. Her mouth opens in an "o" as she dabs at her eyelashes. I climb in, tucking my backpack by my feet and buckling my seatbelt.

"Your timing is perfect." She screws the cap on her mascara and tosses it in a bag. "You ready?"

"For school?" I make a sound like an Orca giving birth. Not that I've ever heard it, but I can imagine.

"Right?" She nods in perfect understanding.

"Plus, yesterday was horrible. I have a million things to tell you."

"Well, it has been almost twenty-four hours since we talked." She reverses out of my driveway and heads toward the school.

It takes me a solid five minutes to recap what happened, the black magic assault, the strange brain fog, and finally seeing The Caster's hand. "As soon as I recognized he was a man, our connection snapped. I woke up in my bed."

"Wow." Her fingers tap the steering wheel, and she navigates the early morning traffic. "He's gone, right? You're good?"

"I think so…"

She hears my hesitation. "But?"

"If I start acting weird, lock me in a closet." I chuckle and playfully elbow her.

Instead of the expected laugh, her lips remain flat. "What should I really do?"

I give the best answer I can, thinking of the one person I know can help. "Take me to Zach."

"Take you to magical lover boy. Got it."

"Ha ha."

The mood lightens as *Meant to Be* plays on the radio. She smirks, turning it up, and we sing along. This is good. Normal. Everyday. My phone buzzes, and Zach's name lights up the screen. A giddy fizz fills my chest.

> ZACH: Is that good?

I scrunch my forehead and look back at my last text, then wince when I read it. *You make me feel like a chocolate chip cookie.* Ugh! Did I really say that? No one should be allowed to text after midnight. Nothing but awkward or cringey comes out in the wee hours. I need to set my home screen to say, "*I do not word after dark.*"

> ME: I was 1/2 asleep. Maybe 2/3.
> Ignore me.

> ZACH: Impossible!

Pink colors my cheeks, and the gooey, melty feelings come back.

"Is that Zach?" Portia glances at me. "Or is there another guy who makes you all blushy? A guy who you obviously didn't meet at drama camp since you were determined to avoid that cliché."

"You're hilarious." I throw as much sarcasm as possible in my tone and roll my eyes. "Yes, it's Zach."

ZACH: So...good thing?

ME: Choc chip IS my fave.

ZACH: My GF is my fave.

Gluten-free? That's weird. He totally ate bread and rolls last week.

ME: No gluten?

He sends a laughing emoji. Followed by a cry-laughing emoji. Followed by a sideways cry-laughing emoji. Obviously, I missed something.

ZACH: LOL! GF = girlfriend. NOT gluten free.

Of course, duh. Is death by embarrassment a thing? I consider throwing my phone out the moving car's window, but that solves nothing. Besides, he knows I'm awkward and has decided to accept me anyway.

He called me his favorite!

ME: *FYI, BF = breakfast food.*

ZACH: Let me guess, OMG is Omelet, Muffin, Grits?

ME: Exactly.

ZACH: BTW (bacon, toast, waffles), can I see u after school? I have ur necklace.

Waffles. He totally gets me. My thumbs start typing an

agreement before I remember needing to meet Dad for the sketch. Delete, start over.

> ME: Gotta hit the police station first. After?

> ZACH: Donut run?

> ME: Obviously. But GTG school. Your house later?

> ZACH: Sure. CYL (crepes, yogurt, Lucky Charms)

Portia smirks as we walk into the school. "If your smile was any bigger, your face wouldn't be able to hold it."

"Fine, I admit it." I hold my chin high, nose upturned. "I got sucked into a cliché drama camp romance. Happy?"

"Of course, I'm happy. You deserve this."

I seriously have the best, best friend.

"Drama camp double couple," she says, pumping her fist.

I take it all back. I have the most annoying best friend. But I love her.

We go our separate ways to first period and the familiar routine of school kicks in. Things are good. Normal. Everyday. Even better with the promise of seeing Zach later. And the infrequent chills and quick flashes of brain fog are just remnants of The Caster. Nothing more.

CHAPTER
TWENTY-SEVEN

MAC AND CHEESE: MONDAY AFTERNOON

Reciting my school ID, I pay for lunch and head toward Portia. She's sitting already, content with Cheetos and a Diet Coke from the vending machine. Holding her phone, her thumbs move across the screen in classic texting form. Probably Devin.

"CeCe LeBlanc." The shrieky tone of Julie Jolley's voice plucks the feathers from angels' wings. "I need to thank you."

I just want to sit next to Portia and eat my school-issued mac and cheese, which already slinks into its mushy demise. Fluorescent lights glare, and an ache strains behind my eyes. The crowded cafeteria hushes as I spin to face Julie, my fingers clench around the scratched lunch tray.

She's with the J-Crew, Gemma and Jaelynn standing on either side. Gemma gives me a subtle wave, disguising the gesture by fixing the white flower barrette in her dark hair.

"What do you want?" The passive-aggressive back and forth irritates me, and I refuse to play anymore.

"Someone woke up on the wrong side of the bed." She purses her red lips. "I'm trying to show my gratitude."

Don't ask, don't ask.

"Why?" The question pops from my mouth.

"For getting to Zach first. I'm so relieved I let you have him. Can you imagine dating the son of a murderer?" Her eyes widen, and her mouth opens in mock surprise. "Oh, I guess you can."

"Julie, don't." Gemma's face pales, and she takes a step away as Julie and Jaelynn laugh.

Jaelynn flicks her braids over her shoulder and eggs Julie on. "Do it."

"That's right," Julie goes on, loud enough for the cafeteria and the neighboring classrooms to eavesdrop. "We all saw your boyfriend's mom arrested. She killed two people. What a psycho."

My temper snowballs in a cold fury and the pounding drums reverberate. This beat isn't calm or compelling. This beat is power. Black magic rushes to the surface, mocking my illusion of freedom. Letting go of my grief helped me gain control, but it was too late to completely disentangle from The Caster. The connection has been inside all along, waiting for a trigger like Julie Jolley. Her taunting spurs my growing desire to squash her with magic.

She raises her voice, putting on a performance. "You were always creepy and weird. Now you found a freaky boyfriend. Two pathetic losers with no mamas to raise you right."

Vengeful shards of ice flow in my veins, a cold front building and spilling from me. The Caster knew we'd be more powerful together, and now I feel it too. He whispers in my head, promising retribution against Julie.

"You need to walk away," I say, fighting the magic trying to escape.

"Or what?" She takes a step closer.

"Just leave her alone." Gemma tugs at Julie's sleeve but gives up in favor of hugging herself as the air around me grows colder.

"You're a joke." Julie flings her hand, tipping the cup on my tray.

Water spreads, trapped within the beveled plastic, and my power escapes in a wintry burst. The clear liquid turns opaque, white trails weaving through as ice forms. Cold pours out, and my grip tightens.

Julie bites her lip, a hint of fear glossing her eyes.

Yes, I think. *You should fear me.* The Caster is my own private cheering section, urging me on.

The macaroni disappears off my tray, and I turn to see Portia holding it.

"Allow me." She hurls the entire contents of the bowl, and it splats in Julie Jolley's face.

Swollen pasta clings to her cheeks, forehead, and hair, several chunks plopping to the floor. Despite the icy tray, the macaroni managed to stay goopy enough to stick. The outraged gasps of Julie and Jaelynn echo in the cafeteria.

"What's wrong with you?" Julie screeches. Leaning forward to protect her clothes, she swipes at the cheese sauce decorating her hair.

"You thought you could pick on my best friend, and I wouldn't retaliate?" Portia gives her a pitying look. "Bless your heart, girl."

The assistant principal walks in, eyeing the commotion.

"Time to go," Portia says, tossing my tray on a table and dragging me out the rear doors of the cafeteria.

She holds both of our backpacks, but it doesn't slow her

down as we run like criminals on the lam. Energy vibrates along my nerves, needing release, and I clench my teeth, trying to keep it inside. Drums pound in a static rhythm, The Caster strengthening the link between us.

We bang through the metal doors leading to the parking lot, and the bright sun assaults my eyes. Portia opens the passenger door of her Fiat and stuffs me in. The engine revs and tires squeal, the soundtrack of our hasty escape.

"Never thought I'd save Julie Jolley by throwing mac and cheese in her hair." She drives out of the parking lot, and pulls over to grab her phone. Her thumbs fly as she texts. Normally, I'd ask about it, but all my energy stays focused on not losing control.

Signaling back on the road, she keeps talking. "Hopefully Mom and Dad won't find out I skipped class, especially after drama camp last week. I have to be back in time to grab Peter and take him home. But the afternoon is yours."

I desperately think about how I felt this morning—the singing, the texting. The normal. But the floodgate of magic opened, and I take shallow breaths, my muscles tense as I fight against the deluge.

"Are you okay? Or are you going to freeze the upholstery?" She pats my hand and grimaces at the contact. Directing the vents at me, she turns the heater on full. "Don't worry. We'll be there soon."

"Where?" I ask through gritted teeth.

"Zach's house."

Zach? The black magic swirls, sending icy spikes under my skin. The pounding beat turns faster. Panicked.

Portia parks at the curb in front of a pale-yellow house with a green door and shutters. Zach leans on the porch rail, his dark brown hair picking up streaks of light from the sun, his blue t-shirt an almost exact match to his eye color. The sight of him makes me thaw. At least for a few seconds until an aching pressure builds in my head, making my eyeballs feel like they might burst.

The mechanics of opening the door become too complicated, and my fingers tremble on the handle. It swings wide without my assistance, and Zach is there, trying to help me from the car. I scream at the fiery hands gripping my upper arms and pull out of his grasp.

"CeCe, what happened?" He holds his hands up, backing away. "You're freezing. I can't believe how deep the magic has gotten."

My teeth chatter, and I can't respond. Black magic swims in my bloodstream. The connection to The Caster has grown. I fight to stay in control.

Portia's gaze bounces between us. "What do we do?"

He looks behind him, eyeing the house. "Can you get her to the porch?"

Portia leads me, half-dragging me up the concrete ramp. I fight against her efforts. The black magic doesn't want me closer to Zach or his house. She persists and lowers me into a chair, keeping her hands on my shoulders and standing behind me.

"CeCe, can you hear me?" Zach crouches to my level and hesitates until I make eye contact. "Black magic is like venom, and the touch of life magic is an antidote. But it's going to hurt."

I shake my head, whispering through chattering teeth. "Don't use magic."

"It's not using magic. Just my touch."

He runs his fingers along the back of my hand, small circular motions covered in flames. My eyes flick down, checking for matches or a lighter. The burning wrenches a scream from me and my muscles spasm. The Caster shrieks —a hunted animal flailing as Zach's motions move up my arms. Portia says something, but her words hide behind the panicked drums pounding in my head.

"Stop!" The word squeezes through my pain. Tears stream down my cheeks, and my body twitches against the heated onslaught.

"I can't, Sugar. I'm sorry." His arms wrap around me, and he draws me closer in an almost hug. Sharp pains stab everywhere he touches. He talks me through the agony, his voice a gentle whisper. "I know it hurts. My Aunt Lucy did the same thing for me once. Hang in there."

The poison claws, trying to hold on, and The Caster grapples to keep our connection. The rope between us tightens, dragging me to him. A fresh wave of cold submerges me in icy water, and suddenly, I'm there. Seeing things from The Caster's perspective.

He sits in a car, clenching a black leather steering wheel. A gold wedding ring circles his finger, and his watch has a brown band. I focus on the details and push to see more. *What kind of car is he driving? What clothes does he have on?* But I'm stuck in this limited scope.

The shifting between hot and cold, Zach and The Caster, gives me whiplash. My body can't decide exactly where I am. I feel Zach, his touch continuing to warm me, but my spirit stays with The Caster, watching. The dizzying duality makes me nauseous.

"Let go," Zach says, hauling me tighter, into an actual hug.

"Wait," I say. But this close to him, pressed to my favorite snuggy place, his warmth finally wins.

My connection to The Caster fades, and the inside of the

car disappears. I flash on something familiar, and I can't quite place it as I come fully back to reality. Holding still, I try to recapture that blink of time.

What was it? Despite my best efforts to remember the tiny flicker, the moment is gone, and I'm left with a heavy impression The Caster is someone I know.

"There's my CeCe." Zach kisses my head, his lips lingering. Excitement dances where we touch, and the rush zings in his every pore. His pulse taps wildly, his body shakes, and I look into bloodshot eyes.

I shouldn't have let him help.

"Thank you." I shiver, and he rubs my back.

"Hey, I'm here too." Portia kneels in my periphery, and she nudges Zach aside to look at me.

I'm awkwardly positioned, sitting in the chair with them crouched in front of me, and I lean down to hug my BFF. "Portia?"

"What?"

"Did you really throw my mac and cheese on Julie Jolley?"

She laughs and gets to her feet. "I should have taken a picture. I knew you'd want to see it again."

"I gotta hear this." Zach stands, a little unsteadily, and offers me his hand. "Let's go and have some lunch. It sounds like you didn't get to eat."

We go inside, talking about the epic mac and cheese toss and being spotted by the assistant principal. He appears normal, laughing at the story, smiling like nothing is wrong. But his fists clench, his breathing speeds up, and his eyes can't seem to settle on anything.

Portia and I sit in the kitchen on barstools at the island. White cabinets reach to meet the tall ceilings, complementing the beautiful gray marbled countertops. The stain-less-steel farmhouse sink is big enough that I could probably bathe in it. Zach moves to the fridge, pulling out sandwich fixings.

"Why aren't you at school?" I ask, realizing he shouldn't be here making us lunch.

"I'm taking a few days off until we figure things out with my mom. Dad's with the lawyers now, and I'm waiting for Mason to get home from his tutoring session." He opens a bread box on the counter, grabbing out a loaf.

"Mason?" Portia asks, swiveling back and forth on her stool.

"My brother."

"How's he doing? With your mom being gone...." I trail off, remembering the moment my dad arrested Jennifer. Grateful Zach doesn't hate me because of it.

"Dad's treated it more like a simple misunderstanding, 'no big deal, we'll get her back in no time.' Which has helped a lot," he says, putting together the sandwiches.

We eat and chat, Zach talking about the progress with his mom's case (possible alibi, sketchy timelines, and lack of motive), and me filling Zach in on the latest (Caster is a man, who wants me to resurrect his dead loved one, and also picked his next victim).

Just light lunch conversation.

As I take the last bite of my sandwich, the front door opens. A younger-looking version of Zach rolls into the kitchen in a wheelchair.

"Mason," Zach says. "Come meet CeCe and Portia."

The kid, who can't be more than eleven or twelve, smiles and winks. "Ah. The girlfriend. We finally meet."

"Hi, Mason." I take his outstretched hand, but instead of shaking, he places a kiss on the back of my fingers. The kid has game.

"I like your pink hair." He waggles his eyebrows. He gives such a good waggle I worry Portia's eyebrows might get jealous.

"Thanks," I laugh, and he turns to Portia.

"Hey beautiful, are you taken?" he asks.

"You think anyone can *take* this? I don't think so." She swivels on the stool. "But I'm dating Devin."

"He doesn't deserve you."

"No one does." She gives an eyebrow waggle of her own.

"Okay, Player, leave them alone." Zach shakes his head, walking over to ruffle Mason's hair.

"What's wrong with you? You're all sweaty and twitchy." Mason gives him a once-over. "Any news about Mom?"

He ignores the first question and tackles the second. "Things are looking good. Mom has no motive and a possible alibi."

Mason nods, and his smile smooths out, looking more natural. "Did you give CeCe the necklace Aunt Lucy made?"

"Not yet. I'll be right back." His steps fade as he walks from the kitchen.

Mason shifts to face Portia fully and turns on the flirt. "Alone at last."

He really does look like a mini-Zach.

"Listen, ladies man. You're too young for me, but I give your skills a solid one and a half thumbs-up," she says.

"How do you give a half thumbs-up?"

"Like this." Portia laughs and holds up a bent thumb.

A chill catches me, and a haze dims my focus. I close my eyes, ready to push The Caster away, but I can't remember how. I know I've done it before.

"Hey, are you okay?" Portia asks.

The magic whispers a promise of power, tendrils of slime oozing across my mind.

Portia moves next to me, holding my hand. "Zach, she's getting cold!"

He's suddenly there, putting the necklace on me. The heavy pendant feels heated, and his touch stings. Not the same burn as before, but uncomfortable. This time he easily chases The Caster back, and I let out a tight breath.

"You didn't tell me she has black magic." Mason rolls closer, watching me, his expression wary.

"She doesn't. It's not her." Zach grips my upper arms, a somber expression on his face. Crimson streaks the whites of his eyes, and he looks exhausted. "The connection needs to be broken. I'll have to fight fire with fire."

"No," Mason says. "You can't do that."

"What do you mean?" Portia asks before I have the chance.

He takes a breath and blows it out. "I'll have to use black magic to sever the link. It's the only way."

CHAPTER TWENTY-EIGHT

IT'S SKETCHY: MONDAY, 4:30 P.M.

Portia has to work. She offered to call in sick, but after taking off last week, I knew it would look bad. The trendy clothes consignment shop is how she affords her habit of fabulous fashion. No way I'd ask her to risk it.

So, Zach is driving me to the police station. My mind wanders as he talks on the phone with his dad. I hear his end of the conversation (all positive progress on getting his mom out), and I rub my new pendant, thinking about how to break my connection with The Caster. *I'll have to use black magic,* Zach said.

I told him when New Orleans freezes over.

There must be another way to sever the link. Not only did I make a promise, but I see how black magic affects him. The way his magic craves the darkness. Even now, he sneaks touches to get a tiny fix, holding my hand, grazing my arm, brushing against me. I wonder if Zach will still want me as his girlfriend if I lose that hint of darkness. Or is having it part of my appeal?

Living with The Caster in my head won't be too bad. The new necklace eases the strain. And when Jennifer's out of jail, she can help. We'll make it work until we find a better solution.

"Sorry about that." Zach sets down his phone and rubs a thumb over my knuckles. The familiar zing pumps excitedly in my blood. My magic has a serious crush on his magic.

"How's your dad?" I ask.

"Doing better. Our lawyer put some holes in the police timeline, and he's hopeful we can have my mom out soon." His dimples wink at me.

"That's great."

"Yeah, we'll all feel better when she's home."

The tall, white columns of the police station come into view, and my stomach dips. So much is riding on my ability to help. A man is in danger. Jennifer's in prison. And the real Caster is loose, willing to do anything to resurrect his loved one.

No pressure.

Zach covers my bouncing knee. "Are you nervous?"

"I am a little." Or a lot.

"Don't worry." Letting go of my hand, he maneuvers into a space and puts the car in park. He turns to face me, his deep blue eyes a balm to my nerves. "I'll be there for moral support."

"You don't have to come in."

"And miss out on seeing a sketch artist in action? No way. Besides," he catches a strand of my hair and runs it between his fingers. "I can help if you need it."

Seriously, chocolate chip cookie feels.

We walk into the station holding hands, and we're led to a room. There's no artwork on the walls, no plants or décor. Plain and minimal, with a rectangular table and six chairs. Nothing else. Zach slides out a chair for me, the metal legs screeching across the floor, and then settles in the seat next to mine. Only a few minutes pass before Detective Rivera pokes his head in.

"Hi, CeCe. Gotten into any trouble lately?" He sits across from us and folds his hands in his lap.

"All sorts of trouble." I smile, but my gut churns with worry he'll recognize Zach. Even though Dad believes in Jennifer's innocence, I don't know what Rivera thinks.

Rivera's gaze flicks to Zach, and a dull recognition lights his eyes, but he doesn't seem to connect the dots. "And who's this?"

"I'm Zach," he says, no last name given, thankfully. "CeCe's boyfriend."

"Boyfriend?" Rivera shakes his head. "You're too young to chase boys, CeCe."

"What'd you say the recommended dating age is? Thirty?" I ask.

"At least. Your Dad agrees." He chuckles and leans back.

Dad picks that moment to join us, walking into the room with a woman who wears black slacks and an oversized burgundy sweater. Almond-shaped eyes and olive skin speak to her Asian heritage. She carries a large case, and Dad pulls out the chair at the head of the table for her to sit. Resting a hip against the wall, Dad stands behind Rivera.

"This is Gina Lee, a forensic artist from the FBI." Dad runs a hand down the pink paisley tie I gave him for Father's Day. I suspect he wore it as a supportive nod to me. "Gina, this is my partner, Detective Rivera, my daughter

CeCe, and..." he pauses for a moment, barely stumbling before finishing the introductions. "Her boyfriend, Zach."

"Nice to meet you," Gina offers me her hand. Her black hair is in a pixie cut, the bangs ultra-short on her forehead. It's pretty on her. I'd look like I lost a fight with a pair of scissors.

"Let's get started," Dad says.

"This will take about an hour." There's something comforting about her calm demeanor. She pulls a thick binder from the case. "We'll begin by looking at photographs. If you see anything that strikes you as familiar to the unidentified man, I want you to point it out. A person in these pictures might have the same shape of eyes, similar jaw structure, or face shape. Study the photos and let me know. Do you understand?"

"Yes, ma'am." I take the heavy binder and open it up. Each page contains 15 pictures of a different man, and I flip through, studying the photos. Every few pages, I have to close my eyes and envision the bar, imagining Ben sitting next to me. Older, with graying hair. Kind eyes. Brown. No, hazel. Small nose, almost too small for his face.

I point out features that seem similar. B-12's eyebrows, D-7's face shape, G-25's lips. Gina sketches on her notepad, the scratching pencil a constant background noise, and the others watch the process in silence. At some point, Zach reaches under the table and takes my hand.

Gina sets down her pencil and pulls the sketchbook upright, holding the image away from me. "This is the initial drawing. First impressions are critical. Picture the man and have that image in your mind as you look it over."

"Okay." I tighten my fingers on Zach's.

"Let me know what needs to be different." She flips the picture around, and I get my first glimpse of the drawing.

"It's...almost right." I hesitate, knowing I got something wrong. "I think the face needs to be thinner. Like, a narrower chin."

Plucking the eraser from her kit, she works on the things I suggest and makes small changes. The drawing gets closer and closer to how I remember Ben. I try to describe the heaviness in his eyes, the sadness weighing down his lids, but capturing it proves challenging.

"What do you think?" she asks.

"That's him. That's definitely Ben." The comparison amazes me. Gina could do this for a living. Which, of course, she does.

"You did great. You remembered details like a pro." She tears the page from her notebook.

"The sooner we get this out, the sooner we find him. I'll take it to the PIO." Rivera takes the drawing and winks at me as he heads out of the room.

"The PIO is our public information officer. He coordinates with the public and the media," Dad explains. "He'll get it circulated."

"This might actually work," I say. All the nerves from earlier dissipate under the promise of hope. My chest feels lighter. I squeeze Zach's hand and bounce my knee under the table, this time from excitement.

"Really nice job, Ms. Lee." Dad moves from his spot holding up the wall to sit in Rivera's abandoned seat.

"Really nice job, CeCe," Zach mimics, whispering in my ear, and I playfully elbow his stomach.

"Please, call me Gina, Detective LeBlanc."

"It's Cooper." He runs a hand through his hair, and his cheeks match his pink tie.

Are they flirting?

I look at Zach, and he bites his lip, trying not to laugh.

Checking out her left hand, which she conveniently placed on the table in front of Dad, I note the absence of a wedding ring. Not to mention Dad's ducked head, Gina's soft eyes and slight smile.

They are flirting. I hope he asks her out.

She scoots her chair back, and Dad stops her. "Actually, I wonder if you could do something else."

"Sure. I'm free all afternoon." She straightens rather quickly and meets Dad's gaze, blinking her brown eyes at him. It's adorable.

"This might be a little unorthodox, but maybe you can run with it?" He glances at me, telling me I need to run with it as well. "It would be a personal favor, not something through the NOPD."

Her lips quirk. "Okay?"

"How are you at drawing landscapes?"

"I'm better at portraits." She shrugs, tipping her head to the side. "But I can try."

"CeCe, maybe Gina can, uhhh..." he works his jaw back and forth and squints, struggling to form words. "Help you retrieve your memory from that car accident." He gives me a laser stare, willing me to understand. It takes a second, but I catch on. Move over, Sherlock. Dad is a genius, hoping to find The Caster through the accident. *If there was a fatality, it's traceable.*

"Right. The details are super fuzzy. My therapist said it would really help to talk it through." My improv skills are far more legit than his.

"Yes." Dad clears his throat. "Your therapist."

Zach's smile tells me he figured out what's up too.

"Oh. Okay." She picks up her pencil and notepad. "I'm happy to help."

Dad gives an overview without revealing anything

about my necromancy or The Caster. He may not have the gift of improv, but he can talk around a subject. She hangs on every word, her expression sincere. If she thinks it's strange we want to learn more about an accident I supposedly witnessed, she doesn't say anything.

Zach's hand warms my knee, his fingers rubbing small circles. "The black magic can help you remember," he whispers in my ear. "Magic holds memory better than a photograph. Let it pull you into the magical plane."

Magical plane? I don't know what he means, but he leans over and takes off my necklace.

Cold blasts my spine, The Caster's presence immediate. Ice jabs and drums pound. He tries to seize control, but with Zach's touch steadying me, I have the upper hand.

"Are you ready to start?" Dad asks.

"Ready." Closing my eyes, I bring the images to mind, remembering what The Caster showed me. The scene is so vivid, like I'm there. And maybe I am. I walk the street, seeing the police lights blink in blues and reds.

Now I understand what Zach means about magic, memory, and the magical plane.

"Tell me what you remember," Gina says.

I shut out the grinding from the jaws of life and the people running around. "It's a one-way street. The police blocked the road behind me, and there's no oncoming traffic."

The pencil scratches on paper. "What's around you?"

"Oaks. Lots of them. And mansions. I think I'm by the Garden District."

"You've been to Lafayette a million times, CeCe." Dad sets his hands on the table, and I feel the vibration on my end. "What part of the Garden District?"

"Ummm...I don't know." Adding my personal experience to The Caster's memory only confuses the vision, and I push my thoughts aside. "The sun is setting behind the accident. So, we must be facing west." I shift my body the slightest degree, as if I'm really there. "Maybe southwest."

The drums beat again. Urgently. Goosebumps break out on my arms, and the snake slides below my skin. Color drips away from the scene, like water washing it clean, and everything shifts into shades of gray. The police lights dim, and the shadows cast by the oaks grow. Darkness crawls, unnatural shapes forming and reaching for me, forcing me to stay silent. It feels like being spirit kidnapped. Pulled against my will.

"How wide is the street?" Gina continues to sketch, and I can't open my mouth.

A chair squeaks beside me, and Zach wraps his arm around my shoulders. His heat chases the darkness, the ice melting from his touch. The gray recedes, color lighting the vision.

"CeCe?" Dad's voice is soft. Hesitant. "Are you okay?"

"We can take a break if you need," Gina looks up from her drawing and the scratching of the pencil pauses.

"I'm fine." I take a breath and squeeze my eyes closed to stay in the memory. "The street is two lanes wide. And the cars have crashed in the cross street. A black car, heading north, smashed into the driver's side door of a blue car."

"Is there a painted crosswalk?"

"Yes." I nod and move my foot so it nudges Zach's. I need the extra point of contact. "And the park strip is dry, the grass burned out. Probably late July or August."

"Two lane street, dry park strip with oaks, mansions, black car, blue car." She continues to sketch, and I listen to her switching pencils, the lead rasping as she colors.

"Retrieving memories is hard, but you're doing great. Can you think of anything else?"

I tip my head to the side, a sound grabbing my attention. But not from the room. From the vision. Metal screeches against metal, a high-pitched whine that can be heard every time the jaws of life pause.

"I hear the streetcar." I know exactly where I am. My heart pounds, and the whole scene comes together. The vision opens, and I'm no longer constrained by The Caster. I see everything. "We're on St. Charles."

I open my eyes and blink back to the room. Gina finishes the drawing, and Zach keeps his arm around me.

Dad stands and walks to the door, calling out. "Officer Menard, I have a job for you."

Exhaustion drags at my limbs, and my body shakes. The necro-shivers surprise me because I didn't use necromancy. Or maybe I did? I don't actually know. Zach holds me tighter, lending me his warmth.

"How's this?" Gina flips the drawing.

I'm amazed at how good it looks. Somehow, she brought the scene to life with my limited details and colored it to match what I saw. "That's perfect."

A uniformed officer, who I assume is Menard, steps in. "Detective LeBlanc?"

"I need some research. A car accident happened on St. Charles, in the Garden District. At least one fatality." He takes the paper from Gina and hands it to the policeman. "This should give you a visual of what you're looking for."

Officer Menard glances at it, and his lips flatten. "I don't need to do the research. I worked this accident. Rivera was with me, and that's something you don't forget."

"Carlos Rivera?" Dad's face loses color, and he goes still.

Missing pieces of the puzzle click in his mind as his gaze sharpens. "This was the accident when he lost his wife."

Menard nods. "Before he was promoted to detective, I was partnered with him, and we got called in. Destroyed him to find out she was killed by a drunk driver."

Dad runs, the door slamming against the wall from the force of his speed. His feet echo down the hall, and Officer Menard hurries after him.

The room spins. Shock flares like a jolt of static. I struggle to draw a breath thinking about the man who's been partnered with my dad for six months. The man with the sweet tooth who always takes the time to check in with me.

Detective Carlos Rivera. The Caster.

CHAPTER TWENTY-NINE

CECE THE PSYCHIC: MONDAY, 6:30 P.M.

I feel sick.

Rivera kidnapped my spirit. He spied on me at drama camp and planted evidence to frame Jennifer. And he definitely knew Zach. His expression wasn't faint recognition; it was annoyance.

Gina puts her things away in the big case. She glances at Zach and me but stays quiet, understanding something big just happened.

Zach moves his arm from around my shoulders and takes my hand. "Are you okay?"

"Rivera always acted like he cared. Once, he helped me with a report for AP History. But all along, he was watching me." The times he talked to me, made me laugh, or asked how I was doing.

"How did he know about"—he pauses, flashing a glance at Gina— "your talents?"

Talents meaning necromancy. I drop my mouth to Zach's ear, lowering my voice. "He knows Dad and I go to the morgue. And Dad always has 'confidential informants' to help solve cases. If Rivera was really looking, which we know he was, he could have figured it out."

He rubs his forehead, a soft *oh* echoing from his mouth. "That first night at the morgue, the first time you met The Caster. He was hunting your...talents."

I let that discovery turn over in my mind, picturing the circle of ash and the red-tipped pins. "But why couldn't I feel it in him? I've done things like shake his hand before."

"It's not something he was born with, so you wouldn't be able to. If you're not naturally *talented*, it's undetectable by touch."

I nod. Black magic is learned and doesn't have a natural source to draw from.

My vision goes fuzzy, and the bond with Rivera draws me in. The room fades, my spirit following the string to join him. I don't try to stop it. He's in a car, driving something different than before. The perspective widens, and I sit next to him in the passenger seat. He's not hiding his appearance anymore.

"You know me, CeCe," he says. "I'd never hurt you."

That's a lie. You'd do anything to get your wife back, even if I ended up dead.

"No, you're safe with me. We can help each other."

I don't want to be a part of this.

"Ben's miserable. He doesn't want to live in a world without his wife." He runs his thumb along the wedding ring he still wears. The brown leather watch band, that I now recognize as the one he always fiddles with, wraps around his wrist. "I can free him from his misery."

By killing him?

"He won't have to slog through his broken life, and we'll have the last organ." He takes a deep breath, and an eerie

237

calm settles on his face. "I'm bumping up the timeline. I need your cooperation."

Bumping up the timeline? Dad knows it's you. They're going to find Ben.

"That's why we have to move fast."

He keeps saying "we," and my disgust spikes. I don't want to be a "we" with him. In fact, I never want to see him again.

You'd never get away. Wanted for murder and on the run from the law. Not to mention the reappearance of your dead wife. It's impossible.

"I've planned for everything, and I know how to hide."

Zach rubs his fingers along my arm. The heat from his magic makes the connection with Rivera fuzzy.

"Stop letting your boyfriend interfere." Rivera smacks a fist against the dashboard. "He can't help us."

Zach slips the pendant on my neck, and the obsidian effectively slams a door on Rivera. I come back to myself in the police station. My pulse races, and I clasp the necklace.

"Rivera's bumping up the timeline," I say, using his words.

"This isn't just a recurring dream, is it?" Gina scoots to the edge of her chair, our knees almost grazing. "CeCe, you're psychic, aren't you? I know a girl who's psychic. She consults with the FBI. On the down low, of course."

"Oh, umm...." I clear my throat. "*Psychic* isn't the right term."

"You can trust me. I won't say anything." She clasps her hands, and a growing smile transforms her face. "I knew it. As you described the accident, I could tell you were really seeing it."

She's not wrong. And right now, I wouldn't mind

having some psychic ability to figure out how this mess with Rivera ends. But... "I'm really not psychic."

"I think it's great Cooper accepts your gift." Her burgundy sweater slips off her shoulder and she pulls it back up. "A lot of people don't want to acknowledge the supernatural, and the fact that your dad does, well, that says a lot about him."

Her eyes take on a dreamy glow, and if Dad plays this right, he'll definitely score a date. But if they become a couple, she should really understand that I can't predict the future.

"I think you misunderstood—" I start, but Dad walks in.

"Rivera's in the wind," He loosens his tie, the pink paisley knot hanging low. "I checked with the PIO, and he never dropped off the sketch. He took it and ran."

Zach's sigh echoes mine, and his fingers tighten on my arm. Rivera on the run is not what we want. *I know how to hide.*

"So...Detective Rivera stole the sketch?" Gina's eyes bounce between us as she tries to follow along.

"Yes. I'm sorry, Gina." Dad moves his hand as if he's going to pat her but he pulls back.

"Did anyone see him leave?" Zach asks.

"No. Why would they notice? He's part of the precinct." Dad takes the seat next to Gina, and stretches out his legs.

"There's something else," I say. An embarrassed pause follows my statement as I realize Gina hangs on my every word. Ugh. If I'm not careful, I'll be consulting with the FBI in no time. "Rivera is going after Ben tonight."

"Tonight?" Dad's eyes go wide.

"He knows it's now or never." I twist the pendant, the black obsidian emanating warmth.

Dad looks at his watch, muttering a curse under his breath. "We're running out of time. It's almost 7:00."

"I can find him," Zach says. "I mean, I can help CeCe find him."

Dad grunts, which means *how?*

I look at Gina, who is clearly captivated. While improv is my thing, talking around the subject is more Dad's territory. "Just trust me, and I'll find him." I put on my confident, easy-peasy smile. He doesn't buy it.

"I don't like this. It's too dangerous." He sighs and runs a hand through his hair. "How will I protect you?"

A wave of tenderness has me squeezing his hand. "You've been training me to solve crimes for a decade. You taught me well."

"This determined streak in you"—he turns his hand palm up, squeezing back— "You're saying it's my fault?"

"Of course, it's your fault. I know the morgue better than I know the mall." I laugh and pull away. "But you need to be ready. Once I find him, you have to arrest him."

He grunts, which I take to mean, *I'll be ready.*

"I can help too." Gina pulls the album of photos and her sketchbook from the case. "I can make a new drawing."

"You remember it?" Dad asks.

"Not exactly." She shows us a paper where she wrote a list. *B-12's eyebrows, D-7's face shape, G-25's lips.* All the way down to *narrow the chin.* "I have a habit of taking notes when I draw."

"You're a genius. I could kiss you." Dad realizes what he said, and a blush covers his face, deep enough it looks like he spent an afternoon in the sun. Gina bites her bottom lip and averts her eyes, her rosy cheeks just as telling.

Adorable.

"We should get out of your hair," I say, linking my arm

through Zach's. "I'll call when I know something. It was nice to meet you, Gina."

"Bye, CeCe. I hope to *see* you again." Heavy emphasis on the word *see*. She really does think I'm psychic.

Dad tips his chin to me, the same farewell he always gives. It means goodbye, see you later, and I love you, all in one gesture.

I respond with my normal farewell. "Bye, Daddy."

CHAPTER
THIRTY

THE STORM: MONDAY, 6:45 P.M.

Zach and I walk to his car, and the gray sky above haunts us. The wind picks up and whips my hair in my face. Humidity thickens the air and weighs in my lungs, heavy with the promise of a storm.

"Rain's coming," he says, driving out of the parking lot. His thumbs tap against the steering wheel in an agitated rhythm, his tension rolling in faster than the clouds.

"Is something wrong?" I ask.

"The black magic gets to me sometimes." He shakes his head and rolls out his shoulders.

I was so involved with the sketch and Rivera, I didn't notice Zach's bloodshot eyes and jittery motions. All the touching and pushing back the black magic took their toll.

"If the magic is too much—"

"CeCe, I want to help." He stretches his fingers, releasing the chokehold on the steering wheel. "I just crave the magic, and my control can slip. But I'm good now."

I must have a skeptical look on my face because he

laughs and rushes to speak again. "I promise, I'm in control."

As if to prove it, he takes my hand, linking our fingers together. My pulse jumps, and I wonder if it'll always be like this. Or once we catch Rivera and figure out how to erase the black magic, will the zing disappear? Will Zach still like me if it does?

I shake off the questions and pull out my phone. Taking my hand back, I text Portia. Even though we spent the afternoon together, a landmine of information detonated over the last hour.

> ME: So much to tell you. Rivera is The Caster. He's on the run. Lives are at stake!

With my dramatic text, I expect an immediate answer, but nothing comes. *Maybe she's with a customer?*

"Portia's not responding," I mutter, after another full thirty seconds.

"Isn't she at work?" A crash of thunder shakes the sky at his words. *Foreboding much?*

"Yes. But I want to gossip-text with her and she's not participating."

Zach laughs as he pulls over, parking on the street. I take a moment to orient myself. We're close to Jackson Square, the clanging of the St. Louis cathedral bells announcing the seven o'clock hour.

"Where are we going?" I get out of the car as he opens my door.

"Mom's store is nearby. She has everything we need." He takes my hand and leads me down the sidewalk. "We got good parking tonight."

My Vans shuffle on the pavement, and I listen to the faint music. A brassy street band plays in the distance and

243

will probably keep going until the rain comes. A loud tuba holds the beat with its robust horn, while a couple of trumpets and trombones hit the melody. Growing up in New Orleans, jazz is a part of life, filling the air as much as the sun lights the day.

Zach pulls a key from his pocket and unlocks a door. I step back to look at the sign. *Black Wren Voodoo,* it reads, in curved lettering. Below that is a circle with the silhouette of a Carolina Wren inside.

His Mom's store is a *Voodoo* shop.

"After you." He holds the heavy wooden door open with his foot, and I walk inside.

"When you said we were going to your mom's store, this isn't what I had in mind." I look around, the vibe less witchcraft and more new age. Clean white shelves line the walls, displaying voodoo dolls and spell books. Different colored baskets hold all kinds of mystical items, from herbs to crystals.

"Just your normal N'awlins shop," he laughs. "My mom and Aunt Lucy opened this place three years ago, and I've worked here since then."

"You started working when you were fourteen?" I sift through a handful of vibrant rocks, letting the cool stones fall from my fingers and plink into the bowl.

"Yeah. Back then, I did magic work, like blessing gris-gris bags and preparing spells. Now I run the register."

"The register? Sounds brutal."

"You know it." He laughs and moves behind the checkout counter. The back wall is lined with bottles and jars. Holding a large glass bowl, he grabs things from the shelf, not even double-checking the contents.

I watch him and lean my elbows on the countertop. "I bet you could gather everything blindfolded."

"Probably. I've been selling things like—" he holds up a jar that he adds to the bowl— "devil's claw since the shop opened."

"Devil's claw?"

"It's a plant from Africa that my mom imports. It has really strong psychic properties." He winks at me. "And you should know, being psychic and all."

"It's not funny," I say, but I'm laughing. "If she starts dating my dad, that'll make for really awkward family dinners."

"They'll be dating for sure. You might want to brush up on your premonitions."

"Ha ha," I deadpan.

Juggling the bowl, now filled with spell materials, he pulls on the shelf, and the whole wall opens.

It's a secret door.

"That's so cool." I step around the counter to peek into the hidden room. No windows alleviate the gloom, and I go inside, letting my eyes adjust.

"Every respectable Voodoo shop needs a casting room." He smiles, and I sense his dimples rather than see them. "Not all rooms are concealed as well as ours, though."

He flips a switch, and dim lighting fills the space. I run my hand along the wood-paneled wall. A permanent circle is carved into the cement floor.

"Is that what this is? A casting room?"

"We need a space to prepare the charms, spells, and dolls. Mom and Aunt Lucy didn't want to bring their work home with them. So, here we are." He sets the bowl down and hands me a canister of salt. "Are you ready?"

I nod. "Let's find Rivera."

"You pour, and I'll set everything up."

Thunder roars, the weather offering an ominous quality

to the night. Salt hisses from the spout as I step along the perimeter, filling the deep etching. He lays out the supplies inside the circle. A large, handheld mirror with a silver handle. A jar of fennel seed. A black candle. A bottle of water. A small vial of oil. A plastic bottle with a blue liquid inside. A spell book. And a jar of devil's claw.

"I researched the Fetter of the Spirit Puppet spell Rivera used, and you'll combine a few reversal techniques to counteract it," he says, then lifts the book. "I also have this to help walk us through."

Rain pelts against the walls, the torrent sudden and urgent. The small room magnifies the sound, thousands of droplets battering the shop from the outside. An angry wind howls and my name carries on the breeze.

CeCe LeBlanc.

The thunder growls again. Quieter. More rhythmic. A steady beat. Not thunder at all. Drums.

"I feel Rivera," I whisper, grabbing the pendant at my neck and rubbing it between my thumb and forefinger.

"Then let's get started."

We sit cross-legged on the floor, and he scoots to put a small distance between us, opening the spell book by his feet. "We need to be careful. I don't want to touch you and dilute your connection to Rivera."

"No touching. Got it."

His lips kick up in a half smile, and he meets my gaze. "Hopefully, I never have to say those words again."

He drips oil over the candle and sprinkles crushed fennel seeds on the surface. Because of the oil, it adheres, the candle coarse with the herb.

"What does the fennel do?" I ask in a hushed tone.

"It's for spell protection and countermagic." He sticks the candle into the built-in holder on the bottom of the bowl. "Will you pour the water? Be sure not to rinse the fennel."

Twisting the lid off, I dump the clear liquid, mindful not to let it splash. The wind howls, shaking the shop, combining with the attacking rain. He pulls out a lighter, handing it to me, and I set flame to the candle.

"This feels super eerie," I say, barely audible above the downpour.

"Storms are the best time for casting. Magic loves a little chaos." He opens the devil's claw, dumping it in the water, and then places the mirror next to me. "Keep the reflection down until I tell you to look."

"Okay. What else?" A clap of thunder causes me to jump, and I cover my heart, clutching the pendant.

His finger trails over a page in the spell book before he nudges a lancet close to me, the kind a diabetic uses to check insulin. "It says we need a few drops of your blood in the water."

I pick up the finger stick, the sharp point reflecting in the candle's glow. Pricking my thumb, I hold it over the bowl and watch the red liquid plop. It spreads, a swirling dance of crimson seeping into the water.

"This spell draws on your unique power to trace Rivera. It's not black magic, but a general spell that utilizes what you have. Through that, you can find and follow the connection Rivera forged with you. Do you understand?" He waits for my nod before continuing. "I don't know exactly how this will work with death magic, so if you're not comfortable with it, we need to stop now."

The words, *what's the worst that could happen,* rest on the tip of my tongue. But tempting fate seems like a bad idea. "Zach, if there's even a small chance we can find him, we have to try."

"Okay." His chest rises and falls slowly with the weight of nervous anticipation. "Take off the necklace."

I lift the chain over my head, setting it beside me. Immediately, I feel Rivera, his desperation dragging me closer. The drums join the rain, heightening the sound reverberating in my head.

"Anytime someone uses magic, it leaves a trace, like DNA at a crime scene. No one can hide it or cover it up." Zach's soft voice pierces through the noise. "You need to find his trace and follow it back to him."

"How?" I force myself to concentrate on what he says and not the drums.

"Umm." Paper crinkles as he turns a page. "Focus on the candle and think of Rivera. Don't let him drag your spirit this time. You pull him instead."

Rather than be redundant, because *how?*, I stare at the flickering candle. The flame wavers, the light alive as it sways. It makes me think of Mawmaw, sitting on the porch swing, smelling the burning citronella candle and enjoying the sunshine. Lemonade cooling my mouth, the drink a little more sour than sweet. The cicadas buzzing, a high-pitched hum in my memory.

But it's more than a memory. I actually hear the cicadas, their voices in sync with my pounding pulse. The insects crowd my mind, growing in strength and overtaking the drums. Loud vibrations drill in my skull. Incessant. Shrill. The cold of my necromancy bristles on my skin. The shrieking insects clamor for attention. I squeeze my eyes closed.

"CeCe, what's going on?" Zach asks, a hint of concern punctuating his tone.

I want to reassure him, but I can't. Covering my ears, I try to block out the cicadas. Unable to because it comes from within me. My brain feels full, ready to burst, all the noise swelling.

"Talk to me." His voice comes closer.

The storm outside howls. The tumult inside me roars. *Stop,* I think, and the Cicadas pause. I slow my breathing, settling my panic, and the cicadas respond. In my mind, I see them, crawling on the drums, so many it stops the beat.

Then I understand. I control them.

"I'm going to put the necklace on you."

"No, I'm okay." I let the cicadas play, a symphony of buzzing, and it tugs at my connection with Rivera.

They lead me, the sound vibrations bouncing along the link. The more I focus on that, the less my head hurts, and I mentally pull at the string, dragging it closer. Instinct guides me, the magic teaching me what to do, and for the first time since this crazy mess started, *I see him.*

Rivera.

He sits in the sloped-ceiling room, dressed in the same long, black robe he wore the last time I watched him use magic. Candles are set on the floor, the tiny flames flickering. He wears black gloves, and in his hand, he holds a voodoo doll.

CHAPTER
THIRTY-ONE

CHASING THE CASTER: MONDAY, 7:30 P.M.

There's no mistaking the doll's resemblance to Ben, thinning gray yarn hair and brown button eyes.

Don't make this hard, CeCe. Rivera speaks in my mind. *We're so close.*

"I won't help you," I say.

You will. He shouts the two words, his fingers clenching around the doll. Then his hold loosens, and his shoulders relax. *You miss your Mawnaw. So much it hurts.*

"Yes, it hurts, but you have to let it go." I have Rivera to thank for that lesson. Clinging to grief can change you into someone unrecognizable.

We'll work together. Neither one of us needs to be alone.

"You already tried this with me. I'm over it." If my eyes weren't closed, I'd roll them. "Especially because I'm not alone. I have Dad and Portia. And Zach."

A sinister smile creases his face. *There are other ways to convince you.*

"What does that mean?" I ask.

He ignores my question and focuses on casting his spell. The lack of response makes my nerves spike, tiny pinpricks of worry poking my chest.

"CeCe." Zach's voice jolts me back to the room and I open my eyes. He sits with one leg propped up, his elbow resting on his knee. The spell book lays on the floor next to him. His dark hair falls on his forehead, nearly covering eyes gone navy in the soft candlelight.

"Look in the mirror," he says.

I forgot the mirror. Picking it up and peering into the glass, I face Rivera again. But this time I see him with my actual sight. And not only that, I see his magic DNA trace.

It streams from the bottom of the reflection in a smoky red line. It's the same kind of line I saw when Rivera tried to trace me from the morgue to Tulane. I stand and shift, noting that the line stays in the same place, a compass pointing north. Or, in this case, to Rivera.

"That's amazing." I twist to the side, watching the line move, disappearing off the mirror for a moment until I turn back. Spinning in a circle, I wait for the line to reappear and stop when I notice a second trace—this one in the opposite direction of Rivera. I move the mirror back and forth, double-checking to make sure I'm not seeing things.

"What does it mean if I see two magic traces?" I ask.

"It means he's set another one." Zach takes a deep breath. "You reversed the trace that leads to you, so it goes back to him. But if there's another, it's probably the one he's using to trace Ben."

"But he knows where Ben is. Why would he need to use a tracing spell?"

"His physical body knows where Ben is. His magical essence doesn't." Getting to his feet, Zach stands next to me, careful to keep space between us. "Rivera's trace will lengthen and get closer to Ben's. Once they connect, Rivera will have him."

"What do we do?" I clutch the mirror's handle so tightly I worry it might crack.

"Who's closer to you, Ben or Rivera?"

"I don't know." I spin back and forth, unsure how to determine the distance.

"You can't tell by looking with your physical eyes." He runs a hand through his dark hair, leaving the strands disheveled. "The magical realm is on a different plane. Send your magic to follow the trace, and you'll know."

"Zach, I've never done this before."

He reaches for the mirror, but quickly stops and folds his arms. "Close your eyes. Feel the magic and let it guide you. You can do this."

"I don't know how." But when I close my eyes, I do feel something. The traces are alive, breathing with energy. I reach out to touch one and realize it's not with my physical hand. My spirit hovers somewhere outside reality, in the place where magic lives. "I can see it."

I study both lines again, running my spiritual fingers through the fog. The traces are cold and clammy, thicker than smoke, and slimier than water. Things work differently in this plane, and I can't get a clear place or time, but the feelings are more vivid, and the intangible becomes real. Rivera prepares the spell. I see him working as if I was there with him. His desperation stabs the air in sharp puffs of pain. I sense Ben drinking at a bar a few streets away. Most likely on Bourbon Street. His grief is so thick I can grasp it in my hand and mold the emotion. "Ben's closer."

"Then you should find him."

I open my eyes, and the weird shift from magical plane

to physical plane leaves me unbalanced. I sit down, crossing my legs. "How do we do that?"

He lowers next to me, close enough to see into the mirror but avoiding any contact. "You follow the trace and pull along that energy. Combining what you know with what you're experiencing is hard. Really hard. But force yourself to focus and figure out where he is. You'll understand what I mean when you're there."

"It sounds like you've done this magical stalking before," I say, trying to wrap my mind around the complex instructions.

His lips turn down. "Yeah. But not in the way you think."

Well, I wasn't really thinking any particular way. Now I'm curious. "After this, will you tell me what happened?"

"Yeah, I will. For now, let's save Ben."

Taking out my phone, I dial Dad. He answers with a grunt, and I get right to the point. "Head to Bourbon Street. I'll keep you on the line and let you know where to go."

"Let's roll," he says to someone on his end. The jingle of keys and shuffling movement fills the line. "CeCe, we got a hit on Ben. A call came in after his picture was on the news. His name's Ben Lund. Age 62. Lives in Metairie. I sent a couple of uniforms to his house, and he wasn't there."

"He's already at the bar." Putting Dad on speaker, I set the phone down and look in the mirror. I know what it's like to be pulled, my spirit traveling without permission. I've never been on the other side—the Puller. The magical stalker.

But apparently Zach has.

The rain continues outside, wind shrieking through the plaster walls. Zach said magic loves a little chaos, and he's not wrong. Power surges beneath my skin, ready to be released. I take a deep breath and close my eyes.

My body vibrates with energy, and I grasp at the trace. Everything else fades. The storm, the casting room, sounds from the phone. I pull along our link, a slow-motion effort. The cicadas sing, quiet at first, until their voices rise like the hammering rain. They lead me with their sound, moving ahead and guiding me. I'm a shadow, dragging down the street and heading closer to the bar.

It's painful being in three places at once. My physical body at Black Wren Voodoo with Zach, my spirit tracking down Ben, and this mental link with Rivera that lets me see and hear him. My head aches, a stabbing agony like my skull will split. My stomach churns, a constant, nauseous tumbling. I don't know how long I can do this, and I fight harder to follow the trace.

Work with me, CeCe. We don't have to raise your Mawmaw. I can give you something else.

Rivera's icy magic holds me back. A circle of ash surrounds him, and he sticks a finger in the soot, smearing a streak across the Ben doll's forehead. I forcibly shift my mind away from him, wrestling through the pain to keep moving along Ben's trace. My body shakes, not my spirit body, but my physical self. The split causes spasms to shoot into my arms and legs. Hundreds of needles stabbing, reminding me of Henry Guillory's pin-riddled body.

"We're about to turn onto Bourbon." Dad's words come from far away, a dull static.

Combining what you know with what you're experiencing will be hard. Zach's words come back to me as I open my mouth to give Dad directions. I struggle to place where I am. The buildings and storefronts make no sense. An intense jab twinges in my brain, so sharp my eyes roll.

Agony stings along my spine. But I force myself to bridge the gap between the physical and the magical. "The bar's on lower Bourbon."

My tongue feels swollen. I want to describe what I see, but Rivera's in my head, slowing me down. I follow the trace, inch by agonizing inch.

"Hang in there, CeCe. You can do this," Zach whispers.

The trace turns, heading into the courtyard of an older building. Lightning flashes, reflecting off the water pooling in gutters, and I see Ben. He wears a blue slicker and black rubber boots, and he props his arms on a table, his face hidden in his hands.

Don't say anything else. You'll regret it.

"Where am I going?" Dad asks.

I shake off Rivera's attempt to divert me. "It's an older building. Cracked gray plaster with red bricks peeking through."

"Sounds like Lafitte's." Dad shuffles around in the background. Then, "Lafitte's. Ahead on our left."

The wailing of police sirens grows close, but Rivera moves faster, the red line nearly on top of me. Dad's too late. I feel Rivera before I see him. The air thickens with black magic, and the ground vibrates with the beat of his drums. Ben lifts his gaze and looks around, nervously reaching for his drink.

"He's here," I whisper.

Rivera's trace blends with Ben's, becoming a solid line, and he appears next to me in the courtyard. The black robe billows around him, his shadowy presence like an omen of death. He clenches the voodoo doll, a physical object hijacked into the magical plane. A strange piece of tangible hidden from Ben's view by Rivera's power.

How can his spirit even hold it?

Rivera toys with a loose string on the side of the doll, and Ben stands, rubbing the same spot near his ribs. His startled gaze flashes around the canopy. I propel myself forward and grab for the doll, the fabric slipping like sand through my fingertips. Everything is different in this plane. I keep forgetting.

Compensating for the strange, sifting material, I cup my hands like I'm trying to hold water and clap them closed over the burlap. I'm clumsy and uncoordinated, but I make Rivera scramble to keep his grip.

"Let go."

"No." If I hold on, I can stall long enough for Dad to get Ben out of here. Then Rivera will have to start the trace over, buying us some more time.

"Your dad's been keeping secrets. Your mom has magic."

His words distract me, and my fingers slip, leaving me clutching at the material's edge. "I don't believe you."

"I can't lie through our connection any more than you can hide your curiosity."

Well, duh, of course, I'm curious. Dangling a secret about my mom is like offering me a role in The Exhibition. Impossible to refuse. And the truth of his words sits heavily between us, more than an elephant in the room. This is the weight of something life-changing.

I want to know.

He answers as if I spoke the thought aloud. "You're powerful like she is. I've never met anyone more powerful than your mom."

Another truth. I feel his certainty through our connection.

I use all my strength to keep hold of the doll. Wasting energy on thoughts of my mom gets me nowhere, and Ben's life hangs in the balance. My spirit pulses like it will shatter, and I jump between the physical and spiritual, my body aching, my essence fading.

"Stop fighting, and this can all be over. It must be excruciating to keep yourself here. Just let go."

"No!"

My physical body twitches, muscles cramping and convulsing. A wave of dizziness twists my world as I lay back on the floor of the casting room. Zach calls to me, wrenching my full focus from Rivera, but I hang on to the doll while keeping my metaphorical foot in this plane with Rivera.

Blinking red and blue lights flash in the courtyard as police cars screech to a stop. The sound of running footsteps turns Rivera's attention from the Ben doll, and I take advantage, tugging it away.

Rivera's startled gaze meets mine, and he shakes his head, his face radiating anger. Worse than anger. Fury. Stepping into the shadows, he disappears.

Dad runs into the courtyard, hair plastered from the rain, his suit soaked. The scene fades from my view as he approaches Ben.

I open my eyes and find myself back in the voodoo shop with Zach. The mirror, which I managed to keep in my hand, clatters to the floor. The voodoo doll somehow came back with me, and I drop it to clench my head. My hands seem to be the only things keeping my skull from cracking open.

"You're amazing, CeCe." Zach pulls me to a sitting position, wrapping his arms around me. The heat from his touch burns and soothes at the same time, a weird duality of hurt and healing. Tasting blood I realize, at some point, I bit my tongue. Hard.

He puts a hand on my neck, rubbing the tension. His

other hand drifts over my arm, holding me together. "Did your dad make it in time?"

My words won't come, but I nod, as much as I can while tucked into Zach. Tears spill down my cheeks, and my breathing escapes in sobbing gasps. The necro-shivers hit and try to tear me apart with the force.

"Hey, it's okay." His hand moves from my neck to rub down my back. Warmth permeates the pain, calming the tremors, his presence soothing the discomfort. "I have something for you. It's a drink my mom makes for magical recovery."

He puts the bottle with blue-tinted water to my lips. The acidic jolt blends with the taste of blood, and I gag when the liquid hits my throat. I manage to choke it down, despite my body shakes and stomach upheaval.

Zach speaks softly, his presence steady. "My mom uses healing magic, and it helps with rejuvenation."

The flavor is herby, like tea, and leaves a bitterness in my mouth. Or maybe that's the blood. Though the drink is cold, it heats a path down my throat and through my chest. The headache eases, the torment fading to a dull throb. My muscles unclench, and I'm able to breathe in deeply.

A violent shudder wracks my body, but I start to feel more human. "Thanks. I think I'm going to live."

"You're going to need a minute. Or ten. Maybe twenty." He helps me take another drink and sets the bottle aside. "I've never seen anything like what you did. Splitting like that, following the trace, and talking to your dad on the phone while watching Rivera. Saving Ben. You even brought back the doll. It was incredible."

"I just followed your directions."

"No, I gave you directions to walk through the spell. You soared." Zach speaks with a mixture of fear and excitement.

"Your magic is a force to be reckoned with. I've only met one person with that kind of power."

That kind of power. The familiar ring of his words, so like what Rivera said about my mom, makes something uncomfortable coil in my belly. I sit up straighter and bite my lip. "Who are you talking about?"

"Her name's Constance." His expression changes from confusion to concern, and he takes my hand. "What's wrong?"

Nausea swells, and a weight crushes my chest. It can't be a coincidence. First, Rivera brings her up. And now this.

"My mom's name is Constance LeBlanc."

THIRTY-TWO

CICADAS: MONDAY, 8:30 P.M.

"Whoa, wait." Zach stills and blinks a few times. "Your mom is Constance?"

"Well, that's her name."

We sit on the hard floor, both of us with crossed legs, our hands entwined. The candle flickers, adding a soft glow. Rain batters outside, the wind and water swirling in a blast of chaos.

"It isn't a very common name." He lifts my chin, his gaze roaming my face. "You look a lot like your dad. Especially your eyes. But yeah, maybe."

"I barely remember her." I wonder what resemblance Zach sees. It never seemed strange before that I don't have a picture of her anywhere. "I'm named after her. Well, both my mom and dad, Cooper and Constance. Each of them passed down their first initial."

"I can't believe she's your mom." He picks up my necklace and slides it over my head. "This is wild. She's actually the person I had to...magically stalk, as you put it."

"You traced her?" The woman who may or may not be my super mighty magic-using mom.

"I told you I got deep into black magic. I met Constance, and she was willing to teach me. For a price. She wanted access to my life magic. Then she bound our power together, very similar to what Rivera did to you."

"I'm sorry. What happened?" I can't wrap my head around the idea that my mom did this to him.

"When I wanted out, she wouldn't let me go. It was... messy. So, I had to trace her." His voice fades to a whisper, a fearful reverence to his memory. "I found her, cut our link, and never saw her again."

She's been moonlighting as a magical mentor. First Zach, and then Rivera. *How long has she lived in New Orleans? Did she ever leave?*

"Wow." The necklace calms me, and I rub the mirrored pendant between my fingers. "What's she like?"

As much as I try otherwise, I can't stop thinking about her when I should be focused on catching Rivera. And why do I even care? I'm not going to suddenly seek a mother/daughter relationship that's been non-existent for the last decade.

"Nicer than you'd imagine—for a scary magic user. But also, intense." He scoots closer and takes my hand again. "And calculating. Like even her backup plan would have a backup plan.

"This doesn't make sense." I shake my head. "I don't believe my mom's some black magic caster. She left because she couldn't handle my necromancy."

Thunder grumbles, the surly sky still dousing NOLA in

heavy rain. It batters the building, thousands of droplets pummeling our otherwise quiet cocoon.

"Are you sure that's why she left?" Zach's gentle tone nudges me to reconsider a fundamental idea I've believed for ten years.

I remember her words, spoken as she cradled my face. The cloying scent of burnt sugar clung to her. I knew she was going to disappear when she cleared out her dresser. I knew when I watched her pack.

And I especially knew when she slipped out before Dad got home from work, leaving six-year-old me to stare into her empty closet and wonder what I did wrong. "Yes. The last thing she said was that my magic is too much."

"You're powerful, CeCe. More than I've ever seen. Your mom's magic is all about balance. Maybe *that's* what she meant by too much."

A loud ringing echoes beside me, and I jump. My phone's screen lights up with the words Chief Daddio.

I swipe to answer. "Hi, Daddy."

"I'm heading to the station. We'll interview Ben and assign a protective detail. He's shaken up." He sounds the siren, a short *whoop whoop*, probably clearing a slow car out of the way. "Any idea where I should look for Rivera?"

I check the handheld mirror lying on the floor. It reflects me. Just me. No magic traces. No sign of a wannabe heart thief. "He's gone. I can't feel him at all."

"I'm not surprised." Dad's deep exhale rumbles in the speaker. "I need you to stop by before you go home. Can you do that?"

"Sure." I glance at Zach, and he obviously overhears because he nods.

"You did great tonight, baby girl," Dad says, and hangs up.

"I guess it's time to go." I make no effort to move, exhaustion weighing me down.

"Not quite." Zach picks up the Ben voodoo doll lying between us and turns it over. A hair sticks to the burlap, and he plucks it off, burning it in the candle. "Ben should be safe now."

"How did I bring the doll back, anyway? It's a physical object." It freaks me out, the way my eyes opened and I held it in my hand. The pounding in my head made it impossible for me to question it, but now I wonder when I suddenly developed the ability to break the laws of physics.

He blows out the wick, and a string of smoke spirals above the candle. "The spell Rivera used is really complex. Because the voodoo doll is infused with magic, it can travel on the spiritual plane. Not just anyone can breach the veil and bring it back."

Yep. Super powerful me who barely understands this world of magic. My thoughts tumble like they're in a spin cycle. I have no words to tackle the imbalance of my conflicted feelings. Instead, I start gathering the supplies laid on the floor.

"Don't worry about cleaning up." He stands and helps me to my feet. "I'll take care of it later."

"Are you sure?"

"Yeah. I'm working extra hours to help run things while Mom's gone." He tips his head as he studies my face. "Besides, we can try tracing Rivera again tomorrow."

The idea of another trace spell sends a round of nausea to my gut. The indescribable pain of splitting. My skull feeling like the Tik Tok challenge to explode a watermelon with rubber bands.

"Sure," I say.

"If you need more time..." His attempt at a smile wavers

at the corners, and he turns away to lead us from the casting room, back into the shop.

"I know how important it is to get your mom released." I put my hand on his shoulder as he presses the secret door closed. "Of course, I'll do it tomorrow."

A long exhale drags from his mouth and his whole body relaxes. "Thanks, CeCe."

We head outside to the still-raging storm. The shop's wooden eave shelters us as he locks up. Buckets of rain pour on the cars lining the street. But nobody chances the barrage. No more jazzy sounds of trumpets and saxophones fill the air, and it leaves the street empty and eerie.

Looking down the block, most of our way is protected by rooftops and second-floor patios. We make a dash for Zach's blue Subaru, my black and white vans splashing on the sidewalk. My chest feels lighter, the stress of Rivera and my mom set aside. If only for a minute. Running through the torrent frees me. Ben is safe, Rivera is quiet, and I'm with Zach.

By the time we make it to the car, Zach's shirt drips, and hair hangs in his eyes. He pulls out his keys, and we swoop in, drenched to the bone. I recline against the headrest, and a blast of pride bursts inside. We just saved Ben's life. Turning, I look at Zach.

His dimples are dimpling, his blue eyes bright like a clear sky, and my breath catches.

"Don't move," I say, pulling out my phone.

"What?" A droplet of rain runs from his temple down his jaw.

The light from my camera flashes, and I capture the image. "I want to remember you just like this."

"Like a drowned dog?" He shakes, water flinging in all directions.

"I'm thinking a sexy billboard for something like cologne or natural mountain spring water." I can't wipe the smile off my face.

And then his phone flashes.

"It's only fair for me to get a sexy billboard picture too."

"Delete that. Now." I self-consciously swipe at my soaked hair while reaching for his cell.

He dodges my attempts to throw it out the window. "Can't. I already marked it as a favorite."

He looks like a model. I probably look like something living on the bottom of Lake Pontchartrain. "Seriously, move it to the trash."

"Your smile lights up the screen. It would be a crime to delete it." He brushes his fingers down my cheek, and the phone drops in a cup holder between us. "You're so beautiful."

His words echo what he said during *Stuck*, in the seconds before he kissed me. I swallow down all the complaints and simply say, "Thanks."

I haven't felt his lips against mine in ages. Crush-time passes differently, like dog years, and I realize it's been for-EVER since we kissed. Suddenly, I want nothing more than to move my face close enough for our breath to touch. Then I could shift the tiniest bit, tipping my head to the right, and he'd tip his head to the right, our mouths a whisper apart.

Before I can finish plotting my kiss-incubussing, he takes my face in his hands, and presses his lips to mine.

Earth moving...

Heavens opening...

Candy bar unwrapping...

Honestly, it's a miracle we don't sit around and kiss all day. Rain shrouds the car in a wet curtain, the discordant roaring of thunder our background music. The storm grows as the kiss deepens, and the wind rattles. Magic sizzles, barely contained beneath our skin. It's hot and bright, and I'm afraid if I open my eyes, we'll both be glowing from the effects.

The kiss exceeds my expectations. Solid A-plus. Plus, plus, plus.

His power trembles, his pulse racing, the same kind of jittery excitement following a taste of black magic. I wonder if it's me making his blood run hot, or if my connection to Rivera gives him a fix of the darkness he craves.

Thunder rumbles again, and on the heels comes the sound of my cicadas. The buzzing grows louder, pumping in time with my heart. A humming chorus of our mingling magic.

Zach pulls back, his shaking fingers trailing down my cheek.

"Cicadas," he says. And then, "Hmm."

"You can hear them?" I ask.

"Of course I can hear them, CeCe. That's the problem."

CHAPTER THIRTY-THREE

SOUND MAGIC: MONDAY, 8:40 P.M.

"They started singing when I traced Rivera. Is it bad?" I pull my hands from where they circle his neck and fold them in my lap.

"No. Just...your connection with Rivera is getting even deeper." His eyes stay on me, and he cups my chin, his hold unsteady. "Calling sound is a potent black magic."

"Calling sound?"

"As you become more advanced, you can develop a vibration of sorts. A sound that adds strength to your magic. It's like hot sauce in gumbo. Something that provides a lot of punch." He rubs my arm, his skin buzzing at the contact. "It's unique to each person."

"Rivera uses drums." I think of their hypnotizing rhythm, the way it drags me under.

"If he uses drums, the cicadas aren't his," he says, pausing for a moment. "How did you even develop sound magic?"

"I don't know, but I kind of like the cicadas. They remind me of Mawmaw."

"No, you don't understand. Rivera's creating an unbreakable connection to you." His lips flatten, and he takes a breath. "I almost couldn't sever the bond with Constance."

"Because she's powerful?"

"Because I didn't want to." He runs a hand through his hair and shudders. "The draw to that power is a constant temptation I have to resist, and I don't want you to have the same struggle."

Silence follows his statement, the rain ticking outside the only sound. The fogged windows encase us, and his words hang in the space between our breaths. Heaviness fills my chest as the fear builds. I see a lifetime with Rivera, me helpless, him using my magic endlessly.

Those thoughts are enough to freeze my blood, but no magnetic lure sucks me in, or tempts me with more power. "I don't feel the addiction like you. Do you think it's because I've never actually used black magic?"

"Probably," he says. "But it's steeped inside you. Even performing one spell could push you over the edge."

"That's what Rivera wants me to do to bring back his wife."

"You can't." He runs a hand through his hair and closes his eyes. "You can't do it."

A loud trilling startles me and I jump. I swipe the screen. "Hi, Daddy."

"We're at the station, waiting. When you get here, come back to the same conference room." Dad's all business, his tone abrupt.

"We're on our way. Ten minutes tops," I tell him and hang up.

Zach takes my hand, his touch softer and steadier now. "Don't worry, okay? I won't let you get sucked in."

"Okay." I smile sadly, wondering how he plans to stop it.

Flipping on the headlights, Zach pulls away from the curb. Rain soaks the windshield and smudges the street-lights in blurry smears. The wipers squeak, and the outside world becomes crisp and clear for less than a second before the pouring rivulets drown the glass.

My phone vibrates, and I assume it's Dad again, ready for another brusque order, but it's not him.

> UNKNOWN: Don't say anything to Zach. I'll know if you do.

A picture pops up, the image so dark I can't tell what it is. A person in a chair? I zoom in, squinting to study it, and then I notice something. My hands shake as I zero in on the distinguishable part of the photo. A pair of red, wedge sandals. The same ones I watched Portia searching for in her pile of clothes at drama camp.

Freezing hands grip my lungs. I check my last message to her, and it remains on "delivered." Not even read. My thumbs type out another quick text to her.

> ME: You okay?

I add an *"SOS"* to let her know it's urgent, and then immediately call.

Straight to voicemail.

Ice races over my skin and settles in my hands, my fingertips going numb. My vision narrows to the picture lit up on the screen. I make a noise. Something between a gasp and a cry.

Zach glances at me and frowns. "Bad news?"

"It's Portia." *Don't say anything to Zach.* The words glow in the car, and I angle my phone away from his view. How much does Rivera see? Can he hear everything? With Portia in danger, I can't risk it. I clear my throat and clutch the pendant. "She...missed a big sale."

"I'm sure she's devastated. Hey, you're really pale." He reaches over, touching my forehead with his wrist. "Do you need a few more minutes to rest? You used a lot of magic."

"I'm okay." I speak through a haze of anxiety. Forget a nervous gut boulder. This is a mountain threatening to crush me.

I type a reply to the number that obviously belongs to Rivera.

> ME: Am I supposed to know what that picture is?

Buy time. Think.

I can't even grasp onto an idea before another image comes in. This one unmistakably Portia. Her curly hair. Deep brown eyes. And a piece of duct tape covering her lips.

> ME: Leave Portia out of this.

Such a cliché thing to say, but she's my best friend, the salsa to my chips, my other amigo. And Rivera still needs a heart.

Hang in there, Portia. I won't let him hurt you.

> UNKNOWN: Take off the necklace.

Once I take it off, I'll be totally open to Rivera. But he found my weakness. He went for Portia.

The station comes into view, and I'm running out of time.

> UNKNOWN: Do you want to see Portia again? Do it now.

> ME: Let her go first.

> UNKNOWN: CeCe, don't mess around. Take off the necklace, leave it behind, and I won't hurt her.

Do I believe him? Do I have a choice?

> ME: I can't in front of Zach. I'll do it when I get out of the car.

> UNKNOWN: Head to the back of the station. Don't let Zach follow. Throw your phone in the dumpster. I left a black Jetta there with the key inside.

Zach pulls over on the street, parking against the curb. Rain pounds the windshield, and he stares at the pooling water. "We're gonna get soaked again."

"No. You stay here," I say, setting my phone in the cup holder next to his, and taking off my seatbelt. "I'll be quick."

Angling toward me, he crosses his arms. "What's going on?"

I go with the first plausible reason that pops into my head. "I want to ask Dad about my mom." The lie blurts out, and guilt nags me. But I think about Portia and swallow the remorse. "It's probably better if you're not with me."

"Are you sure? I could at least walk you in." He unlatches his seatbelt, and I stop him with a hand on his squeezable bicep.

"I'm good, really. Let me do this alone. Please." I reach for my cell, brushing my fingers against Zach's phone instead. Suddenly, I have an idea. Adding a lightness to my tone, I plaster a smile on my face. "If I'm not out by 10:31, come find me."

"10:31? That's an oddly specific time." He matches my smile, glancing at the dashboard. "And definitely not quick."

"10:31's a great time. Think Halloween." I don't give him a chance to respond. Getting out of the car, I hop onto the sidewalk and run. I wonder how long it'll take Zach to notice I took his phone. I wonder if he'll realize I gave him the code to unlock mine.

Rounding the station, I do what Rivera asked, and unhook the necklace. The chain slips to the sidewalk. Immediately I hear the drums, the noise blaring and sudden. Rivera's presence charges into my head, an all-consuming pressure threatening to burst.

Taking the necklace off was a mistake. But it's the only way to find Portia.

Rivera stands in the room with the heavy metal door and sloped ceiling. Portia is there, struggling against the duct tape. She grunts and wriggles, frustrated to be bound, but alive.

The last time he pulled me to this space, I was physically asleep. Deep enough it felt like a dream when he showed me the vision of his wife's accident. This time, he shows me something while I'm wide awake. Nausea rumbles in my gut as I navigate the disorientation. I haven't fully recovered from the last split, and I take a breath to ease the dizziness.

Sprinting to the Jetta, I keep my thoughts on Portia, afraid to give anything else away. The blue dumpster is slick with rain, and I throw Zach's phone inside, the loud metal clang barely audible above the storm.

THIRTY-FOUR

BLACK MAGIC: 9:00 P.M.

I'm going to save Portia. I'm going to save Portia.

I stop in front of a narrow, one-story shotgun-style house with a sharply pitched roof and broken porch rails. This is where Rivera led me. My heart knocks wildly as I race from the Black Jetta and add another layer of wet to my clothes. In my mind, Rivera shows me his casting room and compels me to join him. Drums beat. The rhythm calls to me, pounding in my chest and urging me closer. Out of habit, I rub the spot where the pendant would be, regretting I left it behind, and I step inside the house.

Rain rolls off the pitched metal roof, the sound cavernous from inside. With every step, the ooze of black magic thickens. I struggle to breathe through the waxy filth, and my lungs ache from the strain.

The metal door of his casting room looms ahead, and I step closer, pushing it open. My eyes immediately take in my bestie. She's strapped to a chair in the center of the circle etched into the planked floor. Her head lolls to the side, her curls wild. I run in and shake her by the shoulders. A low groan rumbles from her mouth, and her eyes flutter before pinching closed again.

She's alive! Relief uncoils the knot of dread, and I kneel to work at the tape holding her wrists to the arms of the chair.

"Portia!" Tears build in my eyes as I free a corner of the silver tape. "We have to get out of here. Rivera's The Caster."

A noise creaks behind me and I spin around to see Detective Rivera blocking the doorway. He still wears the black robe, the bottom of it long enough to hide his shoes. A tic flexes in his jaw as he stares me down.

"It took you forever to get here. We have work to do," he says.

His footsteps clomp on the wood floor at his approach, and I stand up, blocking Portia.

"What did you do to her?" My words cut off as he grabs my arm, pulling me forward. A sharp pinch tweaks my shoulder, and I cry out.

"It's just chloroform," he mutters, pushing me down. The chain of a leg shackle is drilled into the ground, and he fights to cuff it on me. I make it as hard as possible, kicking my feet, my shoes squeaking. But I'm no match for his size, strength, and training, clearly not the hardest prisoner he's had to subdue. Slapping the metal around my ankle, he secures me inside the circle.

He dusts off his hands, not even winded, and tips Portia's chair towing her from the room.

"Don't hurt her. I did everything you asked," I yell, yanking against the cuff on my ankle. The effort causes the steel to dig into my skin. The ring moves slightly, and I wonder if I can dislodge the screws, so I keep trying. Again, and again. The pain increases, my foot swelling, but I don't care. He can't take Portia's heart.

I watch his movements through the partially open door. He lugs her into the kitchen and they disappear from view. Rattling drawers and rushed movements echo.

Checking the metal ring, I realize my attempts to loosen it have gotten me nothing except a bulging and bleeding ankle. Dad always tells me, in an emergency, I need to control the panic and use my head. My adrenaline pumps, but I close my eyes to focus. My thoughts are too scrambled to latch onto anything tangible, but I can feel. Power pours through the engraved circle, and with my injured foot dripping blood, my death magic comes alive.

I swipe at the broken and slick skin below the cuff. With blood on my fingers and magic in my veins, I let the power take over. My cicadas call to me. A slow hum that grows in strength and buzzes like a night in the bayou. A flow of energy rolls in the room, a soothing brush of warmth.

It reminds me of Zach.

Thinking of him draws me like a magnet, my cicadas tracking him down. They pull on my link to him. The one that doesn't need black magic or spirit kidnappings. I remember our kiss, the way his power calms me, the way our magic is acquainted. It wraps around me, a comfortable friend, the familiar heat flowing through my veins.

Floating on the magical plane, I drift to the police station. And I see him. I look down, hovering over the conference room where Zach and Dad sit. Dad scrolls on my phone, shouting orders at Menard, who stands in the doorway. Zach slumps in a chair, head in his hands, my necklace clutched in his fingers. He obviously found it where I dropped it on the sidewalk.

"Help me," I whisper.

The cicadas grow louder, and his head snaps up.

"I need a pen. A pencil. Anything." He frantically gestures, and Dad pulls a pen from his suit pocket.

Pushing his chair away, he draws a circle on the floor to focus his magic. Dad watches closely, rubbing the back of his neck as Zach sits in the improvised ring. He closes his eyes and reaches out.

Suddenly, our connection is clear.

Zach.

"Where are you?" His tension pours heavier than the storm outside.

By Pontchartrain. Which isn't super helpful since the lake covers dozens of miles. So I show him.

Picturing my arrival, I retrace my steps in a backward timeline. I show him where I sit, the kitchen and front room I walked through, and then the front door. The dull grayish shotgun house looks gloomy in the shadowed night, and my eyes trace over the details. Leaving in the car, I head in reverse down the muddy lane, approaching Lakeshore Drive.

A sharp crack strikes across my face and silences my cicadas.

"What did you do?" Rivera stands over me, his chest heaving. "I feel your magic."

I rub my cheek and blink to reality. The police station is gone from sight, and the traces of Zach's magic freeze in Rivera's presence. *Did I show him enough?* Trying to hang on to the small link, I grasp for the sound of my cicadas, but Rivera's drums surge in volume.

"Where's Portia?" The closed door blocks my view, and I can't see my bestie anymore.

"Don't ruin this for me, or I'll kill her." His voice drops

to a low, gravelly tone. He grabs me by the shoulders, shaking me hard enough to make my teeth clash together. "I'm so close. My Alice—" his words end on a growl, and he shoves me away.

He stalks to a shelf and pulls down the three glass containers used to hold the gathered organs. One at a time, he places them inside the circle, the kidney first, followed by the lungs. And then the previously empty jar, which now holds a heart.

He has a heart.

Terror crawls up my throat. "Is that...Portia's?" I know it can't be, but I still ask.

"Don't be stupid." He shakes his head, moving back to the shelf and picking up a box. "It showed up on my porch."

Showed up on his porch? What does that mean?

Reaching into the box, he sets out candles and lights them around the perimeter of the circle. Next to each candle, he lays a few Tigers Eye stones and draws a circle of ash around them. The air grows heavier with each addition.

The robe sleeves slide up his arms, revealing his gloved hands, as he lifts the hood to shadow his face. He grabs a spell book from the shelf, tucking it in the crook of his elbow, and the dark cover blends in with his cloak. The drum beat picks up speed and he gets closer. The pounding amplifies enough that it pummels inside my chest, making my body quake. Gone is the detective. Gone is the man with a smile and a sweet tooth. This is The Caster.

Setting the book in front of me, he flips through the old, tattered pages. It's ancient and dusty, a lot like the one Jennifer used to look up the black magic spell.

"Please let us go." Tears spill from my eyes, and I swipe at my snotty nose. "You know this is wrong."

He reaches into his robe pocket and pulls out a knife.

Candlelight glints on the blade, an array of oranges and yellows reflecting on the smooth surface. I know he won't kill me. He needs my necromancy, but seeing the sharpened edge makes my muscles tense.

"Perform the ritual," he says.

"I don't know how," I shout, fear and desperation churning my emotions.

"Read the spell. I'll do the rest." He speaks calmly, twisting the knife in his hand.

"Rivera, this is insane. She might not even want to come back."

His backhand finds my cheekbone. The hit sends my head whipping to the side. It's the second slap in the exact same spot, and I tenderly pat the stinging skin below my eye.

"Read the spell," he says again, using the knife to point at the book.

My hands shake, and I smooth the page, seeing the words *Shroud of Reawakening* across the top. I read the title out loud and clear my throat. The tiny writing swims in my vision, and I blink the tears from my eyes. I don't want to do this. I've never performed a black magic spell, and my head screams with Zach's warnings. In black magic, there is only darkness and addiction. And there is always a price to be paid.

"Please," a sob breaks my voice. "I've made you cookies before. You've eaten at my house."

Rivera wraps my ponytail around his fist, and with his other hand, the knife tip only a centimeter away from my eye, he strokes my cheek. The same cheek that wears the bruise he gave me. A soft smile accompanies the tender motion, and his dark brown eyes stare into mine. The gentle touch scares me far more than his flying backhand.

"CeCe, don't make me hurt you or your friend." He releases my hair and sits back.

"I need to see Portia again. If she's okay, I'll read the spell." I have to stall. Buy myself more time. "I can't concentrate without knowing she's safe."

He grits his teeth, his jaw working back and forth. Agitation flushes his skin, but he rises to his feet, and takes long strides to the door. A loud screech comes from the kitchen, and then he comes back into view, dragging Portia's chair with him. The wooden legs scream against the hard floor, and he stops as soon as she's in my line of sight. Her head tips forward, chin touching her chest, still unconscious from the chloroform.

"Now read," he says, leaving her there and striding back into the casting room. He closes and locks the door before sitting next to me.

I'm out of moves. Stalling more will only get me or Portia killed. Probably both. I browse the words and discover one last possibility. "It says we need an actual bone from the deceased. We can't complete the spell without it."

My short-lived relief withers as he sets a bunched-up handkerchief on the floor. The tip of a finger pokes out of the cloth, the discolored nail peeking from the folds. I draw back, trying to put distance between the bundle and me, but the shackle stops my movement, forcing me to stay close.

From his pocket, he pulls out a voodoo doll, one with auburn-colored yarn hair and blue button eyes. He sticks green-tipped pins, which represent life, into the spots where the heart, lungs, and kidney would be.

"Alice Rivera. Alice Rivera. Alice Rivera," he chants over and over, his words in time with the pounding drums. With the knife, he slices his thumb, and crimson blooms from the cut. Using his blood, he draws a circle around the handkerchief and doll.

He grabs me by the wrist and slices my palm, the sharp blade cutting cleanly. I scream and close my fingers over the wound in a futile attempt to slow the stream of blood. It drips through my fist, and he maneuvers my hand so splashes of red plop on the floor, the doll, and the handkerchief. Every time it touches his circle, our combined blood hisses and turns black, bubbling like boiling lava.

The power and intensity build, threatening to make me buckle. It's suffocating, like sinking further and further underwater. Or under quicksand. A filthy film envelops the room, surrounding me in a heavy ooze. The tension squeezes my head. My eardrums clog. The weight buries me alive, smothering me.

"Start reading." He stops chanting to give me the instruction.

Looking at the words, just reading them in my mind, eases the crushing strain. Zach's caution about black magic has permanent living space in my brain, but I know I need to cast the spell. Either that or suffocate.

Not to mention the sharp knife clutched in Rivera's hand pointed at me.

"Eyes of the grave, blinded by death." I speak slowly, drawing out each syllable. That kind of stalling might only buy me a few seconds, and I wonder if it will make a difference.

I still hold out hope Zach and Dad will find me.

Rivera unwraps the handkerchief, fully exposing the finger. A gold wedding ring hangs loosely below the first knuckle, and the modest diamond sparkles in the low light. "Alice Rivera," he chants quietly.

I don't continue fast enough for him, and a sharp sting pierces my thigh as he pokes me with the knife. "Keep going."

A small spot of red spreads on my jeans, and I press my non-bleeding hand against the wound. "Wraiths of the Shadow, release this soul."

Rustling comes from the handkerchief, a subtle swish giving me pause. Between Rivera's chanting, and the drums pounding in my head, I wonder if I imagined the sound. I hold my breath and lean closer, watching everything inside the circle of blood. And then it happens again. A swishing. The fabric wriggles.

My mouth goes dry, and I watch in horror as the voodoo doll moves. Actually moves. The arms twitch, a stitch pops, leaving the thread to dangle. Even for someone who raises the dead, this is scary.

"Keep going." He grabs me by the ponytail, yanking my head closer to the book.

A grunt of pain slips from my lips, and I whisper the next line. "Unearth the cadaver and defy the corpse."

The doll's legs shudder, another stitch breaking with a muted pop. Then another. It stretches, and the burlap limbs reach wide. The face bulges in a contorted mass, swelling until the seams split and the button eyes pop off.

"Spirit of the darkness rise." I'm disgusted. Horrified. Rivera lets go of my hair to caress the expanding doll, running his fingers down the burlap cheek. The last stitches burst, and a fleshy mass oozes out. It forms a star-like shape that spreads, the bottom edges lengthening into legs, the side points stretching into arms. The yarn hair attached at the top softens and grows long.

My gut clenches and acid crawls up my throat. I shove

the book away, sending it spinning to the edge of the circle. "This is wrong. I won't do it."

"No! You can't stop!" Sweat dots his upper lip, and he scrambles to retrieve the spell book. "Read it, or Portia's dead."

"Look at what you're doing," I yell, pointing at the jiggling mass.

"I'll make you finish," he growls, lunging at me. Snatching my hand, he rubs his bloodied thumb into the open wound on my palm. The blood turns black, bubbling against my skin and seeping into my veins. Icy flames lick like hungry tongues. I try to pull away, but he holds tight, urging the black magic to take over. Pain ignites, my body twitching in response, and tortured sounds eek from my mouth. The ache spreads, the feeling so intense I can't decide if I'm burning or freezing or dying.

I collapse on the floor, huddling in the fetal position. The shackle pulls my ankle, keeping me close and chafing the swollen skin. But an even worse agony is his power, a thick snake moving along the same route as my necromancy. Starting in my right hand, it slithers under the surface and weaves with my magic, from one side of my body to the other, leaving a trail of slimy mucus in its wake.

I fight his influence as the black magic winds around my vocal cords. Just one more line, one simple phrase to finish the spell. He's in my head, compelling me to let Alice Rivera rise. *Who once was dead, let live again.* It's right there, on the tip of my tongue. And I want to say it. I feel the words, tasting them on my lips.

"Say the words," Rivera says.

Say the words, my brain whispers. But it's not really my brain. It's him, stealing my thoughts and telling me what to do.

Rivera pulls me into a sitting position. "Finish it."

I clench my hands, biting my tongue to keep the words from coming out. The fleshy mass wriggles on the floor, waiting for the next instruction. Dark magic rains down like the storm outside, and I wonder how long I'll be able to hold on.

Help me, Zach. Even though he can't hear, the plea runs through my mind.

A loud thump comes from across the room, and I lift my head. Noise echoes on the other side of the metal door, and it shudders in distress. Rivera quickly gets to his feet, flipping back the hood of his cloak.

With a loud bang, the door flies open and hits the wall.

THIRTY-FIVE

ZACH MAGIC: 9:30 P.M.

Dad charges into the room, his body crouched, and gun at the ready. He gives me a quick once-over just to make sure I'm okay. Behind Dad, and stopped in the doorway, stands Zach. Our eyes lock, and his relief is clear. Until he notices the gelatinous body.

In a swift motion, Rivera abandons the knife with a loud clatter and draws a gun from the folds of his robe. His fingers tighten on the Glock, and he aims at Dad.

"Carlos, drop it!" Dad commands.

My heart stops. I've always worried about losing my dad. His job keeps that anxiety constant. I never thought I'd have to watch it happen, though.

"You can't shoot me," Rivera laughs. "It'll hurt CeCe too, and I know you don't want that."

"Zach?" Dad's aim stays steady as he asks for the confirmation of Rivera's words.

"It's possible," Zach hesitates as he steps into the room. "The magic in here is thick."

285

"You've been a constant nuisance. Why can't you stay away?" Rivera shifts to point the gun at Zach, and panic tips my world, spots clouding my vision.

"Don't do this, Rivera," I say.

"You can always bring him back." As Rivera talks, his magic works, demanding I finish the ritual.

"You're a good cop and a good man." Dad holds his gun with one hand and, with the other, urges Zach to retreat a few steps. Rivera tracks the movement, turning his back on me to follow Dad's progress.

The distraction gives me an opportunity to act. But I'm shackled to the floor. I have no weapon and no phone.

Taking stock of what I *do* have, it hits me; In the back of my hair, holding my flyaways, I have a bobby pin. I can't believe I didn't think of it sooner. Pulling it out I bite the plastic tip on the end, removing the little nub. Using the hard metal of the shackle, I bend the pin's tines to the shape I need.

Growing up with a cop meant strange daddy/daughter dates like breaking out of a car trunk or basic self-defense. Right now, I'm grateful for the long lessons on how to escape from handcuffs. Leg shackles have the same kind of locking mechanism, and I gently push and twist the modified bobby pin in the keyhole to manipulate the latch. The satisfying click seems loud to my ears, but Rivera talks over the sound.

"Alice didn't deserve to die. She was better than all of us. I just need CeCe to finish the spell and then I'll disappear." He moves to negotiation, buried deep in his hole of justification.

"Disappearing isn't easy." Behind Dad's voice comes the sound of sirens. Back-up is on the way.

I carefully remove the shackle from my ankle. The

swollen and bloody skin becomes more apparent as I get a good look. It's not pretty. Ignoring the pain, I lean closer to the body. The flesh mass squirms, and I pluck an auburn-colored hair from its head.

Quietly scooting back to the edge of the circle, I pick up one of the burning candles and pour a puddle of melted wax into my unwounded palm. It bites my skin, the burn familiar and strangely comforting. This I know. This is my magic. I form a moon token, hoping I guessed correctly with waning gibbous. Following the moon cycle has never been my strong suit.

I swipe the wound on my ankle with the cooled moon token, painting it crimson. Power radiates from the wax, not the dirty haze of black magic, but the clean vibrancy of necromancy.

Rivera feels the change in our connection and whips around to look at me. My fingers hover above the candle, the auburn hair dangling. Dropping the strand, I let it burn, turning the flame blue.

"No!" He lifts the gun, the black barrel pointed right between my eyes.

A loud bang reverberates in the room.

My whole body tenses, waiting for the pain. My ears ring, the white noise blocking out sound. In the shock of confusion, I struggle to understand what happened. But pieces come together, Dad pinning a bleeding Rivera to the floor. His Glock kicked away as Dad slaps cuffs on his wrists.

It wasn't me that took a bullet, but Rivera's shoulder. It seeps an ugly red, the blood hissing and turning black as it spills to the ground.

Zach crouches at my side and repeats himself twice

before I realize what he says. "You have to take care of the body."

Right. The gelatinous blob that still writhes, waiting for my last instruction.

"Put this—" I lift the moon token and motion to the flesh mass— "on her forehead."

"Okay." He extends his hand, and I give him the wax circle, careful to avoid touching, so his warmth doesn't disrupt my magic.

An IV of ice water travels through my veins as Zach places the token. A crisp breath enters my lungs. My cicadas buzz, and their sound covers the crashing drums. It chases out the oily snake of black magic. Wind blasts, blowing something off the shelf across the room. But the gust doesn't touch anything in the circle.

"Alice Rivera," I whisper. Having her name is important. It connects us, my necromancy to her spirit.

I close my eyes and feel her experiences like a memory. Times with Rivera. Their laughter. Their love. Happiness floods my senses, a lightness filling my chest with helium. Better times when Rivera was a better man. But there's sadness, too. Rivera's obsession and desperation changed him into someone unrecognizable, and she hates what he's become.

Her dread passes through me, alarm at Rivera forcing me to raise her. She wants him to let go, turn the corner on his grief, and allow her to move on. This is something I can give to her, the peace she seeks.

"Alice Rivera, you can rest now." Chills roll down my spine, goosebumps dimpling my arms, and I blow out the candle. The fleshy mass melts into a crystalline veneer that crumbles and dissolves to dust. The moon token falls to the floor. Her finger decomposes as well, leaving behind a circle of gold sitting atop a pile of ash.

"It's over," I say.

Rivera cackles, a hysterical, high-pitched laugh, that projects spittle from his mouth.

"Knock it off." Dad forces his former partner to stand, dragging him by his collar and the handcuffs. "Get him out of here," he yells to the officers charging in.

The shoulder-shot doesn't seem to bother him, and he keeps laughing.

"Look." Zach points to the floor where Rivera's blackened blood crawls. It moves like a snake, a living thing curling around the wedding ring and moon token, forming a circle.

"You'll never get rid of me, CeCe." Rivera's low voice rumbles, and he presses his cut thumb, the same one he rubbed against the wound in my palm. It's like a knife to my hand, and I shriek, the pain surging and spreading.

"CeCe!" Dad yells.

Blinking my eyes open, I glance around in confusion. My legs stretch on the floor, and my cheek presses against Zach's chest. His warm hand brushes the loose hair from my face while Dad checks my pulse.

"Baby girl, you passed out. How do you feel?" Dad examines my eyes, looking from one to the other.

"Confused. Barfy."

In my peripheral vision, I see something move. A slow slither. Skinny tendrils of Rivera's blood branch off and creep toward me.

"It's drawn to your magic," Zach says, watching it ooze closer.

The necro-shivers explode, hitting hard enough to make my body seize. My teeth hurt from the force of their chatter, and a headache engulfs my brain. Zach slips the protection pendant over my head and hugs me. The heat seeps in slowly, stretching like a sunrise. Just as quickly, the cold chases it out, a storm front covering his light and warmth. The drums beat steadily, staccato and chaotic.

"What's happening?" Dad asks, his voice panicked.

"It's Rivera. I have to break his connection to her."

"Zach, no." I clasp the necklace in my hand, but don't feel its power.

The room blurs, and images flood my mind. Alice's broken body loaded on the stretcher. A trembling Rivera, wearing his beat cop uniform, running his fingers over her auburn hair. But it's too late. She's already gone. Tears puddle in my eyes at the onslaught of emotion. Rivera will never let me go. He wants me to feel every stab of pain, every shattered dream.

Zach's arms tighten around me. Almost painfully. "It was always going to come to this."

"You can't use black magic." My reality twists again, Rivera slinking into my thoughts, and overtaking my mind. His grief and anger pulse with a need for revenge.

The pain in my palm twinges, and I cradle my hand against my chest. Zach lifts it to get a better look at the wound draining blackened blood. Shaking his head, he bites his lip and stays silent. He doesn't need to say anything, though. I see the fear in his expression.

"Oh, baby girl." Dad takes my hand from Zach to examine it. "Why is the blood black?"

"Magic," Zach and I say at the same time.

The sensation of floating tingles through my body as Rivera spirit kidnaps me, pulling me to join him in the back of an ambulance. I drift above, looking at him laying on a stretcher. Two paramedics work to stem the bleeding from his shoulder, and an officer stands by. The disorienting split wrestles my headache into disaster territory, and I close my eyes to keep my brain from exploding.

Rivera stares at the ceiling, right where I hover, almost like he can see me. Maybe he can. "Seven words," he says.

"What?" The officer leans closer, but I know Rivera's talking to me.

"Seven words." His voice turns to granite. "She was there, practically risen. And you refused to finish."

The cop shakes his head, muttering, *whatever*.

"CeCe, what's going on?" Zach's fingers are solid in mine, but I'm being ripped in two, unable to escape the ambulance. My energy is spent. My gas tank sapped dry.

"I'm with Rivera," I say. Not to him, but he answers.

"You'll always be with me. Until we bring her back." He clenches his jaw, the tic trembling. "We can salvage this. Her essence is in that wax circle you made. I'll show you what to do."

"She's at rest now." I breathe through the agony. "She doesn't want to come back."

"That's a lie." He clenches his fists, and I feel the grip as if it was actually wrapped around my throat. The breath cuts from my lungs and I fight back, but on the magical plane, I'm helpless.

"CeCe, stop. Stop! You're hurting yourself." Zach grabs my fingers, trying to peel them from my throat. "Rivera's controlling her."

"I'm going to shoot him again." Dad stands, reaching for his holster.

"Wait," Zach says. "Killing him might not release her. It needs to be done through magic."

The pressure increases, Rivera's thumbs crushing my windpipe. I kick my legs, needing to breathe, needing to get free. Switching between the room and the ambulance, I struggle to figure out where I am.

Rivera's voice rings out, telling me he'll never leave me alone. His mocking laughter surrounds me. Consumes me.

"Zach, help," I force through my cramped vocal cords.

I know the promise I'm breaking. The only way Zach can save me is to use black magic. But the connection to Rivera is too deep. It's impossible for me to sever.

"Get outside the circle," Zach says to Dad. "I'm going to help CeCe."

THIRTY-SIX

THE MAGICAL PLANE: 9:45 P.M.

Dad moves to the edge of the room, and Zach's already at work. Removing a pocket knife from his pants, he knicks his thumb. A few drops of blood splat around us, and they hit the floor with a sizzle. He closes his eyes and takes a deep breath.

"It's going to be okay," he says, gripping my hand.

At Zach's touch, silence falls. My physical self fades, and all tangible sensations become invisible. The ambulance disappears, the room vanishes, and I find myself in a strange place. The landscape stretches for miles on a beach that feels wrong. Black and blue sand swirls in the shade of bruises. The sky above glows a deep crimson highlighting the shadow moon. Orange and yellow waves lap at the shore, and a cracked concrete levee holds the ocean back.

It's some kind of magical plane.

Zach sits cross-legged on the ground between me and the water. A colorful aura surrounds him, but it's not bright or happy. More like the filmy reflective light shimmering on oil, heavy and thick with power. He draws shapes on the ground, and blood oozes from his finger, causing the sand to clump in chunks. The power grows, and the waves crash harder, like Pontchartrain in a storm. Pieces of concrete snap off and plunge into the churning ocean.

"Zach..." I hesitate and lower my outstretched hand. Something is different. The darkness in him is kept in check by a tiny thread of control. He's the levee trying to hold back the force of a black magic hurricane.

A frothing surf bursts through the barrier and moves closer.

My cicadas recognize Zach and start buzzing. The bugs actually appear, I see them, and they encompass me. The shimmery wings glimmer in the light and create a forcefield of sound offering protection. But Rivera is here too, right next to me; a hazy version of himself, like he stands behind a gauzy screen. His drums thrum in my chest. The beating produces visible sound waves that shoot in a ripple of air aimed at me. It shakes the cicada barrier and disrupts their energy.

The quaking grows strong enough to knock me off my feet. My balance falters, and I steady myself on my hands and knees. My fingers dig in the bruised sand, and my cicadas fall to join me on the ground. Their bodies tremble, their hum weakening.

A screech pierces the air. And then another. And another. The shrieking obliterates everything else. A heavy haze blows in to cover the crimson sky, and it goes black. Patches of light perforate the murkiness, and I stare above me. It rolls through, and as the darkness closes in, I see wings flapping. Dozens. No, hundreds of them. A deluge of crows shrouding the beach.

The crows descend and fly straight at me. I scream, and curl into a fetal position to protect my face.

The drumbeat dwindles, and the pulsating air settles. The vibration in the ground fades, and I cautiously sit up, my shoulders scrunched. My cicadas circle me, and the crows leave them alone. They leave me alone. Their beaks peck at Rivera and the ripple of drums. He swings his arms, batting at the birds, but there are too many of them. The drums are no match for the power and magnitude of the flapping wings and rasping caw.

In a rush of understanding, I know this is Zach's sound magic. Crows.

The wispy image of Rivera fades, the crows easily tearing his magic apart, leaving no sign of him behind. The link between us snaps, the tether breaking, and I'm free. Like a cleansing breath of fresh air, the layer of filthy power disappears.

The black magic ocean washes close to my feet. Startled, I look at Zach and see him sitting in a foot of water. It's thicker than normal, and it sticks to him, forming tentacle-like arms. The syrupy liquid slowly drags him into the surf.

"Zach!" I scream and lurch forward, my knees sinking in the foaming waves.

His eyes remain closed, his body still. Magic blankets him in a deep trance, and I can't wake him up. I reach for his hand, and a group of crows split off, forcing me back. They drag me, and I flail to chase them away. The closer I get to him, the harder they fight to keep me from the dark water.

"I'm trying to help," I yell at the birds.

Despite the crows' efforts, water climbs my legs and imprisons me in a gluey puddle. The slime clings, and I swipe at it, the sticky honey impossible to get off. My body slides, caught up in the tide sweeping me to the water. Zach's a few feet ahead of me, gliding nearer to the levee. The concrete cracks, and big chunks sink into the depths.

Everywhere the water touches causes small tingles to spread. Tiny pinpricks of calm dotting through me. It relaxes my resistance, making me wonder why I fight to get out. So, I stop. The gooey liquid slinks to my knees, and I want more. I see it in my head, diving into the depths, the blackness swallowing all my troubles, all my resistance, all my pain. Just me floating in an ocean of bliss.

The euphoria nearly captures me, but my cicadas hum. The vibration breaks the pull of darkness, and I watch as the bugs dance against the sticky water. Their iridescent wings flap and catch the light, creating a beautiful kaleidoscope of color. It loosens the viscous liquid and I wriggle from the hold.

I can't get caught in the black magic ocean.

I jar from the stupor, and renew my efforts to free myself.

"Zach!" I scream again.

He lifts his head and looks around, taking in the waves, the crows, and then meeting my gaze. A hazy film eclipses his eyes, and he blinks a few times. The water climbs higher until he sits waist deep in it, and it adheres to him. Keeping him captive.

"We have to get out." I shuffle forward through the thick liquid. This time, with his eyes on me, his crows stay back, allowing me close enough to grab his hand.

A full-body tremble runs over him, and he grasps my fingers. I tug, trying to help him stand while he rips the sticky tentacles with his free hand. They come back, a fierce barrage of waves attempting to pull him in. To overtake me. The crows swoop to surround us, their beaks fighting against the draw of the water. Struggling to his feet, he nearly tips me over. But we take lunging steps to break free, moving away from the shoreline.

My eyes open—my physical eyes—and we're back in the room. The hard floor feels solid beneath me, and a wafting smell of ash tickles my nose. Every ache in my body comes alive, my bruised cheek and cut hand flaring in pain.

I don't feel Rivera at all. His blood stills, puddling motionless on the ground.

His presence is gone. No slithering inside me, no sludgy heaviness. Just the clean residue of me. Only me.

Zach's hand anchors me next to him, and he shakes, the quaking moving up my arm. "Are you okay?" I ask.

"Yeah. I need a minute." He leans forward, inhaling deeply, and sweat drips from his forehead.

I listen to his gasping breaths, waiting for his tremors to ease before I talk again. "What was that place?"

"It's the magical plane I created, a space to dampen the effects of black magic." He speaks in short spurts, his lungs heaving.

If that place dampened the effects, I'd hate to see the full repercussions. The darkness called to him, the vast ocean drawing him closer to falling. I stood at the brink of his addiction, and it scared me. He's powerful. His magic made Rivera look like a dabbling beginner. And I witnessed the line he treads to stay in check.

I squeeze his hand, and his magic responds with an unmistakable vibration. It's distinctly him. Uniquely us. It reminds me of our first touch, a million years ago at drama camp. A gentle warmth passing between us, before everything changed.

Now I have no black magic buzz, no influence of the

darkness he craves. Knowing the intensity of his attraction to it, I wonder if what I am without it is enough.

Dad stands at the edge of the circle. "Do I have to shoot someone? Or is it over?" he asks.

"It's over," I say, hoping it means my link with Rivera and not my relationship with Zach.

CHAPTER THIRTY-SEVEN

IT'S OVER: LATE MONDAY NIGHT

Police still swarm the shotgun house, both inside and out. Having a cop involved in two murders, a kidnapping, and an attempt to force me to perform an evil ritual—okay, they don't know about the last one—the collection of evidence is careful and thorough.

The storm trickles, a fraction of the force displayed earlier. Portia and I sit on the tailgate of an ambulance, each of us wrapped in a blanket. A paramedic treated us both, she for chloroform exposure and minor abrasions where the duct tape rubbed her raw. Me for my cut hand, stabbed leg, swollen cheekbone, and battered ankle.

Obviously, I won the contest of who walked away more injured.

"Rivera marched into my work, flashed his badge, and said there was an emergency. My boss told me to go." Portia's feet dangle, and she digs her red sandal in the muddy grass.

"Oh, Portia," I say.

"I didn't even question the drive out here, or why he asked me to go inside the sketchy house." She shivers and tightens the blanket around herself. "I feel so stupid."

"You're not stupid. I should have called you as soon as I found out it was him." I lay my head against her shoulder, grateful nothing worse happened. "Apparently, I'm not psychic."

"What?" she asks.

"It's seriously been the longest night!" I fill Portia in on Gina, and her assumption that I see the future. The recounting starts somber, but by the time I finish, we both laugh hysterically. One part, *yes it's funny,* one part, *we're still alive after everything and it feels good to break into maniacal giggles.*

"Do you think your dad will ask her out?"

"Definitely." I straighten to meet her gaze. "He blushed. Actually blushed."

"Shh shh." She elbows my side and lifts an eyebrow at my dad, who walks toward us. "Hi, Detective LeBlanc. Thanks for saving my life."

He nods, no big deal, saving people is normal. "Your mom's almost here."

"Did she freak out when she heard I was being held hostage?" She smirks, minimizing her ordeal, but I notice the tremble in her lips. Moisture tickles her eyelashes, and she blinks it away.

"Yes, your parents were upset." He puts a hand on her shoulder. "You okay, kiddo?"

She inhales a shaky breath. "You know me. I always land on my feet."

A familiar minivan pulls up, and Portia's mom steps out, followed by her dad. They make a striking pair. She's tall and elegant, with dark skin, shoulder-length curly hair, and perfect eyebrows. It's easy to see where Portia gets her looks from. Her dad is also tall, well over six feet, and has the powerful look of a professional athlete. People often stop him and ask which team he plays for. He laughs and tells them he works in software development.

"We're sending your folks information about trauma counseling. I think it would be good to look into it," Dad says.

"I will." She stands, dropping the blanket before throwing her arms around me. "Thanks for taking the bait, even though a homicidal maniac waited on the other end."

"Hey, we're the Two Amigos. I'll always come."

She tightens her hold, whispering in my ear. "Are you going to be okay? Do you need me?"

"I'm fine." I look at Dad, and a soft smile touches his lips as he watches us. "Dad's taking me home."

"Good. But you know where to find me if you need anything." She releases me and takes a few steps away, walking backward. "Also, I love you."

"Love you back," I call out, and she waves, rushing to her worried parents.

Dad rocks on his heels and tucks his hand into his pockets. A look of surprise crosses his features, and he pulls out my cell. "I forgot I had this. It was smart for you to leave your phone. Because of that, we were ready to move once Zach knew where to find you."

A proud buzz fills my chest at his compliment.

"Where *is* Zach?" I ask.

"Getting treated by the paramedics. He was wiped out after..." he pauses, searching for the right word to encompass the whole magical juju that went down. "Everything," he finishes and hands over my phone.

Glancing at the screen, I see two texts from an unknown

number. *Maybe Rivera?* My pulse picks up speed as I unlock my phone.

> UNKNOWN: I gave Rivera the heart.

The night stills around me, Dad and the drizzling rain forgotten as I stare at the words. This is what Rivera meant when he said a heart showed up on his porch. I read the second text.

> UNKNOWN: There was a buildup of magic since Rivera didn't finish his spell. I had to restore the balance.

Balance? What does that mean? I hesitate, wondering if I should reply. But a sense of foreboding propels my response.

> ME: Who is this?

The three typing dots appear immediately. Were they waiting for me?

> UNKNOWN: Oh honey, don't you know?

Of course, I don't know. The heart. Balance. Who is this person? My phone vibrates again, and a picture comes through. Me and Zach at the drama camp banquet. Someone was there watching me. Watching us. Taking our picture.

> UNKNOWN: The dress looks better on you than it did on me.

The Dress. The only thing I have left from the woman

who gave birth to me. My hands shake, and my trembling thumbs struggle to type a simple three-letter text.

ME: Mom?

UNKNOWN: Your magic didn't disappoint. I'll be in touch.

ME: What do you mean?

I forget how to pull oxygen into my body. Dots swim in my vision, and my eyes lock on the screen. But my phone stays silent.

"What's wrong, baby girl?" Dad gives my shoulder a gentle shake and sits next to me on the tailgate.

"It's...just read." I give him my cell, letting him go through the messages.

"If she had anything to do with this..." His face shifts from confusion to anger, his jaw clenching. "I'm going to trace this number, see what I can find."

"Wait." I grab his arm, stopping him. "I'm a little freaked out. You have to tell me about Mom!"

Blowing out a breath, he rubs the back of his neck. "She used to live in California, but it sounds like she's here now."

"And she has magic?" I make a rolling motion with my hand, urging him to keep talking.

"Yes," he whispers.

"Dad!" I smack his leg and growl in frustration. "Why didn't you tell me? This is important. Do you know what kind of magic she has?"

"There's more than one kind?"

"Ugh. Of course, there is. I use necromancy." I gesture toward the shotgun house. "Zach has life magic, and Rivera used black magic."

"I don't know anything about this, CeCe." Dad stands and paces in front of the ambulance. "Constance's family has magic. I don't know what kind. But I know she wanted to get away from them. And then she wanted to get away from us."

"You mean from me." I think of her last words, *your magic is too much.* I always assumed she hated my power, but now she plans to "be in touch."

Nausea churns, and I hold a hand over my stomach, my world upended in a matter of seconds. Yes, Mom has magic. Her family has magic. She somehow acquired a heart.

Zach walks toward the ambulance, and his feet drag on the ground. Fatigue weighs on his limbs, a tangible heaviness slowing him down. His smile lifts when he sees me, but it's my dad he approaches. "Hey, Detective LeBlanc. The paramedic told me to come talk to you."

"You feeling okay?" Dad asks.

"Yeah, I'm good. Still a little jittery from the magic."

Dad nods, as if he completely understands. "Thanks for what you did. Your mom's getting released tonight. Menard will take you, and your dad'll meet you there."

"My mom's getting out tonight?" His smile widens. "Thanks for expediting the process. It means a lot to my family."

Dad dips his head, a grateful acknowledgment. "It's the least I could do. Especially after your dad let you help me and CeCe all day with the magic stuff. We couldn't have caught Rivera without you."

"I don't even have the words to thank you, Zach." I can still picture the black magic waves, sucking him in, and even after witnessing it, I can hardly comprehend the sacrifice he made to save me.

"I'll have Officer Menard come by in a few minutes. But

I figured you'd want to talk to CeCe." Dad taps my phone against his leg before slowly handing it over. "Keep this for now in case I need to reach you. I'll be back after I look into a couple of things." With his reluctance to relinquish my cell, I know exactly what he's *looking into*. I have no doubt my phone will be confiscated as evidence tomorrow.

Zach sits next to me, close enough that the sides of our bodies meet from shoulder to knee. The black magic still lingers inside him, and I feel it everywhere we touch. His pulse flutters, a steady thrumming. We watch Dad leave, and Zach takes my hand.

"We did it, CeCe. Saved the day. Stopped the bad guy." He pauses to catch his breath. Even through his fatigue, the energy bounces off him. "We make a great team. But we already knew that and have a valuable plaque from drama camp to prove it."

I can't even muster a chuckle. Guilt over breaking my promise digs under my skin. Here we are, sitting on the tailgate of an ambulance with him on a black magic high. "I'm sorry you had to break my link with Rivera."

"Why would you be sorry? There's no way I'd let you get stuck with that psycho."

"There's something else." Might as well get all the confessions out at once. "My mom gave Rivera the heart."

His foot jiggling pauses, the fidgety energy stalling. "Wow. I wonder why."

Opening my text conversation with Mom, I give him my cell. "What do you know about her magic?"

Light from the phone makes his face glow. It takes him a few seconds of blinking bleary eyes to read. "That's a great picture of us."

"Zach, focus."

"Sorry." He smiles, and the dimpled perfection

threatens to make *me* lose focus. "So, she mentions restoring the balance. That's what her magic is all about."

Balance. Again, with that word. "Like between good and evil?"

"I don't think she sees things as good and evil. More like a balance of energy." He holds his hands out, an improvised scale. "Each kind of magic gives off a different energy. If one side gets too heavy, there needs to be a release or an evening-out."

"She said Rivera caused a buildup," I say.

"The Constance I met would do anything to keep the energy in harmony."

Your magic is too much.

A shiver catches me by surprise. "Would she kill someone for a heart, though? To balance things out?"

He puts his arm around my shoulders and pulls me close. "I don't know."

His fingers rub hypnotizing circles on my skin, and it draws me in. I want to lean on him, let his strength prop me up. But everything's a mess. I asked him to use black magic. My mom caused his addiction. I'm Hurricane CeCe, blowing in and destroying his life. "I get it now. Why you don't date people with magic. I'd understand if you don't want to see me anymore."

"Why wouldn't I want to see you?"

"Because I got your mom arrested, put you in danger, stole your phone, and broke my promise." Saying it all out loud makes me wonder why he even likes me. "Not to mention, I don't have black magic anymore."

"Wow." The circling fingers barely pause at my gut-wrenching admission. "Those are some pretty heavy reasons for us to break up."

"Break up?" Hearing those two words feels like a

sledgehammer to my soul. It hurts, and I resist the urge to press my hand to my chest to keep my heart from falling out.

"You made some valid points. Let's start at the top." His foot touches mine, activating the foot-to-tummy butterflies, and he holds up a finger. "One. You got my mom arrested."

"I did."

"No, you didn't. Rivera planted evidence. He's the bad guy, not you. Why would I be mad at you for something he did?"

"I..." My mouth wants to speak, but my brain sifts through what he says. I begged Dad not to arrest Jennifer. Maybe I don't have to take the blame for this one.

"Two." He holds up a second finger. "You put me in danger."

"Rivera had a gun, and a knife, and magic. I shouldn't have asked you to come—"

"He put us all in danger. Remember, he's the bad guy, and you can't shoulder the responsibility for his actions." He presses a soft kiss to my temple, and before I react, he holds up a third finger. "Three, you stole my phone."

I cross my arms and wonder if he'll blame Rivera again. "Well, that one's true."

"Yeah, it is," he laughs and shakes his head. "But that was smart and resourceful. You are a legit master of amazing, and I'll get it replaced."

I say the only thing I can. "I'm still sorry."

"I know." His voice turns serious, and he holds up another finger. "Four, you broke your promise."

"True again." I drop my head and stare at my hands. *A person who breaks a promise is as useful as sunscreen in a hurricane.*

"No." He lifts my chin, and his palm slides to cup my cheek. His thumb brushes back and forth across my skin, leaving traces of heat. "You promised you wouldn't make me use black magic, and you never did. I chose to use it. I'd do it again if it meant saving you."

Leaning forward, he presses his lips to mine. The warmth and magic flicker, a spark simmering. A slamming car door interrupts us, making him pull back.

Officer Menard stands by his cruiser and waves at us. If he feels awkward interrupting our kiss, he hides it well. "Hey, CeCe. Hey, Zach. I'm ready to leave when you are."

"Thanks. Gimme just a minute?" Zach calls out.

"Take your time. I'll wait in the car." Menard ducks in, closing the door and leaving Zach and me with the illusion of privacy.

"I don't want to go." He lifts my hand, kissing the knuckles.

"Your mom is getting out of jail. You have to go." I pull my hand away, ignoring the tingles that spread like ripples from where his lips touch.

His arm tightens around my shoulder, and his mouth pinches in concern. "CeCe—"

"Don't even think about skipping out on your family." I stand, putting more distance between us. The blanket I'd wrapped around myself falls to the muddy ground. "I'm fine. You should go."

"I know." He blows out a breath but doesn't move, keeping his eyes on me.

"Get outta here." I laugh and help him up. His hand catches mine, pulling me into the snug zone, and I allow myself five seconds in his arms before I let go. "Don't keep Menard waiting."

"Okay, I'm going. But I'll see you tomorrow." He

touches my cheek one last time and walks away.

"I'm sorry, Zach," I mumble, watching as he gets in the car.

Exhaustion pulls at my bones, the chaotic events of the day catching up to me. It feels like I haven't slept in a week. I pick up the blanket from the ground, hoping to wrap up in it, but it drips with mud and residual rainwater.

Would it be crazy to wrap up in it anyway? Probably.

I drop it and sit on the tailgate, leaning my head against the door of the ambulance. My eyes drift shut, and the next thing I know, Dad nudges my arm. Lines of strain crease his forehead, worry heavy on his shoulders. "You ready, baby girl?"

"More than ready." I crack my neck back and forth, stiff from my micro-nap. "Did you find anything out?"

"Nothing yet. We have no idea how the heart got here. So far no fingerprints on anything. Not even a body to analyze." He helps me up, and we make our way to the car.

"Mom's probably gone. Out of our lives as fast as she came in." Only her words linger, *I'll be in touch.*

"Let's hope so," he says under his breath.

The drive puts me to sleep, and flashes of the night creep in. Images of Portia strapped to a chair, a bloody kidney, Rivera yelling at me to finish the spell. And crows. Lots of crows. Flapping their wings and dragging me away from Zach.

When we get home, I shower and spend a ridiculous amount of time in the hot water. Before I get in bed, I pour salt. There's no way I can sleep without a protective circle knowing Mom is out there. I remember the moon token, and I dig through the dirty clothes to get it out of my pocket. Plugging in my wax melter, I drop the moon token on top. "Rest in peace, Alice Rivera."

CHAPTER
THIRTY-EIGHT

ENCORE: SATURDAY

P ounding wakes me. I blink bleary eyes, trying to figure out what the noise means, and realize someone is knocking at my door. The clock says 11:30. I slept in.

"Coming," I yell, dragging myself from the bed.

Portia stands on the porch, a magazine cover model come to life. Her hair is pulled up in space buns. Green cargo joggers cinch at the bottom, and her black and white striped tee hits a half-inch above the waistband of her pants. Taking one look at me, she shakes her head and says, "Nope."

"Nope? What do you mean, '*nope*?'"

"I can't let you go around looking like that?" She motions to my, admittedly, homely appearance. My baggy, gray sweatpants are long enough that I pull them over my toes, and my t-shirt has a picture of an avocado with wings and the words "Holy Guacamole."

"I just woke up. Let me be casual for five minutes." I run a hand through my hair but stall when I hit a tangle.

"Girl, there's casual, and then there's you." Her eyebrows pinch with pity. "Lucky for you, you're getting Portia-fied."

"That sounds terrible."

"It probably will be." A maniacal laugh exits her lips, and I fear for my life.

"You could have called." I open the door wider and let her in. Leading the way to the kitchen, I pull two bottles of water from the fridge and give one to her.

"I wanted to talk face to face." She sets the water down and puts her hands on her hips. "You've been acting weird lately."

"No, I haven't." I totally have.

"You walked away from Julie Jolley without trading insults after she called you a talentless hack. Good thing I was there."

"Thanks for that." My mind has been otherwise occupied with doubt and insecurity. And trying to remember how to breathe without thoughts of Zach intruding.

He calls or texts multiple times a day, but I haven't seen him since Monday night. All my fault. I keep making excuses. The thought of facing him scares me more than the chainsaw dude at the end of a haunted house. The black magic inside me is gone, and all that's left is just...me.

Portia sits me in a chair and goes hunting for supplies, coming back with the works: makeup, brush, curling iron, hair product. Thrown in the mix is an outfit she picked out for me to wear. Denim shorts and a cropped white shirt.

"I'm getting you ready, and then we're going out. Because friends don't let friends wallow in self-pity."

"I wasn't wallowing. I was sleeping."

"Blah, blah, blah. Excuses, excuses." She works a brush through my tangles, none too gently. "Take your complaints elsewhere."

After a solid hour of primping, I'm properly Portia-fied. At least, that's what she declares as we climb in her car. The expertly applied make up covers the fading bruise on my cheek and my pink hair curls in perfect, shoulder length beach waves. She even changed out the bandage around my ankle, finding a fun wrap with music notes on it.

I assume we'll grab beignets and walk through the mall, but she drives past our usual haunts and keeps going. "Where are we headed?"

She waggles her devious eyebrows. "You'll just have to trust me."

The landscape opens as downtown fades behind us. The sun glistens off Lake Pontchartrain, the sparkling surface twinkling like a million stars, the shoreline stretching for miles and miles. Portia slows and rolls down the windows, the humid breeze blowing in the sounds of gently lapping waters. Resting against the window frame, I close my eyes, bright rays kissing my skin with radiant heat.

The quiet drive doesn't distract me enough, and my thoughts turn to Zach. Again. Like they always do. I can't keep refusing to see him in person. But I worry about losing our relationship, and I cling to the remaining threads in a healthy and productive way. By avoiding him.

The car stops, and I blink back to the present. Looking around, I take in the line of palm trees planted in circular cutouts on the long concrete boardwalk. "Are we going to the Mardi Gras Fountain?"

"Close to it." She gets out, leaving me to hurry and follow.

The green space is busy. A family enjoys a picnic, a group throws a frisbee. A small game of football plays out, and there are joggers, walkers, and two yoga enthusiasts. We walk right past them, and I see Devin sitting on the ground, a blanket beneath him. There's also a long carpet runner rolled out, leading to a free-standing, framed door. It's the set for *Stuck.*

"What's going on?" I ask.

If the set for *Stuck* is here, there's a good chance Zach is too. My feet plant into the ground, my roots digging in. But Portia grabs my arm and plucks me out, dragging me forward until we stand in front of the door.

"Open it up." She nods and backs away, moving to sit next to Devin on the blanket.

"Hey, Devin." I wave stiffly, sure my smile looks as forced as it feels.

"Go on, CeCe. Open it up." He winks and throws an arm around Portia.

Ohhh-kay. I'm nervous and anxious, but Heart beats extra pumpy, and Optimism peeks out. My hand reaches for the knob, and I push the door open.

"CeCe, can we talk?"

Zach.

He speaks the first line of the play, a modified version with my actual name. My eyes devour him. Has it only been five days? He wears jeans and a white tee, and I wonder if Portia planned my outfit to match. His dark hair hangs across his forehead. His eyes shine such a bright blue that even the glistening of Lake Pontchartrain can't compare.

"Did we have a performance I forgot about?" I self-consciously run a hand through my hair, brushing out the invisible anxiety.

"That's not your line." He ducks under the door frame

to stand toe to toe. Or at least we would if I didn't take a retreating step.

"Umm, okay." I shake my head and close my eyes for a second. This whole scene is bizarre. But I bring out my best Allie and deliver the dialogue. "I don't have anything to say, and you've already said enough."

"Sugar, please." He speaks with the same volume and intensity as in our performance, and it draws the attention of a few people. The frisbee players and one of the walkers wander over to watch, standing behind Portia and Devin. They probably assume we're putting on a free performance in the park.

Maybe we are. I have no idea.

Eyeing the crowd, which keeps growing, I ignore the confused stares. Mostly because I'm just as confused. "I'm not your sugar."

"That's where you're wrong." He goes off script, and I blink a few times, trying to follow along. "And for some reason, you've been avoiding me."

The crowd heckles like they're watching an interactive melodrama, and Portia's exaggerated antagonizing carries the loudest. I glance to see a few more people have stopped to watch. How sad is my life that there's enough drama to attract an audience?

A gust of wind blows my hair, and I swipe at the strands. "I was giving you space."

"Why? I don't want space." His forehead crinkles and his lips pinch, like he's actually baffled about the distance I put between us.

I tip my head back and stare at the sky. The sun streaks unhampered against the cerulean background, and my real fear pours out. "When we met, you didn't even want to date me. Then Rivera came between us and gave me his black...."

314

I take a breath, hesitant to talk about black magic in front of the growing audience, thinking of a different way to explain. "Licorice. And now it's gone."

"Licorice?" He bites his lip to keep from laughing. "You think I only liked you because of the black...licorice?"

"The thought crossed my mind." To an obsessive degree.

"Well, it's not true."

I glance at our audience, which now includes a few of the picnic-ers. "But I felt the way you crave it."

"It's like a drug. Addictive, dirty, and empty." He sighs, and his voice softens. "You don't have Rivera's black licorice anymore, and I'm glad. This is what I want. You're what I want."

"Are you sure?" I duck my head to stare at my checkered Vans.

His fingers lift my chin, urging me to look at him. "I liked you the minute you called Devin a player."

"Hey now," Devin calls from his spot on the blanket.

Zach smiles, and all the holy angels sing because his dimples come out to play. "I liked you as soon as I heard you laugh. Your eyes get this...sparkle. And I knew I was in trouble when you covered my mouth. I tried not to like you, but I couldn't help it."

"Woohoo!" Portia screams.

"This is so awkward," I say and bury my face in my hands.

"Are you embarrassed? I'm not." He takes my wrists, dragging away my cover and leaving me open. "I met this really amazing girl. She's beautiful, green eyes, pink hair. She's got this courageous spirit."

"You make her sound pretty great."

"Yeah, she is." He leans forward, gently pressing his

forehead against mine. His hands drift from my wrists to my shoulders, and then to circle behind my neck. "CeCe..."

"What?" I ask, holding still in this moment we share. Afraid to pop the bubble he inflates around us.

His cinnamon breath fans across my lips. "I love you."

"Oh, Zach." An explosion bursts in my chest at his words, sending sparkling tingles into my system. I sigh and pull back, meeting his gaze. "It's too late."

His smile melts. "What do you mean?"

"I'm already stuck." Butterflies do an Irish step-dance in my belly knowing what comes after that line.

"Kiss her!" Apparently, Portia also remembers what comes next. She punches a fist in the air and starts a chant, which the crowd picks up. "Kiss, kiss, kiss."

His fingers cup my cheek. Of their own accord, my heels lift, my body drawing closer as I rise to my tippy toes, and our lips meet. The soft brush of his mouth sends a warmth through me that puts the sunlight to shame. It lights me up, fills the gaps.

My power agrees, mingling with Zach's, a welcoming contentment that curls in my veins. It flows through me, hotter than the spiciest gumbo. More exciting than a starring role in The Exhibition. Better than all six seasons of Downton Abbey (*sorry Mawmaw, but you'd totally agree*). The ultimate bliss, stronger than anything the oily darkness produces.

Just like our first kiss, the sound of cheering interrupts us. "Did we just put on an impromptu performance for the fine people at Lakeshore Park?" I ask.

"Yeah. We did." He links our fingers and turns. "Should we take our bow?"

Standing on the makeshift stage, our hands clasped, we dip low, receiving the applause. Portia's piercing whistle makes me laugh, and I hear Zach's echoing chuckle. We look at each other, unable to disguise our amusement.

"Ready for our encore?" He winks and, yep, Heart and Optimism give him a standing ovation.

"With you? Always." I move in, burrowing into the snug zone, right where I belong. My boyfriend's arms wrap tight around me.

Right where they belong.

THE END

ACKNOWLEDGMENTS

It takes a village to raise a book into a well-adjusted tome, and this novel is no different. A giant, titan-sized thank you to Donna Milakovic. My writing spouse, my BFF, my secret keeper, my go-to when evidence needs to be destroyed. May our search histories always stay hidden. And I love you.

To my Rhode Island Red, Haley Peck-Law. Thanks for being a part of our crazy Coop. I couldn't have finished this without you.

I'd also be remiss in neglecting my writing group, Sundays Without Nick. Adam Lund, the voluntold spreadsheet master who keeps me on track (and keeps me laughing). Nick Bright, without whom there would be no "without" in our Sundays. Not to mention being a rock-solid support. And to Barbara Lund, an amazing writer, reliable reader, and the recipient of my violent cuddles. DH + BL forever.

A heartfelt thanks to my publisher and the team behind Monster Ivy. Amy Michelle Carpenter, Caleb Staker, Merrydith Narramore, Caylah Coffeen, Mary Gray, and Lenore Stutznegger. Thank you for believing in me and seeing my vision. To Cammie Larsen, an editing genius, who showed me how to level up my manuscript.

To Miranda Moore, necklace maker, inspired reader, and amazing human.

A big smooch to the best beta reader in the known world, Sydney Holt.

And to my mom, who passed on her love of reading.

I owe a great debt of gratitude to all those who came before. The ones who read my terrible manuscripts and rambling words. The writers' groups of Debbie-past, before I cared about things like sentence variation and proper punctuation. Heroes, every one of you.

To my kids, Megan, Adam, Aaron, and Alex, who have always supported me. You've been patient when my fictional characters stole my attention. You believed in me even when I didn't believe in myself. You encouraged me to put my butt in the seat and work. Y'all are the best!

And finally, to my husband Ryan. For everything and more.

ABOUT THE AUTHOR

Debbie Hibbert is an author, lover of chocolate, and finder of weird things. What kind of weird things, you might ask? There was that one time with the mysterious chimes. The porcelain doll in the woods. The plastic flamingo in the trees. The Hell gates...yes, plural.

When not writing, Debbie likes to explore old grave-yards, drink Diet Dr. Pepper, and solve mysteries with her dogs, Sherlock and Watson. She also likes the beach. Sunny days. Blue skies. Toes in the sand... You get the idea.

She's a Texas transplant that resides in Houston. In a hurricane, during the apocalypse, or through an extended reading of bad jokes on Twitter, she would choose her resourceful hubby and talented offspring to guarantee survival.

Printed in the USA
CPSIA information can be obtained
at www.ICGtesting.com
LVHW011737070923
757555LV00017B/45/J

A NOTE FROM THE AUTHOR:

Stay connected by joining my mailing list. Find it at my
website: debbiehibbert.com.

With the abundance of books available to read, thank you for
choosing mine. If you have a minute, please take the time to leave
a review on Amazon. You will be rewarded with good luck and
positive vibes.

Much love,

Debbie